MR. SMITHFIELD

LOUISE BAY

Published by Louise Bay 2021

ISBN – 978-1-910747-64-3

BOOKS BY LOUISE BAY

The Mister Series
Mr. Mayfair
Mr.Knightsbridge
Mr. Smithfield
Mr. Park Lane

Standalones
International Player
Hollywood Scandal
Love Unexpected
Hopeful
The Empire State Series

Gentleman Series
The Wrong Gentleman
The Ruthless Gentleman

The Royals Series
The Earl of London
The British Knight
Duke of Manhattan
Park Avenue Prince
King of Wall Street

<u>The Nights Series</u>

Indigo Nights

Promised Nights

Parisian Nights

Faithful

Sign up to the Louise Bay mailing list at
www.louisebay/mailinglist

Read more at www.louisebay.com

ONE

Autumn

He was a thirty-three-year-old single father of an adorable four-year-old, and just happened to be the only man I'd ever met who made my insides *actually* quiver when he looked at me. Where would he keep his spatulas?

I'd looked in every single drawer and cabinet in the kitchen and found nothing. All I wanted was an omelet. I'd been looking for about thirty minutes and had found Tupperware, an old Good Housekeeping recipe book from the seventies, and even what looked like a shrunken version of one of those tools to plane wood. But no freaking spatulas. Perhaps the British had a habit of storing vital kitchen equipment in their bathrooms or something? I pulled out my phone and called my sister. Hollie understood the British better than I did.

"Where do Brits keep their flippers?" I asked.

"Like diving equipment?" Hollie responded.

"Yes, Hollie, my stomach's rumbling, it's almost nine o'clock at night, and I'm searching the kitchen for diving equipment." I collapsed onto the soft, navy cushions that covered the long wooden bench that ran the length of the kitchen table. "I just want an omelet."

"Well first of all, they call that kind of spatula a fish slice," Hollie said in her typical no-nonsense tone.

I was pretty sure English was still the language of both England and the United States, but since moving to London a few weeks ago, sometimes I had to check out Wikipedia to make sure nothing had changed. Just being in the kitchen required a translator. I'd discovered that burners were *hobs*. Kitchen counters were *work surfaces* or *sides*. Sides of what? According to a Google deep-dive I wasn't entirely proud of, a "side" could mean any raised, horizontal surface in any room—so precisely not a *side* of anything. And now spatulas were fish slices. "What if I don't want to prepare fish with it? Or slice anything?"

I could almost hear Hollie shrug. "Still a fish slice."

"Well, do you know where I might find . . . *that* in an average kitchen?"

"As far as I'm aware, they keep them in the same place as Americans do. Kitchen, drawer, pot on the counter—that kind of thing."

Maybe Gabriel didn't have kitchen utensils, or maybe he hid them behind that locked door at the back of the kitchen. It was the only room in the house outside of the bathrooms that had a lock on it. Gabriel's clear, unspoken message to me, the hired help, was *Do Not Enter*. And therefore, of course, I desperately wanted to get inside.

"Are you okay?" Hollie asked.

"Well, I'm a little hungry," I said, standing and heading to the fridge. Omelets were off the menu, so I'd have to find something else.

"Gabriel's still at work?"

"Yes." No wonder he needed a live-in nanny for Bethany. He'd left the house just after six this morning and still wasn't back. Everyone had tried to convince me not to take this job. Even Gabriel had tried to discourage me by telling me he needed a nanny who would work long hours for the next few months, as he was going through a particularly busy stretch at work. I'd be working weekends and overnights, too. Still, I wasn't put off. How could I be? Bethany was adorable and Gabriel lived in a mansion that looked like it was something straight out of a Dickens novel, right in the center of London. I could never have afforded to live in Smithfield on a graduate paycheck. Which was another reason why my program being delayed until September wasn't the end of the world. This way, I'd get to enjoy London without the pressure of starting a career at the same time. It was a silver lining I didn't even have to squint to see.

At first it wasn't easy to see a bright side to my program being delayed by six months. The recession that started at the end of last year had thrown so many businesses into a tailspin, even the Fortune 500 company that was going to employ me. I'd been so excited to start, especially since the first assignment was in London. By now I'd thought I'd be having cocktails with my coworkers and laughing about photocopier jams, or whatever it was people in offices laughed about at happy hour. I was supposed to have one foot on the career ladder, rather than one hand wiping a four-year-old bottom.

But taking care of Bethany was a job in London, period. And *any* job in London was bound to be more exciting than *every* job back in Oregon, especially since Hollie and her soon-to-be husband lived here. My sister wanted me to wait tables, be her assistant, or do basically anything other than move into Gabriel's house. But I had pediatric first aid training from summers as a lifeguard at the community pool, plus plenty of babysitting experience. This job came with rent-free accommodation, which meant I didn't need to rely on my sister at all. Hollie had been putting a roof over my head for twenty-three years, and I was desperate to set her free and stand on my own two feet.

Nannying wasn't my first choice, but it could have been a lot worse. I was in London. I wasn't relying on my sister. And my boss was as hot as holy hell. Life wasn't shaping up to be exactly what I'd planned, but it was good.

"Well, maybe you should have an early night," Hollie said.

"I need something to eat," I replied, pulling out ham and cheese from the refrigerator. Gabriel even paid for my food, so everything I earned I could save and spend on travelling next summer. I made a mental note to spend some of my paycheck on a spatula. "And anyway, I'm not tired."

"Of course you're tired. You've been running around after a four-year-old all day."

The truth was, nannying was hard work. I wasn't about to tell Hollie that—I didn't want her to worry. Bethany had an infectious giggle, loved to be tickled, and her curiosity knew no bounds . . . but she had the energy of a cocker spaniel on crack. At the end of every day, I felt like I'd been run over by a Mack truck.

"Gabriel will probably want you out of his hair when he comes in," Hollie said. She was trying to sound breezy, like she wasn't suggesting I keep as far away from Gabriel as possible. Even if I wanted to keep my distance—which I didn't—it was impossible. We lived under the same roof, and he was frequently the only other adult I saw throughout the day. "He'll have worked really hard and will want to decompress. But he'll be far too polite to say so. You should go to bed."

I glanced over at the locked door at the far end of the kitchen. Last night was my first night living with Gabriel and Bethany, and we were all still learning each other's habits. When Gabriel had gotten home, he'd disappeared upstairs and changed out of his beautiful, navy blue suit—the one that made his green eyes light up like he was some kind of god. He'd looked so delicious. So powerful. So like a man who would kiss me out of my shoes. He'd returned in faded jeans that clung to his strong thighs and an old t-shirt that lifted up just slightly when he reached for a wine glass, so I got a glimmer of his muscular stomach. And the hole on the seam of the shoulder was begging for me to push my finger through and find out exactly how hot, how smooth, how touchable his skin was. I wanted to beg him never to wear anything else again. I'd felt my mouth go dry as I tried to find something to say to such a serious, commanding, beautiful man before he abruptly excused himself, and disappeared through that locked door without explanation.

Did he *decompress* behind that door?

And if so, what did decompressing involve when it came to a man like Gabriel Chase?

I could think of a few suggestions that didn't involve him wearing either the suit or the jeans. In fact, esteemed decompress-ologist Doctor Autumn Lumen suggested a shower for two and kissing the nanny for optimal relaxation.

"We should have a talk about Gabriel," Hollie said, her tone shifting when she realized I wasn't taking her trying-to-be-subtle bait. She was using her Sensible Sister voice—the same one she'd used when we'd talked about me dating Darren from Eagle Creek and Stuart from Portland. "He's a father and a very serious lawyer. And he's—"

"You know that we're not dating, right?"

"I know. But I also know that you just moved into his house and you're going to be around each other and—"

"You're worried that I'm going to seduce him and take advantage?" I wasn't quite sure what her problem was. I got it with Darren and Stuart. Back home, she'd been trying to protect me. She didn't want me ending up pregnant by some guy who would never amount to anything, which would lead to me dropping out of college and ruining my life. But I was different now. Gabriel was different. He'd already amounted to something. We were in London, not Oregon. And I was pretty sure I'd have to be having sex with him to get pregnant.

"Hardly. I'm not sure Gabriel ever does anything that he doesn't want to do."

Interesting. I hadn't seen that side of him yet, but I hadn't known him that long. I liked the idea that he had steel-like resolve.

"I'm just concerned because he's . . . you know . . . He's handsome." *Putting it mildly, sis.* "I'm concerned you might develop a crush."

"Oh, don't worry, I can remove any ambiguity for you. My crush is fully developed. But that just means I'm human. I'm sure every woman in London has a crush on Gabriel Chase."

Hollie laughed. "Okay, well that's probably true. I just don't want you to get into a situation you might regret."

I sighed. "Look, Gabriel's not going to be interested in some chick from the wrong side of the tracks who's looking after his kid. I'm well aware of that." I may have resisted changing into my favorite flannel pajamas, and lately my messy bun came with a side of mascara and blush, but I wasn't kidding myself. I wasn't a sophisticated woman of the world who wore five-inch pencil heels, smelled of expensive fragrance even when she wasn't wearing any, and had a weekly manicure at her favorite spa, like most of the women Gabriel was sure to encounter at his law firm. His gaze might light a fire in me that I needed a trip to the arctic to douse, but I wasn't stupid. I was the hired help. My crush was, and would remain, a one-sided fantasy.

Down the hall, the clunk of the three front door locks caught my attention.

My crush was home.

TWO

Autumn

The air shifted when Gabriel came through the door at night. He seemed to carry with him the grey drizzle of the April weather. The constant frown across his brow and the tense line of his mouth suggested a storm constantly raged inside him.

"Hello," I called out. Last night and tonight, I'd spent the hours after Bethany had gone to bed unpacking, getting to know the layout of the house, and studying maps of London's public transportation system.

"Good evening." His voice was almost a growl, and it sent a sensuous shiver up my spine.

I spun around from where I was standing in the kitchen and came face-to-face with my deliciously handsome employer. I didn't know how it was possible but every time I saw him, I wasn't expecting him to be so tall. Or his jaw to be quite so sharp. Or his glossy, black curls quite so touchable. It was as if my memory couldn't handle someone so attractive, so dialed it down until I was faced with reality again. Tonight his glare was a little more intense than usual. "What's this noise?" he barked, shaking the ever-present London rain from his hair and then toeing off his shoes, which I found to be an adorable habit. Who couldn't appreciate a man in a hand-made suit who didn't like to wear shoes?

I wasn't quite sure what he meant by noise and then I realized he must be referring to my phone. I grabbed it and turned down the volume. "A musicals mash-up," I said, wiggling my cell at him. "Sometimes I like to deep dive into the entire soundtrack but sometimes you just want to hear the greats. Am I right?"

He tilted his head as if he was looking at an animal he didn't recognize in a zoo.

"Musicals," I repeated. "You know, like *Showboat. West Side Story. The King and I.*" He still looked blank. There was only one thing for it. I had to sing. "'*The hills are alive with the sound of music*'." Surely that was the one musical everyone in the northern hemisphere had heard of?

He winced. "You're singing."

"Of course I'm singing. Everyone should sing. '*I feel pretty. Oh so pretty. I feel pretty and witty and bright*'." I stopped partly because he didn't look amused but mainly because I couldn't sing a *West Side Story* song without dancing, and I'd learned from experience that I couldn't dance in socks on this floor without falling flat on my face. I shrugged. "I don't know what it is about that song, but I can't be anything but happy when I sing it. Musicals have that effect on people. You should try it."

"I don't think so," he said, moving toward the fridge. "And honestly, with your voice, I'm not sure *you* should be singing either." He peered inside and then pulled out a beer.

"Well, that was rude. Granted, I'm no Idina Menzel, but few of us are."

"I have no idea what you're talking about," he said and set his beer onto the kitchen table while he shrugged off his jacket.

"Never mind," I said, determined not to take offense at his terse manner and his less-than-favorable assessment of my singing ability. "Have you eaten? I was going to make myself an omelet. Can I fix you something?"

"I've got stuff to do."

I glanced toward the locked door at the back of the kitchen. What was behind that door? A dungeon? A man-spa? Perhaps he was an amateur taxidermist. But why did he have to lock it? Was it to keep what was in there from getting out, or anyone else from getting in?

"So, Bethany had a wonderful day. We went to a sing-a-long, as it happens. Presumably, it's okay for your daughter to sing?"

"Well, yes, she's four. And she has rather a good voice, I think. For her age." His eyes widened as if he was waiting for me to agree. The only time his manner lightened was when it came to Bethany. Just talking about her seemed to lift him out of his brooding darkness for a few minutes.

"I love her singing voice. It's delightful. And she has excellent rhythm. She's been invited for a play date with one of the kids from the class. Would that be okay with you?" I asked.

"You'll be there with her?"

"Of course. I'd never leave her."

"Then yes, if you think she would enjoy it."

"And if we can fit it in. She has quite the schedule. We have swimming tomorrow. Gymnastics on Thursday. Music on Friday. And all this on top of pre-school. But from what I heard from the other nannies today, all the kids are sched-uled like they're the Obamas."

He chuckled and I stared at him, fascinated. His smiles were rare and certainly, I'd never elicited one before. Perhaps he just needed to get to know me a little better and he'd warm up.

"I guess it's the same in New York," I said. "Or any big city with lots of pushy, successful parents." A far cry from Oregon, and my parents. They didn't even know if I was in school, let alone keeping up with any extracurricular activi-ties that might have been offered. Which they weren't. There might have been a chess club active for a semester, but chess wasn't really my game. I'm pretty sure that if I'd gotten a job at the trailer park where we lived or in the factory where my sister used to work, they would have been as proud as Idina Menzel's parents when they watched *Wicked* for the first time. Or they might not have noticed at all.

Gabriel pulled open one of the cupboard doors and retrieved a bottle opener from where it was hanging on a rack inside the door.

"Spatulas!" I squealed, spotting the elusive flipper. "How did I not spot these here? You've got them hanging up like they're in a tool shed." Why didn't he just put them in a drawer or something? "You Brits."

"I never thought a fish slice could make someone so happy," he said, looking at me as if I'd lost my mind.

"It's always the little things that feed hope, Gabriel. Always the little things."

He scooped up the fish slice from its hook and held it out to me.

"Are you sure I can't fix you an omelet?" I asked, taking the implement. As my hand wrapped around the handle, our fingers brushed—and it was like a bolt of heat shot up my hand, warming my entire arm. I sucked in a breath.

It was just an accidental scrape of his fingers, but the touch was as intense as if he'd grabbed me and kissed me.

"Sorry," he mumbled. What was he apologizing for? He hadn't grabbed my boob or anything. He cleared his throat. "I must get on."

I glanced at the locked door. Back to stuffing bats or whatever it was he did in there. "If you're busy, I'm happy to keep Bethany's monitor."

"Bethany will have you running around and playing hide-and-seek, riding her bike, and taking her to the park tomorrow. Don't burn yourself out."

I flexed a bicep. "I can handle her." I winced. "I think."

He pulled out a single key from his pocket and slipped it into the lock. A moment later, he disappeared behind the closed door, shutting the entire world—and me—out.

THREE

Gabriel

A crash downstairs drew my attention to the clock on my computer. Shit. Seven thirty. I'd been on this video call for two and a half hours and it was a Sunday morning.

"I'm going to have to go," I said. I'd mentioned having to ring off before seven when I answered the call at just after five. But as usual, Mike Green, my biggest client, liked to push boundaries.

"We're just making progress," Mike said. "I think if we keep going, we can have this deal hammered out by noon your time. You'll get the rest of the day."

"I have a four-year-old, Mike. I'll catch up with you tonight. Just don't engage those useless environmental analysts. I'll find someone else."

"Gabriel, they're the best in the business."

"They were four days late with the last report. They can't be trusted."

"Can you just give me a few more hours? We can get this done."

When I didn't respond, he sighed and gave me a disappointed nod of the head. He'd make me pay for this. People thought that when you made partner at a law firm, you were your own boss, but that was bollocks. Clients ruled my life in a way that other people's bosses made their lives hell. Mike was a dickhead. But he was a successful dickhead and headed up one of the few private equity houses that was still doing deals in this recession. Probably because he had nothing else to do.

I left the meeting and headed out of my office, toward the sound of the crash. Bethany woke between seven and seven thirty every morning like clockwork, and although she normally just played in her bedroom until I came and got her, she may have wandered downstairs.

I walked into the kitchen and instead of seeing smashed crockery and four-year-old bare feet, I found Autumn at the hob, with Bethany sitting on a bar stool.

"Good morning," I said, scrubbing my hands through my hair and then kissing my daughter on the head. "Can we turn that music down?" What was it with Autumn and musicals?

"We're making pancakes," Bethany announced as she continued to stir the mixture in the mixing bowl in front of her. "And singing."

God help us all. Autumn sang like she was drowning in a pit of cats and Bethany was four, so naturally sounded like one of the said cats. The two of them together might be handy as a form of defense if we were fighting off the Taliban, but my eardrums wouldn't survive another chorus of *Let it Go*.

I glanced at Autumn, wondering if she'd heard my request to turn down the music, and she beamed at me. I'd never known a person so happy all the time. I wasn't sure if she was trying to impress me or if she was genuinely, thoroughly enjoying herself. Constantly.

"I picked up maple syrup and blueberries this week, so we're giving it a try. Are you willing to be a guinea pig?" she asked. More smiles. It was seven thirty on a Sunday. What was there to be so happy about?

"Please, Daddy," Bethany pleaded.

"Okay." I had no defense against my daughter's request. I picked up Autumn's phone and silenced the incessant screeching, hoping to dissuade any amateur participation, and took a seat on the stool next to my daughter. I hoped Autumn's cooking was a lot better than her vocal ability. "But I don't expect you to have to cook Bethany breakfast. Or me for that matter. I know it's a Sunday."

"I was awake. And I'm cooking us all breakfast. I hope." She winked. I couldn't remember the last time anyone had winked at me. It might have been the gardener we had when I was a child. These days, I was far too serious for anyone to wink at me.

Except Autumn, apparently.

"Here we go. Are you up for first taste, Bethany?" Autumn slid the first pancake onto a wooden plate. "Not too much syrup and lots of blueberries, please."

"Hot!" Bethany said, staring at the piece of pancake on her fork and giving it an ineffective blow.

Before Bethany had given her verdict, Autumn slid three pancakes onto my plate and handed me a knife and fork.

"Yummy!" Bethany declared. "Daddy, you eat." She jabbed her finger at my plate.

"I'm out of objections," I replied and took a mouthful.

"How are they?" Autumn asked.

I nodded, trying to match her enthusiasm. She'd

accused me of being rude last night, and I didn't have time to look for a new nanny if Autumn decided to throw in the towel. I'd been accused by more than one nanny of being hostile and unappreciative.

"Secret family recipe," Autumn said as if she'd just served up a Michelin-starred dish.

"Daddy, bear soldiers today, 'member?" Bethany said.

"She's been talking about soldiers non-stop," Autumn said. "I'm a little concerned you're signing her up to some kind of teddy bear army."

"I've promised I'll take her to the changing of the guard. She thinks the busbies they wear make them look like bears."

Autumn swallowed a mouthful of pancake. "Changing of the guard? Like Christopher Robin and Alice?" Her face was plastered in sheer delight, like someone had just given her the moon. "Does that actually happen?"

"Of course it does," I replied. Why would she think it wasn't real?

"Can I come?" she asked, pouring more pancake batter into the frying pan. "That poem—" She shook her head as if it didn't matter. "I heard it a lot growing up. I'd love to actually see how it all works. Does the Queen come out?"

I hadn't expected company today. Weekends were for me and Bethany. I didn't see my daughter much in the week, so I tried to make weekends count.

"Yes, Autumn, come! Please, Daddy!"

My daughter had me wrapped around her finger. And it wouldn't hurt to be nice to Autumn so she wouldn't leave me high and dry and without a nanny. Again. Work was manic at the moment and it was going to get worse over the next couple of months. Autumn was due to stay until the end of July, when all my clients went on holiday and I'd have time to find a new nanny. "Of course, Autumn is welcome, darling. But she might not want to come because we won't see Her Majesty. Just a lot of busbies and tourists."

Autumn shrugged, her eyes sparkling like sunshine hitting water. "I can't wait. What time do we need to leave?"

Instead of disappearing until it was time to go, Autumn pulled out Bethany's rucksack and started to pack.

"Here," she said, pulling out a laminated sheet. "I prepared a list of everything we need when we're going out for the day."

"You laminated a list?" It was strange having help at the weekend. It had been a long time since Bethany's mother had left.

She shrugged. "Of course. That way you don't forget anything. I have one for going to preschool, too. I find it's best to be prepared in life. It frees you up to deal with the unexpected."

I wasn't sure what she was talking about, and I was concerned if I asked her to explain, she'd just confuse me more.

Thirty minutes later, Autumn greeted the cabbie as we piled into the cab. "Thank you for taking us to the Palace." She did know he was getting paid, didn't she?

"Tip up. Tip up. Just like Paddington," Bethany sang to herself as she pulled down the tip-up seat and clambered on. I leaned to fix the seatbelt and my hand collided with Autumn's. A flash of energy chased up my arm and lit me up from my center, starting in my bollocks. Jesus. I thought when I handed her the spatula last night, the spark of electricity between us had been a fluke. Apparently not.

Autumn gasped as she pulled back her arm.

Had she felt that? It was like some kind of explosion.

"Are you okay?" I asked, not looking at her but finishing securing Bethany in place.

"Yes," she said, quieter than I was used to. She'd also felt something then.

Autumn was an attractive girl. I'd seen it the first time I'd ever laid eyes on her. I'd stopped noticing women after Penelope left, swearing myself to a life of celibacy. I wanted to focus only on the things that deserved my attention: my daughter, work, and the five men who were more my brothers than my friends. Autumn had interrupted that focus for a split second. But that's all it had been—a momentary intrusion. She'd been unmistakably striking and beautiful and a little haunting, and something in my physiology had reacted. But that moment had passed. Hadn't it?

By the time we pulled up on the Mall, I'd put our collision out of mind. Autumn likely had too, with all her chattering on to the cabbie. I was surprised she hadn't been invited to the man's thirtieth wedding anniversary coming up next month. She'd made fast friends with him as she peppered him with questions about his celebrity passengers and near misses when it came to women almost giving birth on the back seat. Her sunny nature didn't appear to have been put on for my benefit. Or if it had, it was extended to the cabbie as well. She seemed genuinely happy. All. The. Time.

At least she hadn't broken out into song.

We stepped out of the cab onto the street, and I lifted Bethany onto my shoulders like we normally did. This time of year, the crowds wouldn't be too bad, but I wasn't taking any chances. Bethany was safe and also had the best view.

"Could there be anything more iconically British then going to see the changing of the guard in a black cab?"

Autumn asked, her wide smile lighting up a very dull April morning.

"Bears!" Bethany said, pointing toward the palace.

"Let's go," I replied. "We need to get a good spot." There were just a few people here right now but within ten minutes, thousands would appear from nowhere like ants on ice cream.

I felt the vibration of my phone in my pocket before I heard it and my gut swirled like week-old gravy. I knew it would be Mike. I wanted to dump him as a client but with the economy in the ditch, he was the only person making sure I wasn't pushed out of the firm. I pulled the phone from my pocket, holding both of Bethany's legs with one hand. Even with my daughter's splayed hands across my forehead and one eye, I could make out that it was indeed Mike.

"Work?" Autumn asked.

"Yeah," I said. "I have one particularly demanding client. Doesn't have kids so doesn't get wanting to be away from the office."

"But, man, it's the weekend."

"Says the woman who's hanging out with her boss and her charge."

She laughed. "I suppose. But this is fun." She clapped her mitten-covered hands together and turned to Bethany. "I can see the bear soldiers!"

If she was having fun, she'd stay for her full term. Bethany seemed to like Autumn, and other than her love of musicals, she wasn't a terrible lodger. I was barely at home anyway and when I was, I spent most of the time in my workshop. For me, our arrangement was a perfect fit.

We got to the palace gates and huddled into one of the

remaining slots in front of the tall black railings surrounding the palace.

"Honestly, I've been waiting to see this since I was nine years old," Autumn said.

"The changing of the guard?"

"Yes. And London. And the world," she said, tilting her head back as far as she could, as if she was trying to make out Jupiter.

"You've always wanted to travel?" I asked.

"Always. And when Hollie got to come to Europe first, I knew I wouldn't be far behind. I can't wait to see the Colosseum. The Eiffel Tower. I want to go and watch the . . ." She made pincer movements with her fingers. "You know, in Seville."

"Flamenco?" I suggested.

"Gah," she replied, closing her eyes and inhaling as if she was breathing in a bouquet of summer flowers. "I can't wait. I thought I'd have to wait for paid vacation but turns out not having my job start until next September means I can spend the whole of August travelling. Things have turned out for the best."

"Poor gold lady. She can't see," Bethany said, interrupting my tumble of thoughts. She patted my head and pointed at the statue of victory on top of the Victoria memorial.

"No, darling, she's looking in the wrong direction," I replied.

"I think she's making sure everyone is happy," Autumn replied. "And I'm sure someone will show her photos."

"Yes!" Bethany said. "The Queen."

Sometimes I wondered what thoughts raced around Bethany's head in between her random statements. Did she think the statue came alive when the people had gone, and

Victory joined Her Majesty for tea and a giggle about the ceremony? Being a father was the most rewarding, confusing, challenging thing I'd ever done and despite Bethany's mother leaving us, I'd do it all again exactly the same in a heartbeat. Bethany was a constant reminder that someone other than myself was at the center of everything I did. It was an important reminder—one that kept me focused and determined even in the face of nightmare clients like Mike.

"Spin," Bethany demanded, and dutifully, I turned around three hundred and sixty degrees on the spot. Bethany tilted back as she always did when she was on my shoulders, and I tightened my grip on her ankles. "Again." This time I went the other way twice. Soon I knew I'd been crouching down and springing up and rocking my shoulders left and right like I was Bethany's own personal fairground ride. Anything to hear that giggle.

"You two are wonderful together," Autumn said, grinning up at us both.

Someone tapped me on the shoulder, and I turned to find an older woman, pulling one of those baskets on wheels that elderly people transport their shopping in. "Excuse me for interrupting you, but I have to tell you that you three make a very good-looking family."

I couldn't have been more shocked if she'd told me I'd unknowingly come out in my boxers. I was lost for words. I glanced at Autumn, who I expected to interrupt and correct the woman, but she seemed to be studiously focused on the preparations behind the railings.

The woman looked up at Bethany. "You are going to turn out just as pretty as your mama."

She thought Autumn was my wife. That she was Bethany's mother. Couldn't she see I was far older than Autumn? That I was the man who signed her paychecks?

She patted me on my arm. "You have a beautiful family. Take care of them."

If only she knew.

I'd spent five years with Penelope trying to create a beautiful family. I was now certain there was no such thing. Apparently, I hadn't learned that lesson from my father. My ex-wife had to burn it on my soul.

I wouldn't make the same mistake again.

Now I was determined to the best father I could be to Bethany. That meant I lived my life with very exacting standards. I would be a role model for her. A provider for her. And most of all, I'd be her anchor—an unbreakable tether that would give her consistency and certainty. I knew what it felt like as a child when the ground was constantly shifting beneath you and you didn't know whether your parents would both be there when you woke up. Bethany's mother had cut herself loose, but that just made me bind myself more tightly to my daughter.

That meant no overnight trips for work, so I was always there if she woke in the night. It meant no women in my bed, since a relationship might confuse or hurt Bethany. And it meant I had to stop burning through nannies like stationery supplies. Whether she knew it or not, Autumn's place with us was a sure thing for as long as she was in London.

FOUR

Autumn

I wouldn't normally take so long to get ready for a Saturday night dinner with my sister. I certainly wouldn't have bought something new. But I was in London now. It felt like a fresh start even if I was in a kind of limbo until my real career started. Plus, Hollie ran in the kind of circles now where people's sneakers cost more than my entire closet. It might just be dinner with my sister, her husband, and some of their friends, but it was in Knightsbridge. The only person I knew who was richer than my future brother-in-law was my current boss, which meant dinner at Dex's warranted a new dress.

Especially because the aforementioned uber-wealthy boss would be in attendance.

It wasn't like I was trying to impress him exactly. But I suppose I did want Gabriel to think I was pretty—because I thought he was heart-stoppingly gorgeous. Yes, he was cold and standoffish when it was just him and me, but when I saw Gabriel with his daughter, I could see the man he was beyond the gruff exterior. And it made me melt like snow in the Sahara.

The dress I'd picked wasn't fancy. It was plain red jersey that hit just above the knee with a tie waist. As I turned in the mirror, I couldn't decide whether I should wear the slash neck off one shoulder or not. I'd decide on footwear first.

I owned four pairs of shoes and had brought them all to London. Flip flops—even if the weather was better, I couldn't wear those to a Knightsbridge dinner party—sneakers I might have gotten away with had they not been as scuffed, a pair of heels I got on sale for six dollars at Century 21, and finally a pair of black knee-high boots I'd saved for three months to buy and had had for years, though they looked almost as good as new. I settled on the boots. If I wore the heels, my sister would think I was trying to impress someone. And she'd think that someone was Gabriel. And it would become *a thing*.

"Are you ready?" Gabriel called up the stairs. Even though we were only going together because he was one of Dexter's best friends and not because he was my date, his question triggered a ripple of excitement deep in my belly. Like my body thought he was my boyfriend, even if the reality was I'd barely seen him since we'd watched the changing of the guard nearly two weeks ago. He had softened that day. Now he was back to being in a perpetually bad mood. Warm, friendly Gabriel was reserved for whenever Bethany was around. Even when he hid that part of him away, I knew it was there. And I wanted to know why it was buried so deep.

"Coming," I replied, picking up the wrist wallet Hollie had bought me for Christmas.

As I got to the bottom of the stairs, I waited while Gabriel finished giving instructions to the sitter.

"I should be babysitting," I said as Gabriel closed the front door behind us.

"No," he said in a way that left no room for argument. "You should be having dinner with your sister. It's Saturday night."

"But nannies are supposed to do babysitting and we agreed that—"

Gabriel opened the door to the cab waiting at the curb.

"You do plenty of babysitting," he said as he took a seat next to me, scanning my dress. I followed his gaze as it rested on the slit up the side of my thigh. God, was it inappropriate? I'd had dinner with Hollie, Dexter, and their friends before, and thought I'd chosen well. Was my choice of outfit totally off-base?

"The dress is new. I thought it would be okay for tonight," I said, almost embarrassed at his apparent disapproval. What did I know about London dress codes? I grew up in a trailer park. Paper napkins with printed designs were fancy to me.

He kind of growled before he looked away. "You look beautiful," he mumbled to the window.

I tried to bite back my smile. Rather than disapproving of my outfit, had he been checking me out? Heat pooled between my thighs and I swore I could feel the warmth of his body across the foot of space between us in the cab.

"Thank you," I whispered, half breathless from joy at being thought beautiful by a man like Gabriel, and half wondering why he looked so pained to give the compliment. Was it difficult for him to be nice to anyone but Bethany?

He sighed and shook his head like the words tortured him.

"Are you okay?" I asked.

"Fine," he replied, still fixated on the view outside the window. "I shouldn't have said it. I'm sorry."

"I'm not offended," I said. "It's nice to get a compliment. Especially from you."

"*Especially* from me?" He glanced at me and then back to the window, as if he were trying not to look at me.

Especially from someone so impossibly handsome. Someone so worldly, so clever and caring and careful. Someone I had a huge crush on. "Yes," I replied, simply. He must know that every woman within a mile radius had a crush on him. I was no one special.

"How was Bethany yesterday?" he asked, his tone changed as if he'd been sleep talking and had just woken up.

"She's adorable. I took her swimming, like I said. She loves the water." I didn't mention that I thought there should have been a lifeguard on duty even though there had been two instructors. I knew I could be overcautious about stuff like that because of my lifeguard training, and I didn't want him to worry.

"I took her to Greece last summer and she just wanted to be in the pool the entire time."

"Greece?" I asked, imagining whitewashed villas and bright pink flowers contrasting perfectly with the blue of the sea. "I've always wanted to go. Is it wonderful?"

"We didn't see much of it outside the pool. I thought you said you wanted to go to Paris and Rome."

"I do," I said. "Greece too. I want to feel the Mediterranean breeze through my hair and white sand between my toes, not just have *Mamma Mia* as my point of reference. Same goes for Paris."

"Let me guess . . . *An American Werewolf in Paris* is your current point of reference?"

Had Gabriel Chase just made a joke? I felt honored.

I grinned in silent victory. "I was thinking more *Moulin Rouge*."

"Never seen it."

"Stop. You've never seen *Moulin Rouge*? It's non-stop Baz Luhrmann genius. Like, it could be my favorite of all time. And *Mamma Mia* is a musical as well, if you didn't know."

"Yeah, never seen that either."

I wanted to reach for him, turn his face in my direction so I could see his expression and know he wasn't joking. *Surely* he was teasing me. The entire world had seen *Mamma Mia*. I shuffled forward in my seat to see as much of his face as I could. "Holy shit, Gabriel."

He turned to me, his broad shoulders taking up half the width of the seat. "Is it a federal offense in America not to like musicals?"

"Absolutely," I said, incredulous. "I see I'm going to have to broaden your horizons. One night when you're not back too late, I'll begin your musicals education. Oh God—"

"What?" he said, glancing ahead of us as if I'd spotted something.

"Are you telling me you've deprived Bethany too?"

He rolled his eyes. "I think she watched *Mary Poppins* with her last nanny. Or it could have been *The Wizard of Oz*."

I snorted. "Amateur stuff. She's *four*, Gabriel. *Four*. She should have seen *Singin' in the Rain* by now. And *An American in Paris* and—"

Gabriel's frown softened, his shoulders seemed to lower, and he looked at me. Really looked at me, as if he were trying to read my instructions or something. Was I so odd to him?

"I have work to do," I continued, grinning to myself. "Leave it to me and I'll make sure Bethany isn't forever deprived."

"If you say so," Gabriel said, back to his crotchety self.

I tapped the side of my nose just as the cab pulled up in front of Hollie and Dexter's house. Before we were out of the cab, Hollie had opened the door, a grinning Dexter behind her.

"It's so nice to have you here." She pulled me in for a hug and squeezed so tight I was concerned she cracked a rib. "Hey," she said, releasing me and looking me up and down. "I like your dress." She paused while Gabriel kissed her on the cheek and followed Dexter inside. "Are you trying to impress someone?" She had moved on from Sensible Sister voice and was now firmly in Concerned Older Sibling mode. Previously, I'd confidently been able to tell her that despite my crush on Gabriel, nothing would ever happen. I wasn't in his league, and he didn't seem like the type to tumble the hired help. Given his demeanor whenever I was around, I was sure he barely noticed me. Until tonight.

Tonight? He'd definitely noticed my dress. And he definitely told me I looked beautiful. But he also looked like it had been painful to admit. What was going on in that big brain of his?

"It was on sale at Uniqlo, Hollie." I sighed.

"Sorry. You look beautiful. You've always been able to make anything look like it cost a hundred times what it did. I just expected you in jeans. That's all."

"Maybe I'm reinventing myself," I replied. "Can I come in now? I'm cold."

"Yes. Come and help me get drinks. All the boys are

here and they're on whiskey—well, apart from Beck. What can I get you?"

"What've you got?"

She shrugged. "Dexter brought up some champagne," she said, her eyes twinkling conspiratorially.

"Who from the Sunshine Trailer Park would believe this is our life?" I linked my arm through hers as we headed to the kitchen.

"I know. It's like I'm engaged to royalty or something."

"Dexter doesn't have a stick up his ass like most of the royals do." I glanced to where Dexter and Gabriel and their friends sat by the fire. Gabriel sat back, his arm resting on the back of the couch as Tristan, the most gregarious of the bunch, made hand gestures that looked like he was describing a bomb going off. Gabriel looked so calm. So in control. As if he was taking everything in and not letting anything of himself out.

"How's it going?" Hollie asked as she pulled out a bottle of champagne from the ice bucket on the linen-clothed table set up with drinks. "With Bethany."

"Good." It was always the answer I gave her when she asked me about college, too. Even when things weren't exactly going to plan, an all-encompassing "good" accompanied by a smile seemed to stop her worrying. "Bethany's lovely. And I've been getting to see more of London as we go to her different classes and groups. We're going to the Barbican on Monday. Although, I'm not entirely sure what it is. Someone said a theatre and another person said it's a library, but people live there? Apparently, kids love it. Sounds weird but—"

"Who gave you that idea? Gabriel?" Hollie pushed the first filled glass toward me.

"No, one of the other nannies from Bethany's nursery."

"Do you see much of each other?" She held up her glass and I clinked mine to hers. "You and Gabriel, I mean." My sister's subtlety hadn't improved since the last time she'd warned me about her fiancé's best friend.

"Not really. He works a lot. But we message each other about Bethany." That was true, but it was also true that it *felt* like I saw a lot of him. Everywhere I turned in the house, I was confronted by some little piece of him. The inexplicably passionate literature beside his bed. His pictures from school and university. His cologne that stayed in the air long after he'd left, and smelled as moody and complex as the man himself. Every reminder of him was a morsel of temptation that made me hungry for more. The small snippets of him in person left me famished. I'd make sure I had a great view when he reached up to get something from the kitchen cupboard. Or when he bent down to scoop up his briefcase. And the way his voice was almost a growl still made me shudder. I collected all the pieces of him and put them together in my imagination. In the dark of my bedroom. Under my sheets. It was Gabriel I thought of when I touched myself.

"That's good," Hollie said, taking a sip of her drink and pretending she wasn't fishing for information.

"Is it?" I loved my sister. She'd provided a future for me that I couldn't have dreamt about without her sacrifices, but sometimes she needed to back off and not worry about me so much. And if I wanted to fantasize about a man like Gabriel, that was my prerogative.

"You know, it's good that you're not in each other's pockets."

"I don't know what you're so worried about."

"With your job being postponed and you having to be a

nanny and everything, I don't want you to have any more disappointment. I just want everything to work out."

I grabbed her hand. "It will. It always does. We make lemonade out of lemons. That's what the Lumen sisters do." There was no point in focusing on the bad that had been or could be. Whatever was coming would come whether or not I worried about it first. Better to make the most of the good stuff in between, so the not-so-good stuff would be slightly more manageable. I placed a kiss on her cheek and took a sip of my champagne, wanting to change the subject. "Although I'd take this over lemonade every day of the week."

Hollie might have been taking care of me for her whole life, but I could take care of myself now. And a crush on my boss wasn't the worst thing that was ever going to happen to me. I didn't have to tell her that I was pretty sure he'd been checking me out earlier. It had been a momentary chink in his armor that would have healed over by now.

"So, have you assigned seating?" I asked, sure that she would have placed Gabriel and me at opposite ends of the table.

"No." She glanced at her watch. "We should take a seat. That way Howard won't get irritated."

"Howard?"

Hollie winced. "The chef. Dexter insisted we take him full time."

I laughed. I couldn't help it. The idea that my sister now employed a full-time chef, when growing up we worried about having enough food to eat, was so bizarre.

"I know. I've told Dexter it's completely ridiculous." We wandered toward the dining table, which was beautifully set with endless sparkling flatware and about six glasses per place setting. It looked like there would be a lot of washing dishes after we'd left. Presumably Dexter insisted on someone taking care of that, too.

"You don't need to be embarrassed. I think it's amazing that you don't have to worry about cooking, let alone whether you're going to be able to make twenty dollars buy a week's worth of groceries for both of us. Are these flowers real?" I asked, bending to take in the scent of the peonies arranged in mini goldfish bowls dotted about the table. Yup, they were real.

"It's a different life, that's for sure," she said.

It was an easier life. One with less expectation of disaster hiding around every corner. And I couldn't have wished anything better for my sister.

Hollie took a seat at the head of the table and I sat on a chair right at the other end. This was a close-knit group of friends, and I didn't want to just crash into the middle of everything.

Gabriel and Dexter were the next to the table. Dexter took a seat next to my sister and to my surprise, Gabriel sat next to me.

"You okay?" he asked in a half whisper, his gaze only meeting mine for less than a second.

Goosebumps scattered across my body like dropped change onto marble. To an outsider, it was such a barren question, but from Gabriel? To me?

It was all intimacy.

All I could do was nod. How could I be anything but okay? He was sitting next to me.

The spell was broken as the rest of Dexter and Hollie's friends took seats around the table and a waiter came around with wine. At least *he* knew which glass he was using, because that was at least three levels above my paygrade.

As the evening went on, the waiter in charge of the wine managed to use each of the six glasses. My glasses—and Gabriel's—were the only ones that remained mostly untouched.

"You're not drinking," he said, without looking at me. It was the first time he'd spoken to me since he'd first sat down.

"*You're* not drinking," I replied. The rest of the table seemed oblivious to our conversation as they continued to banter and laugh.

"I have Bethany to think about," he said, still staring straight ahead. "You're off the clock. You should be able to enjoy your evening with friends."

My evening with friends? Is that what this was? I didn't really know anyone around this table other than my sister. "Are we friends, Gabriel?"

His chest expanded as he pulled in a breath, and as he exhaled, he pressed his thigh against mine and left it there. This was no casual brush of hands or inadvertent nudge of my knee. He was pressing his body against mine in answer to my question. And it was as erotic as if he was trailing his tongue over my breasts. My breathing grew shallow, my pulse drummed in my wrists, and the heat rose in my cheeks like he'd worked his fingers into my underwear.

I couldn't control my body's reaction to him when we were both fully clothed. What would become of me if Gabriel Chase and I were ever naked together?

FIVE

Gabriel

I rehearsed the conversation I'd have with Mike in my head as I sat in the back of the cab heading home. We were going to have diametrically opposing views on how we wanted to spend this weekend. I wanted to hang out with Bethany. Mike would want to work. I peered out of the raindrop-speckled window, fascinated with the people milling about on the streets. Where were all these people headed at just gone three on a Friday afternoon? Was I one of thousands heading home early? Was it what the rest of the world usually did while I stayed chained to my desk?

Before I left the office, I'd gotten to the end of the draft contract I'd received overnight on one of the Mike Green deals. Other than a couple of drafting issues and a correction on a tax point, I knew this was where we'd end up. I also knew Mike was going to try to make me negotiate it for the next sixty hours straight. If I lost our battle, I wouldn't get to go home for two nights and kiss my sleeping daughter. I'd miss the entire weekend with her, and I'd risk Autumn being pissed off. So I'd jumped in a cab before Mike had a chance to call me. That way, at least I'd get to see Bethany this afternoon.

My phone buzzed in my hand. Mike could fucking wait. I flipped it over to see Gillian Jones's name flashing on the screen. My stomach sank to my feet. I wasn't expecting a call from her. She was my personal lawyer, and I hadn't spoken to her for months. There would only be one reason why she'd call.

"Gillian, what can I do for you?"

"I've heard from her lawyers."

She didn't need to tell me who *her* was.

Her was Bethany's mother, my wife, and the woman I'd thought I was going to spend the rest of my life building a family with. When she'd walked out nearly three years ago, I'd been devastated, blindsided. Heartbroken that our family was shattering into pieces and that Bethany had been left without a mother.

Now I was just numb.

"Her lawyers have sent over the paperwork to start off the divorce proceedings."

It wasn't pain I felt exactly. More the memory of pain. A bruise reminding me what had happened; a shadow that would never fully disappear.

"Good," I replied. "If I hadn't been so busy, I would have started the process before now." She'd filed for a legal separation almost immediately after leaving, but this was the first I'd heard about divorce. "What does she want?" I asked. My father's money had made me a wealthy man. But Bethany was the most valuable part of my life. One, she was welcome to. The other, I'd fight to the death to protect.

"Nothing," Gillian said.

Relief swept through me. She could have had the

money. She must have known that. She could have had enough never to work again. But she didn't want anything? It was the best possible outcome for me. It also added a layer of clarity. She'd never seen our family the way I had, never loved our daughter the way I did. She couldn't have. Otherwise, she would have never walked away. But I should have learned that lesson already. I knew some people weren't capable of loving their children in a way they needed. I just wished I'd realized Penelope was that kind of person before I'd married her.

"Good. Well, get it done."

"I'll courier a document over for signing."

I hung up and dialed a familiar number. "Gordon, the Globe-Wernicke piece that I looked at a month or so ago. Is it still available?"

"The bookshelf you said needed too much work?"

I ignored him. "Is it still available?"

"I sold it yesterday. I'm due to ship it out this afternoon."

"I'll double whatever they paid. Have it delivered to the house in the next hour."

"Absolutely," Gordon replied.

I'd bought a number of interesting pieces of furniture from Gordon over the years. He had a great eye. Best of all, he was a man of few words.

My next call was to Mike. I wasn't in the mood for his bullshit, and I was going to bring the fight to him.

"Mike, did you see the agreement?" I asked when he answered.

"I've just finished going through it. It's outrageous. I can't believe they've asked for a retention and there's no—"

"Nothing they've asked for is unreasonable. Other than a correction on a tax issue, this document is signable."

Mike started his usual expletive-ridden tirade I'd endured during every other phone call I had with him. I ran through my emails and ignored him. When he quietened, I turned back to the phone.

"It's a waste of our time and your money to argue these points. The cost outweighs the gain."

"I don't care. If they've offered this deal, we can get better—"

"No, Mike. They've offered this deal because they don't want to fight over non-material issues for the next week, only to end up exactly where this draft puts us. If you want to negotiate this contract any further, then you need to do it yourself or get another lawyer."

Silence filled the cab before Mike chuckled, his furious mood seemingly having passed. "You're refusing instructions?"

"If you won't take my advice, there's no point in us continuing like this." For the last year, I'd put up with Mike's demands and outbursts and I was at the end of my tether. I'd been through the terrible twos with Bethany, and it felt as if I were back there with Mike. The difference with a toddler was that they grew out of the phase. I'd accepted Mike's attitude to keep the work coming in, but I was done. I was an excellent lawyer who gave great advice. If he didn't see that, then he could go elsewhere. That might get me fired from the firm, but if I could survive Penelope walking out on our family when Bethany was just a year old, I could survive anything.

"You really think this is as good as we can get?" Mike asked, his voice bristling at the edges.

"I do. And you know it's fair. It's what we both thought you'd end up with."

"I suppose that's true."

I didn't try to convince him. Mike knew I was right.

"Okay. Let's get it done. This way I suppose it means I can still take my wife to dinner tonight."

I hadn't realized he was married. "You can thank me later."

"I'm not sure my wife will thank you. I'm sure she would have preferred the jewelry I'd planned to buy her to make up for missing dinner."

I chuckled. "I'm sure she'll be delighted to meet you again. No doubt it's been awhile. I'm going to get this deal done and then we can enjoy our respective weekends. Have a good one, Mike."

I tucked my phone in my pocket and found the tickets I'd bought and pulled them out. Two tickets to the matinee of a *Sound of Music* singalong this coming Wednesday. I stared at them, not quite recalling why I'd bought them. I'd never made suggestions of activities for Bethany to previous nannies she'd had, but I knew when Autumn saw these tickets, her eyes would light up like I'd just made all her dreams come true. She was unlike any woman I'd ever met. Overenthusiastic about everything. Always smiling. She seemed happy just to wake up in the world. She was also stunningly beautiful. I couldn't remember the last time I'd noticed what a woman wore, but I couldn't ignore her red dress last Saturday night. The dinner at Dexter and Hollie's was also the first time I'd seen her a little unsure of herself, and I'd found myself feeling oddly protective of her. I didn't want her spending the night fending off the competitive flirting between Joshua and Tristan.

I felt an urge to shield her from that.

But I shouldn't have touched her. For a few seconds I'd forgotten myself and given in to the desire I had to feel her —just my leg against hers. The call from Gillian was a stark reminder of why such behavior was foolish. I wasn't going down that path again.

The cab came to a halt outside the house. I settled the fare and took my keys from my pocket.

I could hear the sounds of strangled cats before I'd even opened the front door. I stood in the hallway, trying to make out what they were singing about. Oh yes, even I'd heard the dulcet tones of Dolly Parton, belting out "9 to 5." I just hadn't heard it overlaid by the two worst singers in history.

I opened the door to the main family area. "Good afternoon," I said, a little taken aback by the scene in front of me. Autumn's long dark hair was divided into various bobbles and clips and bows, and her face was blobbed with color. Was that paint?

"Daddy!" Bethany screamed as she ran toward me and jumped into my arms.

My daughter's face looked like she was also in training for clown school, although her hair seemed to have fared better than Autumn's.

"What's going on in here?" I asked, needing an explanation for why my daughter looked like she was starring in a Steven King film.

Thankfully, Autumn turned off the music before I had to ask.

"We're playing makeup parlor, Daddy. Do I look pretty?"

Bethany was the only person in my life I lied to. "You look gorgeous." *Somewhere underneath all that color.*

"And Autumn looks pretty, doesn't she?" Bethany pointed at her nanny, clearly wanting me to agree with her.

The fact was, it was easy to see past the smeared lipstick, comically red cheeks and lopsided hair that made her look like she'd had a fight with a puppy. There was no doubt Autumn was more than pretty.

"You like my eye shadow?" Autumn asked, grinning at me. "Bethany's a natural, isn't she?"

"You both look pretty. Very . . . colorful."

Autumn laughed and took Bethany's hand from around my neck and wiped it of something gloopy. I wasn't sure whether or not it was perfume, but Autumn's scent reminded me of sunshine. Of spring blossom and roses. She winced and dabbed my shirt collar. "I think she got you," she said, pressing her fingertips into my neck. "Sorry."

"It's not a problem." It had been a long time since a woman had touched me that way. Our eyes locked. We were just a few centimeters apart, so close I could feel her body heat, feel myself wrapped in her scent. For just a moment, those promises I'd made to myself years ago and reminded myself of just a few minutes ago in the cab disintegrated. I wanted her.

Autumn looked away first.

"You think your Daddy would like a makeover?" Autumn asked.

Bethany's eyes went wide. "Yes!" Before I had a chance to object, she'd slid out of my arms and was pulling my hand, trying to guide me to the sofa. "You sit here, Daddy. You need lipstick."

"No, Bethany. You're not putting makeup on me." I shrugged out of my jacket and loosened my tie. I needed to breathe. "Men don't wear makeup."

"Not true," Autumn said, shooting me a smug smile. She knew she was setting me up. "And I think it should be encouraged. If women have to go through all this, I don't see why all men shouldn't make more of an effort."

"Aren't you supposed to be on my side?" I asked Autumn as she began to gather and tidy.

"I'm on the side of developing Bethany's motor skills. I'm surprised you're not encouraging her to develop in all areas."

I sighed and took a seat on the sofa. I'd won my battle with Mike this afternoon. I suppose it was only fair I lost this one. "Okay. Maybe a little lipstick won't hurt."

"You'll feel like a million dollars when Miss Bethany's through with you," Autumn said. "It will relax you. You might even start singing along and enjoying show tunes with us."

"Speaking of," I said, reaching for my jacket. "I got you two these for next week."

I handed a ticket to each of them.

"What is it, Daddy?" Bethany asked, looking at the ticket.

"Are you serious?" Autumn asked, a grin the size of Ireland stretching across her face. "Really? You bought this for me? For us?"

Anyone would have thought I'd just bought her a small private island. "It's just theatre tickets."

She held her hand up in a stop gesture. "These are not *just* theatre tickets," she said. "Bethany, we get to go to a musical sing-along. Have you ever heard of anything so wonderful?" She sighed and collapsed onto the velvet footstool as if her legs had given out. "This show came to Portland once but we—" She stared at the ticket, shaking her head. "I can't believe I finally get to go." She fell into silence as she held the ticket in her hand as if it were made of gold. Finally, she glanced up at me. "No one except Hollie has ever done anything so nice for me."

I swallowed, completely taken aback at how delighted—

moved even—she was at the tickets. The idea that she'd never had anyone do anything nice for her troubled me. Why not? Surely she'd had parents. Boyfriends? "Well, I don't want to be accused of neglecting my daughter's education, now do I?" I was rarely the one to lighten the mood, but the situation called for it.

Autumn looked at me, a small smile creeping over her face. "As if you'd neglect anything when it comes to Bethany. You're an amazing father."

A ball of heat burrowed into my chest. There wasn't a better compliment. It was the only thing that meant anything to me in this world.

A knock on the door interrupted my imminent makeover. That would be the Globe-Wernicke—my distraction from my impending divorce. Except that I hadn't thought about it once since I'd gotten home.

SIX

Gabriel

I pushed the door into the Mayfair pub around the corner from Beck's place. It had been his turn to choose the venue for the regular gathering of my brothers in everything but blood. This place felt like an old school gentleman's club with good beer, friendly staff, and comfortable leather armchairs. We didn't need anything else.

"Did you know that the only time you're on time is when we meet on a Sunday night?" Beck said, pushing a pint of Guinness toward me as I took a seat at the round polished table.

Joshua clinked his glass to mine. "You okay, mate? You look weirdly rested."

I nodded. The weekend with Bethany had been just what I needed. In the end, I'd escaped lipstick and managed to go two full days without a call from Mike. It had been blissful. "I'm usually late because I'm at work. I just managed the weekend off."

"You're always so busy. I thought we were in a recession," Joshua said.

"Not for me," Tristan replied.

Joshua, Andrew, Tristan, Beck, and Dexter were as close as it got to family. Dysfunctional, frustrating, and more than a little irritating at times, but unquestionably loyal and one hundred percent in my corner. Being as busy as I was, I would have skipped our weekly drinks if they'd been held during the week, and it felt good to be able to make it. Even if we sat around and talked about nothing, I knew I'd walk away feeling like I had a spine of steel.

"Yeah, and not for me either," I said. "I have a round-the-clock job attending to Mike Green's arsehole, apparently."

"Why is it that when Gabriel says something like that, it's like hearing my dad swear?" Tristan asked.

"I wouldn't wish arsehole-attending on anyone," Joshua said. "But Mike Green? What did you do to deserve that?"

Mike Green was known as the client from hell. And Joshua knew better than most, because if it wasn't for Joshua, I wouldn't be working with Mike. "Yeah, I must remember to thank you for introducing him to me," I said.

"You have to get rid of him. Walk away," Joshua said. "I've never been so happy to lose a client."

"Easy for you to say. If I wasn't doing three deals for Mike, I wouldn't have any work. Law has been hit hard in this recession. Especially M&A."

Tristan mumbled something in Dexter's ear and Dexter just shook his head.

"Ever thought about retiring?" Beck asked.

"I'm thirty-three. You want me to take up golf and bowls?" I took a sip on my pint. As if I was just going to give up my career. Law was long hours, that was just how it was. And it wasn't like Beck left the office at five thirty every day.

"No, but you could give up law," Tristan said.

"I like my job. It's Mike Green I don't like."

"At least you have a reliable nanny for Bethany now though, right?" Dexter said, quite obviously changing the subject.

"Oh yes, how is *Hot Autumn*?" Tristan asked. "That red dress on her the other night looked incredible."

I tried not to crack my jaw as I clenched my teeth. *Tristan had better keep well away from Autumn.* "Bethany likes her a great deal, and it's nice not to have to worry about finding someone." I tried to keep my tone even, but I was sure it sounded like I wanted to wipe that lecherous look from his face. With a hammer.

"You seem tense when I mention her, mate. Protective. Has anything happened between the two of you?" Tristan said. "Have I missed something?"

"No," I barked.

"If you even look in her direction, I'm going to have to kill you," Dexter said.

I glanced up, ready to reassure Dexter that no lines had been crossed. But he was addressing Tristan, not me.

"So do me a favor," Dexter continued. "Just don't ever mention her again. And don't even think about asking her out."

It wasn't as if I was about to ask her out, but I wondered if she was off limits to me too. Dexter probably thought I was so responsible, I'd never even consider making a move on Bethany's nanny. Or that my manhood had shriveled up and fallen off. But it hadn't and . . . there was something about Autumn. Something compelling that drew me to her. Something that had me buying tickets to musicals to make her happy. Something making me sit next to her at dinner parties. Autumn just had me thinking about possibilities far more than I'd done before. Far more than I should be.

"Fucking hell, what is the matter with everyone?" Tristan asked. "I was talking about a hot woman that I'm sure all of us around this table would happily bang. Why am I in the firing line?"

"Why do you make every relationship between a man and a woman about sex, Tristan?" I asked. "It's like you never grew up past fifteen."

Tristan looked as if I'd slapped him. I instantly felt bad.

"Sorry," I said. "I got draft divorce papers by email this morning."

The obligatory *I'm sorrys* followed and I nodded as if their condolences helped. It was just good to be with people who knew me.

"What has she asked for?" Dexter asked. "Can you say yes to it to get it over with?"

"Nothing," I replied. "She wants nothing—not her daughter, not her husband, and not any of his money." That's what I'd assumed when she'd first gone. That she'd been a gold-digger all along. I'd been stupid enough to be in love and hadn't bothered to ask for a postnuptial agreement to protect what I'd inherited from my father. But when she didn't ask for anything during the legal separation, I'd started to wonder why she'd left. I'd never come up with an answer.

It was like Bethany and I had been some huge mistake she'd rather just pretend never happened.

Erasing me from her past was one thing, but her daughter? Her own flesh and blood? Penelope was abominable.

"You know what I think?" Joshua said, his voice brightening. "It's about bloody time. It's not like you'd take her back anyway, is it?"

"Of course not." That ship had sailed the moment she'd walked out without discussion or explanation. And anyway, she wasn't about to come back. She hadn't been in contact other than through her solicitor since she left. Each special occasion after she'd abandoned her daughter, I braced myself for a phone call, a letter, even a surprise appearance. But every birthday, Christmas, and milestone passed in silence. She'd disappeared. And now she was just a ghost. Not even a memory for Bethany.

"Have you met Gabriel?" Andrew asked. "He's hardly the guy dishing out second chances to anyone who turns up on his doorstep."

"So, it's good," Joshua continued. "This way, you can move on."

"I've moved on already. What choice did I have?"

"You've put one foot in front of the other," Joshua said. "That's not moving on. That's surviving."

Joshua liked to think he gave tough love—so he called it. I called it bullshit. "Whatever, Joshua."

"I'm saying this for your own good," Joshua said.

"So, what in your learned opinion would constitute moving on as opposed to surviving?" I asked.

"I'm saying you need to get out and fuck another woman."

I'd been given this talk by the guys before. Hollie had tried to set me up with a girl she'd met at a photoshoot. People didn't understand—I wasn't going to date. Maybe not ever but certainly not until Bethany was grown. I wouldn't subject her to it. I clearly didn't have good judgement when it came to choosing a woman. I'd gotten Penelope so wrong. Even when she left, it wasn't as if I suddenly understood who she was and why things hadn't worked out. Even three years later, she had the ability to surprise me by not asking for anything from me financially.

I didn't like surprises. And I wouldn't risk more. I'd had enough to last a lifetime.

"Thanks for the advice, Joshua."

"He's got a point," Dexter said.

Autumn had been the only woman I'd even thought about since Penelope. I didn't know what it was, but something about her drew me in. She was beautiful—that went without saying. She was bright and sunny and saw life how I'd like to see it—all birdsong and fresh mountain air. But there was more to her than that. Her reaction to those theatre tickets had been proof. It was as if she was trying to out-sing some dark melody forever playing in the background of her life.

"Gabriel's a lost cause," Tristan said. "But Autumn shouldn't be. I don't see why I can't have her number."

"You haven't got a chance, mate," Dexter said.

I couldn't have put it better myself.

"How the hell would you know?" Tristan asked.

"Because when Hollie told her not to go near you, she burst out laughing and said you weren't her type."

Warmth settled in my gut. And I desperately wanted to know what Autumn had said when Hollie had warned her off me.

"Bullshit," Tristan spat. "She was just covering it up well."

Something told me Dexter wasn't lying. Tristan wasn't Autumn's type.

But I was beginning to wonder whether I was.

SEVEN

Gabriel

All the signs were there—the whiny voice, the hands balled into fists, and the clock about to strike seven thirty. We were about to enter Planet Meltdown.

"Where is he, Daddy?"

"I don't know, darling. What about Audrey?" I asked, holding up a faded grey donkey who had seen better days.

"I want Bear Bear," Bethany said, talking about the grotty-looking bear Joshua had bought her when she was born that she wouldn't be without.

I tossed Audrey aside and pulled out everything and everyone from her soft toy box. Again. I'd done it three times, but I was grasping at straws. "I know, but Bear Bear's not here. Where did you last have him?"

"He was here before," she said, peering under her bed.

I knew I shouldn't call Autumn. She was having a well-deserved day off, and she'd been talking all week about doing some kind of walking tour. I didn't want to interrupt.

But shouldn't it be over by now? It was late. And I didn't want to have to deal with Bethany losing it.

"Let me check the bathroom again." I padded out into the corridor and into Bethany's bathroom. No sign of Bear Bear. "Did you go up to Autumn's room with him?" I called out. Would it be bad to go up there and check? I didn't want to invade her privacy. I hadn't been into her room since she arrived. But I was slightly curious to see how she'd arranged it. Did she have photographs up or keepsakes by the bed?

"No," Bethany said from behind me.

I spun around and pulled my phone from my pocket. I was going to have to call her.

She answered on the third ring. "Hi," she shouted over the background noise. Where was she? It sounded like a football match.

"I'm looking for Bear Bear," I said. "Any idea where he might be?"

"I can't hear you," she shouted.

"Bear Bear," I said, raising my voice. "Do you know where he is?"

"Autumn," a man in the background called. "I don't mind," she called back. She hadn't said anything about meeting a man. Did she have a date?

"Where are you?" I asked.

The sounds became more muffled. "I just came outside. Some of us from the tour are just having some drinks. Such a cute little pub in Whitechapel called The White Hart."

Was there such a thing as a cute pub in Whitechapel?

She was having drinks with friends. That was to be expected, wasn't it? It was good for her.

"Well, I'm sorry to interrupt. We're looking for Bear Bear."

"Oh, yes. Last place I saw him was in the playhouse. He needed a nap apparently."

I headed toward Bethany's castle-shaped playhouse and dove inside. There Bear Bear was, tucked up as cozy as a bear could be. I unceremoniously pulled him from his bed.

"Found him," I said.

"Bear Bear!" Bethany called.

"Thanks," I said as the noise on the other end of the phone increased.

"Glad you've got him," she said. She was interrupted by the sound of breaking glass. A woman's scream pierced the line.

"You okay?"

The phone went dead. Bloody hell. I called back but it rang out.

"I'm tired, Daddy."

I followed as Bethany padded across the room and slid under the duvet. I pressed a kiss onto Bear Bear's forehead. "Goodnight," I said as I kissed Bethany's cheek, wondering whether Autumn was about to call me back.

I dimmed Bethany's bedroom light and headed out. Before I got to the top of the stairs, I hit the call button again.

Still no answer.

I tried to think back to just before the line went dead. It hadn't been her screaming, had it?

I scrolled through the phone and called Joshua. I didn't want to call Dexter because it was probably fine, and I didn't want Hollie to worry. Plus Joshua was closer.

"How are you?" he answered.

"Can you come over?" I asked.

"Now? Tristan's here. We just ordered pizza."

"Yes, now. Please hurry." I needed someone to watch Bethany. Autumn had grown up in the middle of nowhere from what I'd gleaned. She was young and wasn't used to a big city. And she sure as hell didn't know Whitechapel. If she was caught up in the middle of a bar fight—if it had been her screaming? Dexter would never forgive me if I didn't go and find her.

I SCANNED the heads of the crowd of people in the pub. There was a circle of people in the corner in motorcycle leather. I couldn't imagine they'd been on a walking tour. Then there was a couple of old guys in the window who looked like they were in the wrong pub, and beside them a crowd of cool kids who were no doubt vegans.

"Have you tried calling her again?" Joshua asked.

"Yes. She's not picked up since the scream," I replied, craning to see if I could spot her.

"And it was definitely her you heard scream?"

"Does it matter? If she's in a situation where there's screaming involved, there's a problem. Can you imagine if Dexter found out that she was in some pub where there was screaming, and I just left her there?"

Joshua didn't reply. When I looked around, he was ordering drinks.

"What are you doing?"

"If I'm going to be your wingman, I need a drink."

"My wingman? What are you talking about? We're here to make sure Autumn's okay."

"Right," Joshua answered, handing me a pint of Guinness. "Couldn't possibly be that you have a crush on Hot

Autumn, and you've lost your bollocks and won't ask her out on a date, so you're following her around."

I put my beer back on the bar. "You're being ridiculous. She doesn't know London. She grew up in the middle of nowhere, never been to a big city before. She could be in trouble."

Joshua didn't look convinced. "If you say so."

I didn't have time to argue with him.

"Gabriel?"

I snapped my head around to find Autumn looking quite bewildered. "Thank God. Are you okay?" I asked.

The corners of her mouth lifted slightly, offsetting the slight frown she wore. "I'm fine. What are you doing here?" Her gaze flitted to Joshua, who raised his pint at her.

"I heard a scream and a crash, and I was concerned," I said, feeling a little foolish now I'd found her and she was patently fine. "I couldn't get hold of you and I thought something might have happened."

"Where's Bethany?"

"Tristan's babysitting. You seem fine though?"

She glanced back at a table of people over on the other side of the bar. "Yeah, fine. Someone dropped their drink. That's all. Come and join us."

I was an idiot. I shouldn't be here. I'd chased across town to check on a grown woman who was completely able to look after herself. I glanced over at Joshua, who I expected to be wearing an I-told-you-so expression, but he was too busy talking to the barmaid.

"No, thank you. We're going to go. Just didn't want you to be in any trouble. You've not been in London long and Whitechapel isn't the most . . . Well, it's not Mayfair."

She rolled her lips together as if she was editing what

she was going to say next. "It's very sweet of you to check up on me."

I shrugged. "I thought you were in trouble. That's all. You're a good nanny . . . and Bethany likes you."

Autumn laughed. "Oh yes, right. Wouldn't want to lose a good nanny."

"That came out wrong." I couldn't find the right words. I'd heard the strange voice then the scream—had I put two and two together and come out with nineteen? It would seem like it, but better to be safe than sorry. Right? I tried to think whether I would have done the same for any of the other nannies we'd had over the years.

I doubt I would have noticed a man's voice in the background of any of the phone calls I'd had with them. Or a scream. Or breaking glass. I would have been entirely focused on Bethany and getting her to bed.

But Autumn wasn't like the other nannies we'd had before.

Maybe Joshua hadn't been so far off.

"Well, we should go," I said. "As you're fine." I tried to catch Joshua's eye, but he was too busy flirting.

"You could buy me a drink," Autumn suggested.

I looked at her, making sure I'd heard her right. It was like she was daring me to step over some unspoken line in the sand. She held my gaze as if she were willing me to set my foot down.

No. I wasn't here to have drinks. Flirt. Touch. I shouldn't be here at all.

"We're leaving. Now it's clear there's nothing wrong. There's no reason to stay."

"Are you sure?" Autumn asked.

I nodded. "Joshua," I called out. "We're leaving."

What had I been thinking coming here? Autumn was a

grown woman. I had no business running after her in the middle of the night and leaving my daughter. I needed to remember the promises I'd made to myself to stay away from women. My life and my daughter didn't need complication, disappointment, and disruption.

EIGHT

Autumn

As I wrestled with Bethany's pink and blue swim cap, I had a pang of homesickness. It didn't happen very often, but the summers I'd spent lifeguarding back in Oregon had been fun—perhaps the only fun bit of life in Oregon. I was bummed I wasn't going to be in the water today. Bethany's swimming class didn't have parents and caregivers in the water with the students once they'd reached four.

An image of Gabriel in swim trunks flashed into my brain. Perhaps I should suggest both of us take Bethany swimming some time.

Neither of us had brought up the way he came after me last weekend. He'd been in bed when I'd gotten home that night, and I'd barely seen him this week. When we crossed paths in the kitchen after Bethany was asleep, he'd grunted at me before heading straight to his locked door, still without giving me any clues to what he was doing in there.

I had a bad case of Gabriel Chase Whiplash. One minute he was caring and intimate and a little flirtatious.

The next he was all cold and haughty and brick walls. I wasn't sure which one was the real him. But I bet they'd both look great in a swimming pool.

"There," I said, tucking the last of Bethany's hair up into the cap. Her hair was going to look like she'd been back combing like an extra in *Hairspray,* but we'd cross that bridge when we came to it.

"You're going to watch me?" Bethany asked, crossing her hands over her chest and hopping from foot to foot.

"Of course. Wouldn't miss it, and I'm going to take lots of photos for your daddy." I gathered up Bethany's things, put them in a locker, and then grabbed my bag. "You ready?"

She shivered and then grinned. "Yup."

I cloaked her towel around her shoulders, took her hand and we made our way out to the seated area where the parents and nannies stayed to watch. I glanced around, hoping that this lesson there would be a lifeguard on duty.

"You need a drink?" I asked, as I dumped my bag on a seat nearest the steps.

"No thank you. I don't want to wee wee in the pool."

"If you're thirsty, you should have a drink. You can just ask your teacher to excuse you if you need to wee wee."

"I'm not." She shook her head, and I made a mental note to encourage her to drink in the lead-up to arriving to her next lesson. I didn't want her dehydrated. It was only a forty-minute lesson, but she needed to be alert the entire time. "I really want to dive from the edge again. You'll take a picture of me jumping in for Daddy?"

"I will, Bethany, but I want you to listen to your teacher and only dive when she tells you to."

She nodded excitedly and I smiled, glancing around for that lifeguard I kinda knew wasn't going to arrive. The lesson only had ten children and two instructors, but it niggled me there wasn't someone outside the water who was looking over everything.

The children filed out one after another and lined up at the edge of the pool. It was such a shame Gabriel wasn't here. He'd be so proud of Bethany. She was confident and sensible and when she dipped to whisper to the girl who was standing next to her, I knew she was encouraging her. She was a good kid. Well behaved. Kind. And she loved her daddy.

The same as last week, the class started with some basic safety reminders similar to the kids' lessons back in Oregon, and then just like last week, the instructor in the swimsuit slipped into the pool, while the other kept her red shorts on and stayed poolside.

Bethany glanced over at me as the kids at the far end of the line began to jump into the pool from standing up. I nodded, trying to be encouraging. I knew she'd prefer to try a sitting dive, but she'd get a chance later on.

She jumped in and I got the perfect, mid-air shot that Gabriel would love. He'd told me a couple of times that the next best thing to being with Bethany himself was getting the pictures I took. And while being a nanny wasn't exactly what I'd had in mind for a job, getting feedback like that— helping a father enjoy his child—was far more rewarding than I expected. I was lucky to know Bethany and Gabriel. Lucky to get to spend time with them both. Being paid was a bonus.

My phone buzzed and I glanced down to see a message from Hollie. I'd pick it up later. I wanted to focus on Bethany and her lesson and . . . I just felt better knowing I had my eye on her at all times.

They started the lesson having each student take turns

collecting a colored band from the bottom of the pool. The water came up to their chests, so they were never out of their depth, but it was a good exercise for water confidence from what I could tell. The kids were well-behaved and seemed to be enjoying themselves, taking huge breaths before they sank below the surface. Next was five-meter swimming. When it was Bethany's turn, she swam like a champ, albeit a champ with a haphazard doggie paddle. As soon as she touched the side, she looked over at me, checking I had seen her. I grinned and gave her a thumbs-up.

The boy who was up next swam half of the five meters underwater and almost reached the side before changing course and swimming into Bethany. He began pulling at her in a slightly panicky way. I was already on my feet when the instructor in the pool lifted the boy up and out of the water, sitting him on the side.

I exhaled and sat back down. Jesus, I wished I was just in there with her. I might talk to Gabriel about taking her swimming at weekends or something. The sooner she swam strongly, the better.

Bethany waited patiently until the last fifteen minutes of the session, which was when they started the sitting dives. She'd been so excited last time when she'd managed to go headfirst into the pool that she'd been talking about doing it again all week. Only a few kids had managed it last time. Some had just refused and sat and watched. Others had tried but ended up inelegantly shuffling into the water feet first.

"Hands either side of your ears and lay one hand over the other." The instructor in red shorts on the side of the pool wandered from one end of the row of ten children to the other.

The first child got the go-ahead to dive, and I kept my eye on Bethany, who would be one of the last to go. She looked like she was chatting to herself and kept positioning her arms and then relaxing them, practicing her form. She was so darn cute. She did it again and this time, her body started to move forward, almost as if she was going to go into the water, but she shifted and brought her arms down.

Sit back, I wanted to shout. *Be patient and wait your turn.*

My eyes flitted to the other end of the line-up of four-year-olds sitting on the side, and another child plopped into the pool, taking the attention of both the instructor in the pool and Miss Red Shorts on the side. The instructor in the pool helped the child who had just dived out of the pool while the instructor on the side coached the one about to enter the water.

Bethany brought her arms up again into position and leaned forward, but this time she'd gone too far. I could see the moment her balance failed her. She glanced at me as I stood up, horror splashed across her face—not because she was in danger, but because she knew she was about to go into the pool when it wasn't her turn. She tried to regain her balance, turning awkwardly, but instead of regaining her feet, she slipped into the water, hitting her head on the side with an almighty *clunk* on the way in.

Time slowed and it felt as if everything had been covered in molasses. I dived into the water from the other side of the pool and felt her tiny body in my arms before she hit the bottom.

I was vaguely aware of shrieking as I broke the surface.

"Miss Lumen, what do you think—"

I ignored everything but Bethany, lying her on the edge of the pool. She was unconscious. The blow to the head had knocked her out. I leapt out and rearranged her. People came toward us—I didn't know if it was children or the instructors—and I was vaguely aware of someone screaming.

"Call an ambulance," I yelled.

Bethany's chest seemed to rise and fall but I put my hand on her belly to make sure. She was breathing, thank God, and I moved her onto her side, pulling her head back so she didn't swallow her tongue just like I'd been taught.

"Why isn't she moving?" I heard a child ask.

"Has someone called a goddamned ambulance?" I screamed.

NINE

Gabriel

I nearly tore off the sliding door at the entry to the hospital as it seemed to take an interminable time to open. Finally, I raced up the corridor toward pediatric accident and emergency. I'd been here once before when Bethany had fallen off the bed when she was four months old; I hadn't realized she had learned to roll over, and while I'd grabbed a new nappy she went right over the side. I'd had the same bitter taste of bile in my mouth then as I did now. The same panic running through my veins. Except this time was worse. I hadn't been with her. I couldn't hold her. I couldn't feel her warmth.

"Gabriel Chase. My daughter's been brought in by ambulance," I said to the receptionist who seemed to be on another call and not in any hurry to do anything.

"Just take a seat, and I'll be with you in a moment," she said in a slow, drawn-out reply.

"I will not take a seat," I bellowed. "I want to see my daughter."

"Gabriel," someone called from the other side of the room.

It was Autumn. The adrenaline chasing around my body pulled me toward her, noting how very sad, serious, and bedraggled she looked.

Please don't have bad news.

Please let Bethany be okay.

I'll do anything. Give up everything.

Was it too late to strike a bargain with God?

"How is she? Where is she?" I said, searching her forlorn face for clues.

She pulled at my arm and we raced around the linoleum corridor, past a nurses' station. Autumn ushered me through a curtain.

There sat Bethany, in a hospital gown but fully conscious and smiling, a nurse by her side taking her temperature.

"Daddy," she said, beaming at me. "You're here. Not at work."

Relief erupted in my veins at the sight of my beautiful daughter. Nothing was better than this, I said to myself. Being with Bethany was everything I needed. It was why I put up with work, why I vowed not to date. Why I breathed in and out. It was all about this little one with the gangly legs and shiny curls.

"They say she's fine," Autumn said from beside me.

"I want to speak to a doctor," I muttered before stepping toward the bed and lightly pressing my lips to Bethany's forehead. She looked okay, but I had to push down the urge to scoop her up and hold her as close as possible.

"How are you feeling, my darling?"

"Do you have snacks?" she asked.

Well, that was a good sign.

"She's fine, Mr. Chase. Just a bump to the head is all," the nurse said cheerily. "We're going to keep her for a few hours just for observation."

"I want to speak to the doctor."

"They'll be in when they're free." The nurse smiled, filled in something on a chart, and then left. Bethany smiled, glanced at Autumn, and held out her hand for something.

Autumn glanced at me. "I gave her the iPad. The doctor said it was fine. I know she's not supposed—"

"It's okay," I replied.

Autumn handed Bethany the tablet and she set about doing whatever she did on it, which always seemed to involve feeding cartoon food to cartoon dogs.

"What happened?" I said, taking a seat next to Autumn, trying to show her and myself that I was fine. Calm. Relaxed.

"They were all lined up, sitting at the edge of the pool, ready to do sitting dives—"

"I fell in, Daddy," Bethany said, looking up from the tablet.

"She tried to stop herself from falling and ended up turning and banging her head on the side," Autumn explained. "Then she went down."

The bile in my stomach rose again. I should have been there. "No more swimming lessons for you," I said. I might even look into home schooling. I needed to keep her safe.

Bethany looked up from the tablet. "I like swimming," she replied, frowning.

Autumn's phone went off beside us and she opened up a message. "It's from Hollie," she replied. "She's nearly here. She's bringing me some clothes."

I turned to look at Autumn properly and noticed her hair plastered to her head. "Are you . . . wet?"

She shrugged. "From the pool."

"I thought you didn't get in the pool with her?" I asked.

She shook her head. "I don't usually. I saw what was happening. Bethany was practicing her diving position but was getting closer to the edge. The instructors were preoccupied with the student diving." Her eyes started to fill with tears and then she cleared her throat. "She should have swimming lessons. It's important for her safety. But I don't want to take her back there."

I glanced from Autumn to Bethany, but Bethany was preoccupied by her virtual dogs. She wasn't taking any notice of either of us. I took a closer look at Autumn. It wasn't just her hair that was wet. Her clothes were soaking. "You went in after her."

She nodded. "I knew I could get to her first."

"And thank goodness she did," a woman said from behind us as someone opened the curtain. "I'm Doctor Todd," she said and stepped into bay. "The fact that Bethany was breathing when she was pulled out of the water means she's going to be just fine. We need to keep an eye on her, but you can take her home soon. She's had none of the indicators of severe concussion other than her being passed out for a minute or so. She was conscious by the time the ambulance team arrived." The doctor glanced at Bethany and then focused on me. "You don't need to worry."

"Then humor me and tell me what makes you say that."

"She didn't inhale any water. Didn't require resuscitation. She's had no bleeding or fluid leaking from her mouth or ears. She hasn't been sick and doesn't feel sick. She's alert. Lucid. No headache. No bruising. She has none of the symptoms of a severe concussion apart from a lump on her head and a brief moment of unconsciousness. But as I said, we'll keep her under observation for the next few hours and then you can take her home."

"Please may I have snacks?" Bethany asked.

"I'll get someone to bring you something," the doctor said.

"She can eat and drink as normal?" I asked.

"Absolutely. Like I said, if she'd inhaled the water when she went into the pool, it might be a different story." The doctor swept out and I turned to Autumn.

"You saved her," I said.

"I just knew I could get to her first."

This woman beside me wasn't just beautiful. And kind. And funny. She'd saved my daughter. I would never be as grateful to anyone else, for anything else, for as long as I lived. "You saved her," I said again. And by saving Bethany, she'd saved me.

TEN

Autumn

I tried to decide between the racing car and the dog. It was a tough decision. Gabriel had already picked out the top hat, which was just perfect for the surly British gentleman he was. I liked the dog and all, but it would have definitely been Hollie's first choice. I needed something new. "Okay, I'm going for the car," I said.

"Fine," Gabriel said from where he was sitting opposite from me. He was studiously tidying his piles of money, which he'd lined up in front of him on the sturdy oak dining table in the kitchen. "At least you didn't take long to make that decision," he grumbled.

I laughed. I wasn't used to sarcasm from Gabriel. "Oh look, the Strand," I said, spotting the familiar name on the board. "That's where you work, right?"

"Near there, yes."

"I have to try to buy it. Then you can work for me and I'll reduce your working hours." I grinned at him and he just shook his head like I was the most irritating person he knew.

I was going to win him over and relax him if it killed me, and then I was going to talk to him about Bethany.

"Is there a Smithfield?" People referred to the area where Gabriel lived as lots of different areas. Smithfield. Farringdon. Clerkenwell. But Gabriel always used Smithfield, so now I did too.

"No. We're not cool enough over this side of town."

"It's super cool around here," I replied. "Especially when we're actually allowed out," I said, dropping a hint as subtle as a knee in the balls.

"Do we have to do this?" he asked, ignoring my hint the size of Montana. "I hate Monopoly."

"Yes, we absolutely have to do this." It wasn't my favorite game, but I needed common ground and a way of stopping Gabriel from just stalking off into his private, locked lair, which he had been doing more than usual in the last few days. Anyway, I was used to the New Jersey version of the game. It would be kinda fun to play with the London street names. "Think of it as you giving me a tour around your city."

"There are plenty of tour buses that have stops a hundred meters away. You could see the real thing."

I sighed. "It's warmer to do it like this."

Gabriel hadn't been himself since Bethany's accident. He'd insisted on working from home and she and I hadn't been allowed to leave the house so Gabriel could check on her regularly. It had been five days. Work seemed to be stressing him out and I knew he'd cancelled drinks with Dexter and his other friends tonight. Enough was enough. I was going to talk to him about getting things back to normal. But I had to get him in the room long enough to be able to bring it up. If Bethany wasn't around, as soon as I walked into a room, he walked out. Mainly through that locked door to who-the-hell-knew. Tonight I'd insisted on taking him on in a game of Monopoly, and somewhere during the game I was going to tell him he needed to back off. Go back to business as usual or Bethany was going to become a timid little mouse. I also wanted to ask him why he was avoiding me, but that might take a bottle of wine and a win at Monopoly for me to get the courage up. Did he blame me for what had happened? I wouldn't hold it against him if he did. I was so angry at myself for continuing to take her to lessons despite not being one hundred percent happy with the safety of the classes. I should have said something.

"Ladies first," he said, nodding toward the dice.

"I vote for equality. Highest throw of the dice goes first."

"Highest number on any one die or highest number when the results of the two dice are added together?" he asked.

"Wow," I said, narrowing my eyes and looking at him like he was a fossil in a museum. "Do you ever stop being a lawyer?"

I swear the side of his mouth curved up a fraction. "Details are important."

I grabbed the dice and tossed them onto the board. They both came up as sixes. I shrugged. "Sometimes they are. And sometimes they're not."

He chuckled and threw the dice after me. He got a three and a five.

"And in this instance, they weren't," I said, feeling rather smug.

When he didn't say anything, I looked up to find him gazing at me in that intense way he had for what felt like the first time since the accident. "You know you're asking for trouble," he said, his voice so low the timbre reverberated in my knees. "I'm going to have to beat you now."

It felt like a challenge. A frisson of excitement shot up my spine. "You don't stand a chance."

He shook his head and I threw the dice again.

I started counting his smiles—in my tally a little flicker at the corner of those lips counted—and I swore when we got to six, I was going to pluck up the courage to say something. It was my lucky number of the night, after all.

"Kings Cross station," I said. "I'll buy it because it's right by my favorite station, St. Pancreas."

He smiled. "What are you going to pay for it with? A kidney?"

He seemed pretty happy with himself, but I didn't get the joke. "What did I say?"

"I'm being cruel by laughing. It's kind of cute."

Gabriel was handsome-grumpy after three nights without sleep. I could testify to that because he'd worked overnight for three nights in a row the week before Bethany's accident. But when he smiled? He was like a goddamned movie star. How was this man a lawyer? He should be plastered on a billion teenage girls' bedroom walls. Hell, I wasn't past sneaking a snap on my camera phone and pinning it up over my bed.

"As much as I kinda like that you find me cute, can you clue me in on the joke?"

He held my gaze like he was deciding whether or not to say something. Was he going to deny he called me cute? Tell me he didn't mean it like *that*. Or maybe he was deciding whether he should kiss me. I'd vote for C.

"You added an e," he said finally.

"I did what now?"

"Pancras. Two syllables. Not pancreas, like the organ."

I started to laugh. "Oh my God, I had no idea." I shrugged. "And I always so liked that it was named after a body part. But it was worth making a fool of myself to see you smile."

He stared at me for one second, then two. "You couldn't be a fool if you tried." His tone had turned from teasing to low and serious. "You saved my daughter's life." He glanced down at the board and mumbled to himself.

I reached over and grabbed his wrist. "She's fine, you know."

"If you hadn't been there," he said, squeezing his eyes shut for a second before he reopened them. "If you hadn't been watching like you were."

"But I was, Gabriel. You can't torture yourself with what ifs."

"She's never going swimming again," he said with a resolute shake of his head.

"You know that's not the right decision to make. Give it some time, but she needs to go back in the water."

"I don't want anything happening to her again. And the easiest way to ensure that happens is not to let her swim."

"You're a clever man, Gabriel, and we both know that's bullshit. She'll be safer as a strong and confident swimmer."

He kinda growled at me. At least he didn't bite.

"You can't wrap her in cotton wool all the time," I continued. "You have to let her be a four-year-old. You don't want to keep her home like there's something wrong with her when quite the opposite is true."

"I should have been there," he said.

"And that's another thing. You need to go back to work."

"What are you talking about? I *have* been working."

"But you need to go back to the office. One day she'll leave home and go off to college and if she's not developed her independence by then, what will you do?"

"Easy," he said, as if I'd been peppering him with trivia

questions and just picked his specialty. "Never let her go to university."

I laughed. "You're completely ridiculous."

He sat back against the chair and regarded me as if he were examining a rare object. "I can't remember ever being called ridiculous before."

My heartbeat thundered and a siren of panic filled my ears. I'd taken it too far. I'd offended him. "Oh God," I said, covering my mouth with my hand. "I'm sorry, I just meant—"

He smiled, almost as if he had been embarrassed to admit it. "I didn't say it was a bad thing."

I rolled my eyes. "I don't want to get myself fired here but I'm telling you, I didn't mean it as a compliment."

He shrugged. "Maybe I took it as one. Well, not that I'm ridiculous—that's just patently not true. But the fact that you'd call me so. I appreciate it."

"You like people calling you names?"

"Not people. You. And not names—just the truth."

I didn't know what to say. The way he said it suggested that I was . . . special somehow. "You like me telling you the truth?"

He nodded, looking pained by the confession.

"I'm sorry she got into the accident, Gabriel. I should have told you sooner that I didn't like the setup there."

"It's not your fault. You weren't in charge. And if you hadn't been there—if you hadn't gone in after her . . ." He closed his eyes and inhaled sharply as if he were trying to bear the pain of even the thought that something worse would have happened.

"They should have had a lifeguard on duty—someone who wasn't involved with the class who was just watching over everything."

"I guess you fulfilled that role."

"I'm just pleased I got to her. And she's fine." I smoothed my hand over his, trying to reassure him. "Will you let me take her swimming? Just the two of us. I can teach her. She'll have my complete attention."

He glanced at my hand over his. I was making him feel uncomfortable. When I pulled my hand away, he said, "No." Then slid his fingers between mine. A wave of release pushed through my body and I exhaled.

This.

This was what I'd needed from him.

I'd needed him to touch me.

"I know I'm being overprotective," he said, his thumb stroking the palm of my hand, setting off tiny firecrackers in my underwear. "I just worry."

"I know," I said, half surprised anything came out when I'd tried to speak. I'd expected his touch to take my words away.

We sat in silence for long moments, me getting pulled closer to him with every rhythmic stroke of his thumb. "I shouldn't be touching you."

"I know," I replied.

"We shouldn't be holding hands," he said.

I nodded. "I don't want you to stop."

"I know," he said with such confidence that if I'd been on my feet, my knees would have disintegrated and I would have fallen. "I've tried to stay away."

My heartbeat rammed on my ribcage like a freight train. He'd wanted me?

With this confession, he slid his hand from mine and shoved his fingers through his hair. "It's not right. For a million different reasons."

Nothing he was saying wasn't true. He was one of

Dexter's oldest friends and my employer. He was a father and a serious lawyer, as Hollie loved to remind me. I was . . . just starting out.

But I wanted him.

And now he'd touched me, I knew I couldn't even pretend I didn't.

He pushed his chair out from under the table and stood. Was he leaving? Was he about to disappear behind that locked door?

I stood up too, trying to find the words to ask him to stay. To tell him all the reasons why he shouldn't kiss me would be there tomorrow, but for tonight we could just put them to one side. We could forget about everything for one kiss.

"I should go," he said.

Of course, he was going to pull down the shutters and retreat into his bat cave. What could I say to make him stay? Before I thought of the words, he stalked around the table, took my head in his hands, and pressed his lips to mine. My entire body buzzed as if his kiss conveyed life-giving energy, hot and urgent. I slid my hands up his arms and finally got to feel the hardness of his muscles that I'd seen moving under his dress shirts and semi-exposed by his tees. His skin was as hot as lava and the low moans he was making as he kissed me made every part of me vibrate. I wasn't sure I wouldn't climax right there from just a kiss.

I pushed a little on his chest, concerned I was about to be overwhelmed.

"You want me to stop?" he asked.

"You need to give me a minute," I said, trying to float back down to earth, but it was difficult when I was so close to him and my lips still hummed with the feel of him. "I never know what I'm going to get with you. One minute you're telling me how it's a terrible idea to be near me and then you're kissing me."

"I'm capricious." It was a statement rather than a question.

"You are. But you can't kiss me like that and change your mind. I'm resilient but not unbreakable. Don't shut me out again."

He nodded and cupped my face in his hands. "I'm sorry. I won't do it again." His gaze was determined and focused and fixed on me, and I believed him.

ELEVEN

Gabriel

As soon as I'd touched her, I knew I was sunk.

For days now, I'd had to rehearse all the reasons I shouldn't make her mine over and over in my head, like a mantra. Hoping that somehow, they would sink in and neutralize the urge I had to press my hands, my lips, my body against hers.

But my mantra was silent now. I couldn't focus on anything but her. The feel of her, soft and precious under my fingers. Her scent, warm and inviting. Her large brown eyes, looking at me as if I had all the answers.

My need for her had developed over the months like fine wine, and all the fantasies I'd had of her funneled into this one moment.

She tasted just as sweet as I imagined. I groaned as I pulled my mouth away, wanting to revel in the feel of her lips against mine for days.

"Gabriel," she whispered, smoothing her hand up my chest.

How I'd longed for her touch. Even my name sounded better on her lips than from the mouth of any other. I pulled her closer to me, not ready to let go yet, enjoying the way she molded to me.

I pushed my knee between her legs and she gasped as if I'd lit her on fire.

"Gabriel," she said again, more urgently this time.

I brushed her chin with my thumb and then kissed her again, my dick growing harder by the second. I felt like a kid, unable to shift my focus and keep myself under control. I'd wanted her for so long. Since she moved in a month ago. Since I first laid eyes on her over a year ago. It felt like forever. I'd never just looked at a woman and had an urgent need to *touch* before Autumn. It was as if she existed on a slightly different plain to anyone else, or she'd cast some kind of spell over me.

She wrapped her hand around my neck and twisted her hips slightly, which pushed her against my leg. She moaned, soft and throaty.

This couldn't happen. I couldn't let this woman hump my thigh when I knew I could make her come much harder with my fingers, my tongue, my cock.

She pulled back from our kiss. "Oh God," she said. "I'm dry humping your leg." She laughed at herself, never afraid to be exactly who she was.

Didn't she realize? Everything she did was utterly intoxicating. If only she hadn't been wearing jeans. I wanted her wet pussy streaking the denim on my legs.

I stroked up her back. "Are you wet, Autumn?"

It was the first time I'd ever seen her shocked, but I was done holding back.

"Between your legs." I dipped my hand between her thighs. "Underneath your jeans. Tell me."

She nodded.

I wasn't sure whether or not it was lust or relief that chased through me. Relief that she wanted me. That this was happening. Or perhaps the reprieve of my red, raw hands now I'd finally conceded the tug of war I'd been fighting so hard to win. Defeat had been inevitable. If I'd had any chance at victory, it had slipped from my fingers the first night she spent under my roof. I'd lain in bed with my dick in my hand, imagining how she'd feel under my fingers, between my teeth, and surrounding my cock.

"Show me."

She held my gaze and without looking away, she undid her trousers and pulled them down over her bottom.

I tensed my jaw as she held her underwear away from her, giving me space to see her sweet pussy.

"I'm not sure that's quite wet enough," I said, pushing my fingers into her underwear and between her folds.

"Oh God," she said, unsteady on her feet, grasping at my arms.

I leaned her back onto the table as I explored her. Christ, I couldn't wait to taste her. Couldn't wait to coat my cock in her soaked pussy.

With my free hand, I pushed off her underwear as I worked around her clit, stroking and pushing before delving into her with two fingers.

"Shit," she cried out, and I put my mouth on hers to cover her sounds. I curled my fingers into her, pushing and pulling, circling and pressing, trying to take some of the heat out of my cock, trying to calm myself as much as satisfy her. "Gabriel. I'm. Stop. Gabriel. You're going to make me come."

I stilled. "You want me to stop?" I asked, smirking at her. I knew the answer, but I was going to make her say it.

She couldn't catch her breath. "No. Well, yes. I'm going to come so quickly if you don't."

I pushed back into her, feeling her tense around me. "I know," I whispered. "And you've wanted this for so long, haven't you?" I asked, stroking her between her folds, around her clit, delving deep. "You've wanted me to feel you, to touch you like this, to make you come?"

"Yes, Gabriel." Her confession brought her to the brink, and she began to shudder. I slid my free hand over her mouth to muffle her cries and I held her gently as she floated down, free of weeks of pent-up frustration.

Her cries had only ratcheted up my need and I pulled off my t-shirt, wiping my hand on it before discarding it and working on my jeans.

"Well, that should be illegal," she said, hazy-eyed and pointing at my chest.

"What?" I glanced down.

"You know. All the muscles and stuff. I've never even seen you work out."

"It's all the manual labor," I replied. She laughed but I wasn't joking. The planing and polishing. The lifting and sanding. It was all the exercise anyone needed.

"This is my favorite outfit you have," she said, unbuttoning her blouse like we were in a race to see who could undress first.

Her confession made me grin. I liked the idea that she noticed what I wore, noticed my body. Why did she like it?

"You only wear it when you're about to disappear into your secret dungeon." She shrugged off her top and started untangling her trousers from where they'd pooled around her ankles.

I paused before pulling off my jeans. "My what?" With

a nod of her head, she indicated the door of my workshop. "My workshop?"

"What do you do in there?"

"Stuff you do in a workshop," I said. She stood before me in just her underwear. "God, you're beautiful, Autumn. So *bloody* beautiful."

She reached for me and pulled at my neck and I dipped to kiss her. There was no going back now. I was careering down a one-way street with no way out. I'd vowed never to touch another woman after Penelope left. And of all the people I broke that vow for, it shouldn't have been for a woman who was so much younger, was my best friend's future sister-in-law and my daughter's nanny. But this pull I had toward Autumn was stronger than every objection that existed.

"Turn around and bend over," I said. I wanted to see her beautiful skin against the rough oak of the table. The oak I'd sanded and oiled and given new life to. I wanted every part of me to possess her. She lay forward, the dark strands of her hair falling onto the wood as if she were wrapping herself over it.

She looked like a goddess. I kneeled, peeling her underwear off and down her legs, catching a glimpse of her plump, reddened pussy, shimmering for me. "Beautiful," I said, admiring her, pushing my thumb inside her. Unable to be so close without having a taste, I leaned forward and pressed my tongue against her.

Her nails scraped against the wood and her knees buckled. She was sweet—like amber honey— and her pussy quivered on my tongue like it was so close to climax it just needed the slightest touch.

Later.

I stood and pressed her firmly against the table. "Hold on."

She did as I asked and gripped the edges of the table while I rolled on a condom and took position behind her. I took a final look at her, spread out like a feast for me. Legs weak, pussy wet, breath heavy. It was just how I'd pictured her a thousand times, but so much better. Because tonight, it would be her cunt and not my hand that my cock got to push into.

I growled and grabbed her hips, holding her in place. "Are you ready?"

"Please," she whimpered.

I inhaled at her plea and summoned up strength to continue.

In one swift movement, I pushed in, right up to the hilt. I fought against my need to close my eyes at the tightness because I couldn't deprive myself of the sight of her. Her luscious bottom that I stood behind. The smooth, pale white of her back. The tumble of black locks. She was gorgeous and now I was inside of her, just where I'd longed to be since I'd seen her that first time.

I spanned my hand across her back and pulled out, dragging a groan from her, and then thrust forward. Did I ever think it would be like this? That her skin would feel like silk? That my cock would feel so good filling her up? I leaned over her so my chest was flat against her back, just to feel more of her—I wanted to be surrounded and consumed by this moment.

Shifting up again, I began my rhythm. Slow and relentless, just like the desire I'd had for her for all these months. It felt so fucking perfect that I couldn't believe I'd made it this long. If it had been inevitable, why had I not given in sooner and enjoyed this moment months ago? "I've been wanting this for so long," I choked out. "I've needed to plow into you and show you how good it could be."

She pushed back against me, sending me farther into her if that was even possible. She screamed into her folded arms. "So deep."

I increased the pace, needing her to understand how desperate she'd made me all this time.

"Please. Gabriel. You're. Please. Yes. Please. Please."

The begging was more than I could have ever hoped for. She was always so sure of herself and now this was my chance to make her sure of me.

"You want more?" I pressed again and again. "You think you can handle it?"

I reached around under her and pressed my fingers into her folds. She was gone on a single touch.

Another victory. But I wasn't going to stop.

I slowed as her body shuddered with her second orgasm, then pulled out completely, making her whimper before moving her heavy, slow limbs so she was facing me. I lifted her onto the table and opened her legs.

I wasn't sure what was going to happen after tonight. I couldn't think about it now. I just had to make the most out of every second I had her right now. I unsnapped her bra and discarded it on the floor. Her breasts were perfect. Firm and large and so fucking soft. I weighed them in my hands and then took her nipples between my thumb and forefinger, giving them a short pinch, making her yelp, and then I pushed into her again. She covered her own mouth as she groaned, her head tipped back as if helpless.

"You're mine tonight." And I was going to claim what was mine in every way possible.

"Yes," she whispered, something so reverent in her tone

that I had to stop and look at her. "Yours," she said, sweeping her finger over my eyebrow and down my cheek.

She shifted, pulling me out of the trance she'd put me in with a single word, and I kissed her rough and hard before lifting her up and moving to the nearest seat. I sat down so she was astride me and looked up at her.

So fucking beautiful.

I smoothed my hands around the curve of her arse and lifted her slightly, then pulled her down on my straining cock. As I was about to start moving her, she took over, raising and lowering herself over me.

"It's even deeper like this," she panted. "How?"

I brought my hands up to explore her breasts, rolling her nipples between my thumb and fingers, tightening my hold then releasing her if it interrupted her pace.

"It's so good," she said.

"You like my cock," I replied. "I knew you would."

She moaned and slowed, tightening around me. But I wasn't ready to let her come again. Not yet. I stood, her legs wrapped around me. I strode across the kitchen and leaned her up against the wall.

I slammed into her over and over, pinning her to the spot. I fucked and fucked and fucked as if I'd been deprived of water for weeks and was finally able to drink.

"Oh God, Gabriel," she cried.

"You're going to have to be quiet," I said through a series of grunts. "I'm going to make you come so, so hard, Autumn." I thrust into her again as if to make my point. "But you're going to have to be quiet."

Her head fell to my shoulder and as I continued to fuck and fuck, she cried out into my skin, the vibrations from her moans reverberating over my sweat-sheened skin in a sheet of pleasure.

From underneath her, my fingers found her folds and barely a touch sent her spiraling yet again.

I wasn't going to withstand her contracting around my cock this time. I'd held on for so long. So many weeks.

"Autumn," I cried out. Every drop that I thrust up into her was a part of me. I was giving her everything. My abstinence, my composure, my self-control.

In a few moments, I'd taken a hammer to everything I'd carefully constructed over the past three years.

I'd ripped up the rule book for Autumn.

I'd have to deal with the consequences tomorrow.

TWELVE

Autumn

My limbs were stone-heavy and I wasn't sure I'd ever have the energy to walk again. Sex with Gabriel had been . . . I knew it would be good. I just hadn't expected it to be so completely life changing. And I hadn't expected him to be so filthy. I'd loved it.

"Do you concede at Monopoly?" he asked, fastening his jeans.

I glanced at him with a frown. "Absolutely not. Do you?"

"No, of course not."

I tried to bite back a grin. I liked that the serious, almost gruff side of Gabriel was back. It wasn't as if that wasn't him during sex. Just that he was . . . more. He was open and far less guarded. I liked it all. I just hoped I wasn't about to get a case of whiplash again. There had been a number of times when I thought my attraction to him was reciprocated and then he receded into being my boss and a man I happened to live with. After tonight, I wasn't sure I'd handle it from him.

"So, do we have to have a talk now about how this shouldn't have happened?" If that was the way this was going to go, I wanted to know now. I liked Gabriel and the sex had been the best I'd ever had. Whatever I'd been doing before couldn't really be described as *sex* anymore. There was no real comparison. "Because, it has happened. And I can't regret it, Gabriel."

He pulled me toward him, circling my waist with one arm. "That's not how this is going to go. I like you, Autumn. There's a connection between us that I can't ignore, however hard I try."

"But I don't understand why you've tried so hard." I wasn't a virus to be avoided.

"There are a lot of reasons. Dexter. Hollie. You're young. A great nanny. All that, and my last relationship didn't go so well. I don't want to hurt you, Autumn. And I don't want . . . Bethany's life disrupted."

Gabriel usually said so little, but right now he seemed to be sharing almost everything on his mind. I didn't want to push things too hard. I wasn't angling for a ring. Honesty and openness were all I wanted.

"I'll tell you what it will take me to concede at Monopoly," I said, wanting something from him that was beyond words. "Show me your workshop." I'd been wanting to get behind that door since the moment I moved in. And now I'd seen him naked, it seemed suddenly unfair that he was keeping it from me.

"Now?" he asked.

I shrugged. Seemed as good a time as any. He looked deliciously rumpled, softer somehow in the afterglow of the best sex I'd ever had.

He shoved a hand deep into his jean pocket and pulled out a key.

"Okay," he said, like it was no big deal.

I wasn't sure if my heart was racing like a greyhound out of the gate because I would finally get to see where Gabriel disappeared to every night, or because he took my hand, kissed me on my knuckles, and then slid his fingers between mine. "Don't touch anything, mind."

The click of the lock sounded, and he bent to kiss me before he turned the doorknob and pushed open the door.

I didn't know where to look first. "It's a . . . workshop." A huge wooden island sat in the middle of the room, aged with layers of bumps and scratches. Clamps were attached around one edge and a couple of machines were set on the other side. Beneath my feet were bare floorboards littered with wooden boxes full of . . . implements. The walls on two sides were covered in green racks of chisels, hammers, and lots of other tools I had no name for, sitting over built-in wooden cabinets. Along another wall was open shelving, stuffed full of books and cans of paints and tubs and jars. It was like I'd walked into a small factory. How was all this hidden behind that door?

"I told you it was a workshop."

"I know you did," I replied, stepping inside. "But I didn't expect it to be this kind of workshop." Gabriel Chase, the serious, soulful lawyer, was a secret carpenter on the side. Who would have guessed?

He glanced down at his feet. "I've never shown anyone."

I snapped my head toward him but didn't say anything, feeling sad for him that for whatever reason, he hadn't had anyone to share this with. I was honored to be the first.

"So, you use all this stuff?" I asked, trailing my free

hand over a smaller side bench that was up against the near wall. I liked the idea of him in those worn jeans, flexing his delicious muscles as he sanded, painted, and chiseled. It was so earthy. So freaking sexy. And I thought he was sexier than any man I'd ever met *before* I'd known what was behind his secret door.

"Yeah. I'm surprised you've never heard me."

Now that I thought about it, I had heard banging from time to time, but I'd assumed it must be the neighbors. I wasn't exactly used to living in silence at the Sunshine Trailer Park, so I'd just accepted it.

"What kind of thing do you do in here?"

He dropped my hand and moved to the far side of the room. "This is my latest project," he said, pulling off the plastic cover from a huge bookcase, taller than even Gabriel. "I haven't really started yet but it's a Globe-Wernicke," he explained, and his chest lifted with a hint of pride as he spoke.

"It's nice," I said, unsure what to make of the reddish-brown, hulking piece of furniture.

"It's not really. Not yet. And I overpaid for it." He sighed. "I'd wanted to do one for ages."

I grinned up at him. "And when you say you want to do one, what exactly does that entail?"

"Well," he said, bending and running his fingers down the edge of it. "See here? The beading has been knocked. It's splintering all down this side. And this . . ." He pinched the brass knob on the front of one of the shelves. "This is my favorite part."

Each of the six shelves had a glass front and he lifted up the door on one and pushed it back on itself so it stayed up. "Isn't it great?" he said, turning to me, a grin across his face.

"These little up and over doors . . . It's perfect. Or it will be. Two of the shelves are broken."

"So you're going to fix it?"

He nodded. "I haven't decided whether or not I'll sand off the entire thing. I doubt it. I'll probably just polish it up. You can't plan too much with these things because there's always something that comes out of left field and surprises you. But if I was going to take the lacquer off and take it back to the wood and then re-stain and re-coat it all, it would take me years. Between work and Bethany, I don't get too much time in here."

"I've imagined a hundred things that could have been behind this door," I said. "But I didn't suspect anything like this."

"Are you disappointed?" he asked, smirking and lifting me by the waist up onto the workbench island.

I smoothed my hands over his shoulders, taking in the room from this change of viewpoint. "I should have guessed. I mean, I know you're good with your hands."

He chuckled and pressed a kiss to my forehead. "This place saved me after Penelope left."

He'd never mentioned his wife before tonight, but apparently she was a shadow that loomed over him. Was she an ex-wife? Hollie had explained she'd walked out without any warning when Bethany was a baby, but I didn't actually know if they were divorced.

"Distraction is a good thing," I said, trying to keep neutral and not wanting to open a can of worms marked *ex*.

"It didn't work so well with you," he replied with a grin.

I shrugged. "I'm relentless," I said on a yawn.

"We should get to bed." He checked his watch. "It's late and I've got a busy day tomorrow." He took me by the waist and set me down on my feet. "You were right, though. I need to get back to the office."

"Good. Remember this so that next time I don't have to sleep with you to convince you to see it my way."

"Okay," he said, grinning as we filed out of his workshop. "But maybe I like having you convince me."

"Yeah, I don't mind that part so much either."

He smiled one of those rare smiles I liked enough to count. I pushed my hands through his hair. "Thank you for showing me this," I said. Gabriel unlocking that room and sharing it with me felt like a turning point between us. More than the flirtatious glances and the illicit touches. More even than the sex. Him showing the workshop to me was him letting me in. And I wanted to stay. But I knew better than most that real life didn't have many happy-ever-afters. It had for Hollie, and there was no one more deserving, but there was no way London could be my salvation too, no matter how hard I wanted it to be.

THIRTEEN

Gabriel

It had been almost a week since I'd been with Autumn, but I'd barely seen her. I couldn't wait to get home tonight. I'd have missed dinner with Bethany, but I would get to put her to bed at least. I unlocked the door, went inside, and was greeted by music coming from the living room. "Hello," I called but no answer. It wasn't bath time yet. Where were they?

I set down my things and took off my coat and went to investigate.

I poked my head around the door to find Autumn sitting on the floor, her back against the sofa, surrounded by pillows and a duvet over her. She was grinning up at Bethany who was dancing in front of the TV.

"Good evening," I said, wondering what the hell was going on.

"Daddy!" A pajamaed Bethany squealed and ran into my arms, officially making it the best part of my day so far.

"We weren't expecting you so soon," Autumn said, smiling at me.

"It's movie night," Bethany explained. "We have popcorn."

I glanced at the coffee table, covered in plates and drinks.

"We made it in the mic-wave."

"This is very cozy," I said as Bethany put her arms around my neck and squeezed. I swear the girl was half-human, half-anaconda.

"Come join us," Autumn said, patting the floor next to her.

"Yes, Daddy. Eat popcorn. Please stay and don't work."

How could I say no to an invitation like that? "Okay but you've got to tell me what I'm meant to do."

Autumn laughed. "You need instructions to relax, watch a movie, and eat popcorn?" She shook her head. "It seems we have some work to do on your daddy, Bethany."

"In my defense, it looks like you have more going on here than that."

"You want in?" She lifted the duvet.

"Yes, Daddy. You *have* to be under the duvet if you're sitting down."

Autumn shrugged. "The rules are the rules." She offered me the bowl of popcorn and I shuffled under the duvet and took it from her.

"This was dinner?" I asked as I toed off my shoes and took a seat next to Autumn, making sure I wasn't touching her in case that freaked Bethany. I didn't want it to look like I was deliberately *not* touching her either.

"We had an early dinner," Autumn replied. "This is Friday night after-dinner snacks. We have a fruit platter as well. You don't need to worry."

"And hummus crunchies," Bethany said, trampling over our outstretched feet, finding something that looked vaguely like a crisp, and bringing it back and handing it to me. "They're yummy."

I took the crisp and took a bite. Not because I was hungry or curious but because my daughter wanted me to. "Yummy," I said. "So what's the film?"

"You have to call it *movie*, Daddy. Like Autumn."

"Okay," I said, smiling at her. At this rate she'd have an American accent by the end of the month. "What *movie* are we watching."

"Singing and Dancing," Bethany said, and I groaned. Not a musical.

"*Singin' in the Rain*," Autumn said. "Like I said, she's four. She should know these songs by heart."

"Yes, I remember. I'm a terrible father for neglecting her musicals education."

Autumn's smile was like a physical touch. It filled her face, lit up the room, and warmed my soul. "Well, at least you're aware and willing to put things right. Or at least have me put them right."

"I might leave you to it," I said, shifting to get up. There was always work to do. "I hate musicals."

"Sit your butt back down," Autumn said.

"Butt, butt, butt, butt." Bethany started jumping on the spot.

"No one hates *Singin' in the Rain*," Autumn declared. "It's impossible. And if you've never seen it, you can't say you hate it."

"It's sooo good, Daddy."

"I can hate it," I said. "I got dragged to see *Cats* once when it was in the West End. Was up there as one of the worst experiences of my life."

"Well, Jiminy Cricket, Bethany, what a terrible life your father has had. But what he doesn't know is that movie musicals are different from stage musicals. And *Singin' in the Rain* is the best movie musical of all time." She turned to me. "You hated the show *Cats*. It doesn't mean you hate all movie musicals. You can't write things off like that."

"Why would I waste my time? It's not like I'm Sam I am. I've tried them. I just don't like them."

Autumn burst into a laugh. "That's a perfect name for you—Sam I Am."

I wanted to grab her and kiss her senseless for teasing me. No one ever dared to tease me. "I'm the opposite of Sam I Am. I've already had green eggs and ham." Oh Christ, I was rhyming now.

"Nope. You saw one musical. One time. Broaden your horizons. Give them another shot. The genre deserves a second chance to impress you."

She was relentless. I loosened my tie and resigned myself to at least half an hour of hell. After that, surely she'd agree I'd eaten my green eggs and ham. "Okay then. Do your worst, put it on."

"You'll stay?" Bethany said. "You don't have to work?" She landed on my lap with a thud, and I pulled her so she was leaning against my front.

It pinched at my heart that Bethany assumed I'd have to work rather than stay with her and watch a film on a Friday night. I wanted to provide for her and be a good role model, but she should know that I'd rather hang out with her than do anything else in this moment.

"Only if I get some popcorn," I replied.

"You can have all of it. Can't he, Autumn?"

"Yes, he can," she replied.

"You're going to love this movie so much, Daddy."

What I was going to love was sitting with my warm, snuggly daughter in my lap, next to one of the most beautiful, bright, kind women I'd ever met.

Every now and then, Autumn would glance at me and smile, seemingly glad that I was making the effort to stay and enjoy the film. Intermittently, Bethany would get up and dance to the music and we'd applaud her and she'd curtsey.

Just as we were getting toward the end, Autumn sat up straight. "This is it. Are you ready?" She glanced at Bethany. "Fingers on lips."

Dutifully, Bethany put her index finger across her lips and drew her knees up to her chin.

Gene Kelly and Debbie Reynolds gathered in a doorway to shelter from the rain. Apparently something important was about to happen.

We all held our breath as Autumn stared dreamily at the screen.

"Gah," Autumn said as music started playing. "That is the most romantic line in movie history—'This California dew is just a little heavier than usual tonight.'"

Gene Kelly was dancing his way down the rainy street. "Is that romantic?" Maybe I was missing something.

"Not that line. The next one when he says 'Really? From where I stand the sun is shining all over the place.'"

I didn't laugh because I could tell she was serious, but it took some effort.

She glanced at me and then shifted toward me when she saw I didn't agree. "What? You don't think it's romantic?"

"You don't think it's a little . . . cheesy?"

She groaned as if I was the stupidest person on earth. "It's not cheesy if you're so in love with someone that you can't even tell it's raining."

"I think if you're out in a rainstorm like that and you can't tell it's raining, you need to go to the doctor."

She shook her head and folded her arms. "Such a cynic."

We watched the rest of the movie in silence, and I couldn't tell if she was completely engrossed or smarting at my comment.

"You see," Autumn said, as the credits started to roll. "Wasn't it just the greatest?" She grinned as if she was having the best time of her life.

"It's not as bad as *Cats*," I said, hoping that would be enough to placate her.

She rolled her eyes. "It's a phenomenal movie."

She was phenomenal.

"Although, second time around it looks like it put your daughter to sleep," she said.

I glanced down at the comfortable tangle of limbs in my lap. She hadn't fallen asleep on me like that since she was a baby. It seemed like yesterday and at the same time, so long ago. That first year of Bethany's life I thought I'd finally got the perfect family and now here I was, a single father.

"It's late," I said, looking at the clock. "Just gone eight."

"Another wild, crazy Friday night."

For a brief second, I wanted to ask her what her Friday nights were like back in America. Had they been wild and crazy? Is that what she wanted? Parties, being up all night? I stopped myself. I shouldn't be thinking about what Autumn was looking for. I could deal with right now and not a moment in the future.

We'd not talked about the fact that we'd had sex. I'd

been tied up at work and we'd barely seen each other. And I didn't know what to say. For so long I'd kept that side of myself locked away, but Autumn had come along and bulldozed her way into my life. Into my heart. And although I had a thousand reasons why I shouldn't touch her again, whenever I was near her, none of them seemed to matter.

I reached out with one hand and cupped Autumn's face. "You look beautiful," I said, stroking my thumb against her cheek. She slid her hand over mine.

"It was nice that you stayed. Thank you."

"How could I say no?" I asked, wondering if I could dive into those deep brown eyes of hers.

I removed my hand. "I need to get this one to bed," I said as I stood. "Can you bring Bear Bear?"

"Sure," she said, scooping the toy up and following me as I headed upstairs.

I laid Bethany in bed and pressed a kiss against her cheek, tucking Bear Bear under her arm. God, I loved her so much. All the pain with Penelope was worth it to have such a miracle in my life every day. I was so lucky.

"She's beautiful," Autumn said from behind me. I turned and headed over to where she was leaning against the doorframe.

"She certainly is. Thank you for taking such good care of her."

"I have the best job ever—eating popcorn and watching musicals with the cutest kid alive."

I chuckled as we shifted and I closed Bethany's bedroom door.

"I've been thinking about the other night," I said, not quite sure what was going to come next.

Her shoulders slouched and she groaned like it was the

worst possible thing I could have said. "Don't say it, Gabriel."

"I haven't said anything," I replied, confused.

She turned her back and headed down the landing to the stairs.

What was happening? "Autumn," I said, catching up with her and putting my hand on her arm. "What did I say?"

She stopped and turned and she looked so sad, so disappointed. It felt like a blow to my chest that I might have caused that. "It's not what you said, it was what you were about to say. You were going to say how it wouldn't happen again and it's not right and—"

I pulled her toward me, pushed my hand into her hair, and dragged my lips against hers. I delved into her mouth with my tongue, my skin buzzed at her sweetness, my chest lifted at the feel of her. She just felt so *right*.

She pulled away slightly. "Did I jump to conclusions?"

I wasn't sure why a woman who seemed to live on life's bright side would expect me to go back on my word. Her assumption hinted that perhaps the woman who was all sunshine was in fact constantly expecting rain. "You don't need to doubt me," I said. "I was just going to suggest you might not want to broadcast what happened between us. Until we have a chance to figure it out." I didn't know what was happening or how I felt, and I wasn't going to lie to Autumn and pretend I did. But I also knew some kind of watershed had been crossed and there was no going back. More than that, I didn't want to go back.

"Right," she said, smoothing her hand up my chest. "I haven't told anyone."

"I just got my divorce papers recently. I have a kid. A demanding job. I can't—"

"Your divorce papers?" she asked.

"Yes. It's been years but the paperwork hasn't caught up."

She swallowed and nodded. "So there's no chance you'll be getting back together with her?"

Were those the rainclouds she was looking for? "We were over the moment she walked out, and I haven't seen her since. The divorce is just procedural. But it's something I need to get done. Between Bethany and my job, my plate is full. And I'm not sure what I can offer you. I won't make promises to anyone and I don't expect any in return." It was as honest as I'd ever been with anyone. I wasn't sure how to fit her into my carefully constructed, fiercely protected world.

"I'm not asking for anything," she said. "Let's just deal with right now."

Somehow Autumn always knew the right thing to say. I nodded and she brought her hands up my arms, trailing a shiver across my body.

"And right now," she said. "I have a huge crush on my boss."

I chuckled. Yes, that would do for now. A mutual crush. Something that would pass or fade without drama or significance. I would take her advice and just deal with the moment right in front of me. And all I could see was a beautiful woman I was helplessly attracted to, saying she wanted me too.

I pressed my thumb over her lips in a straight line over her chin and down her neck and between her breasts. "I want to taste you."

She took my hand and linked her fingers through mine. "I'll warn you now, I'm sure I taste like hot, buttered popcorn." She seemed to have an almost magical ability to turn a difficult moment into something easy, to create light where there was dark. Perhaps she'd be able to breathe life into a cold, damaged heart that had been in hibernation for a very long time. And perhaps I'd be able to shield her from any impending rain clouds. Just for the time being.

FOURTEEN

Autumn

I was surrounded by racks and racks of white tulle. At my feet was five-inch-deep pink carpet and when I looked up, all I saw was sparkling crystal. This must be what it was like to live inside a cloud. Or heaven. Or unicorn throw-up.

"I don't even know where to start," Hollie said. "Maybe I should just buy something online."

"Don't you dare," I replied. "You can't buy your wedding dress online. I think it's illegal or something."

"Prison's got to be better than spending the entire afternoon trying on a million dresses. And I can't believe I dragged you here. I'm sure you have much better things to be doing than babysitting me."

It was typical of Hollie to feel bad about trying on wedding gowns. It was my job to get her to enjoy herself today. I'd make it happen if it killed me. "Are you kidding? I get an excuse to day drink." I took a seat on the cream velvet chair in the ginormous dressing room *suite*, as the sales assistant called it, and sipped from the glass of champagne they'd poured us when we arrived. "And I get to watch my sister look beautiful. What could be better?"

"You're a good sister," Hollie said.

"You're better. Now go into your little hidey-hole and try something on for me to ooh and ahh about."

One of the assistants swept in like she was on wheels, carrying an armful of clouds.

"Just pick out any one of them and take it behind the screen," she said as she added dresses to the rack in front of us. "And then I'll come round and help you get into it. We'll quickly get a feel for what you like and don't like."

"I would be happy to wear my jeans. Or elope," Hollie said.

"This is exciting, Hollie. Just think, a couple of years ago, you would never have thought you'd be in some fancy boutique in Knightsbridge, picking out wedding gowns to wear when you marry the man of your dreams."

"I'm being a Debbie Downer, aren't I?" Hollie asked.

"Yep. Knowing you, you're just feeling bad for feeling happy."

"It's just so much," she said, disappearing behind the screen. "And of course I'm happy, but you're right, I do feel a little weird. Not only did my dreams all come true, but they were surpassed. I never thought this could be my life."

"So enjoy it." I knew she was sighing, even though I couldn't hear it. "You worked so hard for so many years, Hollie."

"I just hope you don't think I'm rubbing it in your face," she said.

I laughed. I loved my sister but she was ridiculous. "How could I ever think that? You spent your entire life making sure I could have a better future. You sacrificed your own happiness over and over. And it worked. I got my degree. I'm in London. Okay, I'm not quite a career high-flyer like you, but it will happen eventually. And in the meantime, I get to look after the cutest little girl and . . ." I could feel the blush start to rise in my cheeks and I knew I had to change the subject before Hollie emerged in her dress and spotted it. "In September I'll start my job. Before that, I'm going to travel across Europe. You and me, we're just at different stages."

"You always put an Autumn spin on things."

"I'm being honest. Life is good, Hollie. I'm happy. You're happy. Mom and Dad are actually working. I graduated college and we don't have to worry about the electric bill or how we're going to last until Friday with half a loaf of bread and a carton of eggs." The weeks where we didn't have enough food to eat were the toughest when I was going through college. It would always get Hollie down. There were a few months in my freshman year where it happened more weeks than it didn't. During those times, I spent a lot of time over at my boyfriend's place. I never told Hollie it was because there was always a slice of leftover pizza in the fridge. Or at least some ramen noodles. That way, Hollie got what we had to herself and didn't have to worry about me. "We need to enjoy how far we've come, and you need to enjoy today."

"Okay, I'm coming out. Are you ready?"

"I'm always ready."

She emerged from behind the screen like a princess in some kind of movie. I half expected cartoon birds to start singing and animated squirrels to join in with the harmonies.

"Wow," I said as she stepped onto a podium in front of floor-to-ceiling, three-way mirrors. "You look really beautiful." It was a proper princess gown, and she would look right at home in the pages of a glossy magazine.

"This is crazy." She shook her head. "But I do like it. I didn't expect to like such a big skirt, but it works."

"It really works," I said, so happy to see her fairytale coming true. "It's like you're going to a ball."

"Is it too much?" She turned from side to side, keeping focused on the dress as it swished with her movements.

"Absolutely not. You are beautiful. The dress is beautiful. You're marrying one of the kindest, richest, most handsome men in London. It's all great. You just need to allow yourself to enjoy it." Whatever happened, she'd never have to worry about being hungry again. That was to be celebrated.

"I need to try on more though, right?"

"Absolutely. I want to stay here until I'm properly buzzed." I raised my glass at her and she stepped off the podium. "Have you decided on a date yet?"

"Well, I wanted to ask you about your plans over the summer. Do you know where you're going or when you're leaving?" she asked as she headed behind the screen to change.

My stomach churned. I didn't want to think about the summer. It was too far off. "It's months away."

"It will be June in two weeks. And you're off at the end of July."

My stomach stretched and contracted like it was limbering up to sprint out of my body. *Just six weeks.* "I'm sure I'll get around to it at some point."

Hollie stuck her head around the screen. "You must have thought about it. I mean, you were so excited to have the entire month of August to travel."

Did I need the entire month off? "Yeah, I'm still excited.

It's just a way off, that's all." I was happy with the now. I didn't want to think about the future. I spent the day with the most amazing kid, hanging out, seeing London, getting to see how the British did things. And then in the evening . . . For the past couple of weeks, in the evening, Gabriel would come home and we were together. He'd make love to me in his workshop. Or on the kitchen table. In front of the fire. We'd talk. I'd make him laugh with my ridiculous stories of life back home. He'd make me swoon with the way he talked about his daughter.

My life was good.

Close to perfect.

I just wished I could tell my sister. But she wouldn't approve and would tell me every reason why he wasn't right for me. And I didn't want to hear it.

Gabriel was a good man. Kind. And thoughtful. He was serious, but he seemed to like me poking fun at him. Yes, he was older, but did that matter? And okay, I had a job starting in the fall that meant I wouldn't be his daughter's nanny, but until then?

Gabriel was right for right now.

"Where do you think you'll start? You still wanting to go to Seville? Maybe Paris would be a good starting point because you can just take the train over."

"Yeah, probably Paris," I replied, wondering whether Gabriel and Bethany would maybe come with me. Even if it was for a few days. Gabriel said he'd been to Paris a lot. Maybe he could show me around.

But I wasn't going to suggest it. Gabriel and I had an unspoken policy about not planning for the future. We didn't talk about next week, let alone six weeks from now.

Hollie stepped out in the second dress. It was even more beautiful than the first, if that was possible.

"It's so glamourous," I said, taking in the fitted corset and sweeping fishtail.

"It looks great. But it's not as comfortable as the other one," she said, stepping up to the podium with a shuffle and a hop.

"It makes your ass look incredible," I said, and Hollie turned around and tried to look at the back view over her shoulder.

"I'm not sure a good butt is worth not being able to breathe. What do you think?"

"I think not breathing is a compromise too far," I agreed.

She nodded and tentatively stepped down from the podium and headed back behind the changing screen.

"Dexter is pushing me on the date, but I want to make sure it doesn't interfere with your plans," Hollie said. "Could you put together some kind of itinerary and let me know as soon as you can when would be a good time?"

I laughed. "You're insane. This is one decision where I refuse to let you put me first. You can't plan a wedding around plans that haven't been made, or a person who isn't the bride. Set your date and I'll work around it."

"What if you're in the middle of Russia at the time we're supposed to be getting married?"

"Well firstly I'm not planning on going to Russia, and secondly, I'll come back." I wish we could get off the subject. There was so much to enjoy about life right now. I wanted to soak in it for a little while.

"I don't want to be responsible for dragging you away from something fun. Can't you just come up with a plan?"

"Okay," I said. I wasn't going to win this battle. Hollie didn't know how not to put me first. I would have to start looking into what I was going to be doing this summer. "I'll look into it." I needed to pull up my big girl pants and start planning. My *right now* wasn't going to last forever, and I needed to embrace the future. I'd spent my entire life dreaming of travelling around Europe, and I wasn't about to be sad about the fact my dreams were going to come true. I just wouldn't allow it.

FIFTEEN

Gabriel

The kind of news I'd gotten today would normally have me irritated. Everyone in my law firm knew that I didn't travel. It was the one rule I'd not broken for the sake of a client since Bethany was born. Apparently Autumn Lumen changed everything, because tonight, I couldn't wait to get home and see the look in her eyes when I told her we were going away.

"Hello," I said as I walked through the door. It was gone eight so Bethany wouldn't be awake, but I tried to make it home before Autumn went to bed. I managed it most nights.

"Hey," Autumn called. As I wandered into the kitchen, I found her at the cooker. "I'm making that meatloaf you liked."

I couldn't remember exactly when Autumn started cooking dinner for me. But for weeks now there was always something to eat when I got home from work. She'd said she was cooking for her and Bethany and so it was no trouble to cook for me too. But she didn't have to, and we both knew it. That was Autumn all over—she always gave more than I expected.

"That's kind of you." I walked up behind her, snaked my arm around her waist, and buried my head in her neck.

"You're back early. How was work?" she asked.

"Good," I said, kissing her neck and then going to the fridge to get a beer.

"Really? That's not normally the response I get from you. Usually you groan and complain about Mike."

I chuckled. "Well he tried to be a dick today but it backfired."

"Really?" she said, putting something in the oven and turning to face me.

"He knows I won't travel. Since Bethany was born, it's a hard line in the sand that I've always had and made no exception for. Today, Mike told me he's looking at a huge telecoms company in Europe, and he wants me out there for a week to look at the parts of the data room that they're refusing to put online."

"Oh God," she said. "What did he say when you told him no?"

I grinned and stepped toward her. "I told him yes. We're going to Rome next week."

Her eyes widened and she grabbed hold of my forearms. "What do you mean *we*?"

"You, me, and Bethany. I thought we could fly out on the Saturday morning. I don't have to be in the data room until Monday. I'm not sure how the week will go, but I thought you and Bethany would like to explore Rome together. I might get some time during the day. But you're probably going to be on your own most of the time."

"Are you kidding me?" It was a sheen of shock rather than excitement that she wore.

"You don't want to go?"

She blinked furiously. "I mean of course. I just need to check about . . . I need to figure out whether I have enough savings and—"

This girl took nothing for granted. "Autumn, you're not going to pay for anything. It's a business expense. But even if it wasn't, I've got this."

She shifted her weight from one foot to the other. "I'm not expecting you to—"

"Autumn, please. You'll be looking after Bethany—you'll be working. And for the record, when I do take you away just for fun, you won't be paying for anything then, either."

"It's important to me that I'm independent, Gabriel. Hollie's looked out for me my entire life. I'm an adult now. I don't want to be dependent on anyone. I need to know I can do life without a handout."

I pushed my fingers into her hair, unable to help admiring her independence. But there was something in me that wanted to show her the world. "Let's not borrow trouble. Rome is a business trip and you're coming as Bethany's nanny. It's as simple as that."

She looked at me like she wanted to argue the point but eventually her frown turned into a small smile. "We really get to go to Rome?"

"You said you wanted to go," I said, my grin as wide as it ever had been as she lifted up onto her toes.

"This is beyond," she said. "We'll get to see the Colosseum. And St. Peters. The Pantheon. Oh my God. Mike doesn't mind you bringing us?"

"I don't care if he minds. Anyway, he won't know. I'll

make sure we stay at a different hotel to him so we get some privacy. And we can stay the following weekend too if you'd like to."

She looked up at me, her hands on my chest. "Are you serious? This is going to be so much fun. Rome."

Before Autumn, I wouldn't have considered going to Rome. I certainly would never have considered putting fun on the agenda. But now? I would enjoy eating pasta and drinking good red wine in an Italian restaurant. I was thinking about something in my life other than Bethany and work. I was looking forward to something. I wanted to share something with another person, purely for the sake of having her by my side. Autumn was shifting everything—what I ate, what time I came home from work and now, what I was looking forward to.

"We need to pack and—" Her smile fell. "What should I tell Hollie? I can't exactly say we're going away together."

Seeing her so concerned about what her sister would say took the sheen off my pleasure. I still didn't know what was happening between us, so I wasn't encouraging her to tell her sister. But the thought that she had to hide something from someone she was so close to didn't sit well with me. "I'm going for work, Autumn. You're coming to look after Bethany so I'm not away from her for a week."

She nodded. "Yes, that's right. That *is* what's really happening." She grinned up at me. "And anyway, she should be pleased. She wants me to travel and I guess I can cross Rome off my list now."

"Your list?" I'd make the week really special. I'd organize a room with a spectacular view and get her a guide to show her around while I was at work. I couldn't remember the last time I'd been away. And there was no one I'd rather go away with than my daughter and Autumn.

"I was just looking at it, actually," she said, pulling away and turning to the kitchen table where a notebook lay open, the pages full of scribbles. "There's just so many places to go. A month isn't enough time to see and do everything."

A month? What was she talking about? We'd be in Rome a week. She slid onto the bench. "Maybe I'll start a new notebook for our trip to Rome rather than use this one."

"So what are you planning in this one?" I said, sliding in next to her.

"Oh just where I'm going in August."

It was as if someone had handed me a cannonball and pushed me into the ocean.

She was planning life after me.

"Hollie's getting stressed about a wedding date and wants me to tell her what my plans are, but I haven't really thought about it. Is that bad?"

It shouldn't have been, but it was a relief that at least she'd not been counting down the days until she'd be leaving me—leaving us. I hadn't been as happy as I was at the moment for a long time. Since Penelope. Before that even.

The year before Penelope had abandoned us, life had completely changed for the better because Bethany had been born. I'd felt soaring pride at being a father but also a pressure that it was my responsibility to give my daughter the kind of childhood I would have wanted—one free of anxiety and worry. One that was all about giggles and laughter and being a kid. I didn't want Bethany to ever have to hear her father berating her mother or hear her mother crying for what seemed like days. I knew what bad was, so I knew how to create perfect for Bethany. When Penelope left, I'd been almost overwhelmed by guilt for not being able to sustain my vision of a perfect family for Bethany. It had eased slightly when it was clear Penelope wasn't coming back, but Autumn arriving seemed to bring back the hope into our lives. She made everything more manageable somehow. She made every obstacle feel surmountable. She was like some kind of joy fairy that came in and made everything better. There was more laughter in the house. More fun.

I didn't like the idea that at some point she'd take her magic wand and move on. But that had always been the deal. I'd always known that was going to be the case. And it was the right thing for her and for us. She was young. She'd never travelled before. She should go out and find her place in the world. And I wasn't ever going to make promises to another woman. That ship had sailed. Our parting was inevitable.

"I can help you," I said, shuffling closer to her. "If you want me to. I can tell you where I've been and what I liked. And what to avoid. Like the *Mona Lisa*—get there early, see it, and then get out. Go and see the other Da Vincis in the same gallery, which are just as spectacular, but everyone wanders past them looking for the *Mona Lisa*."

"That's a really good tip," she said, scribbling away.

"And in Barcelona, make sure you just spend a day wandering in Gaudí's park. It's so beautiful; you won't want to rush it. And in Venice, make sure your hotel is just off St. Mark's Square—you want to be part of the hustle and bustle of the place."

She'd stopped writing. "You're like the best tour guide ever." The light in her eyes dimmed slightly. "It's a shame I can't take you with me."

I nodded, trying my best to make my smile spread to my eyes. "You'll have the best time."

She turned back to her notebook, nodding. "Yes. It will be great."

Until she left, I'd hold on tight to her, and try to bring her some of the joy she'd brought me and Bethany. Even if Autumn's joy meant the end of mine.

SIXTEEN

Gabriel

I'd always enjoyed dinners at Hollie and Dexter's place. It was like being with family—or how families were in my imagination. Food. Wine. Good conversation. But tonight, I'd rather be anywhere else. That wasn't quite true. I'd rather be at home with Autumn. Just the two of us. The fact that she'd be at dinner tonight only made things worse. The bubble the two of us had existed in up until now had disintegrated, and I was being forced to think about all the reasons why I shouldn't be with Autumn.

I paid the cab and headed to Hollie and Dexter's front door, pausing before I knocked. I hated that I was lying to my friends. I'd done exactly what Dexter had warned me not to—slept with Autumn. And worse, I couldn't stop. Even worse than that, I didn't want to. Tonight, being with Autumn seemed so much more complicated that it usually did. Autumn and me, together, was so right. So simple. I didn't want to think about any reason why that wouldn't continue to be true.

She made me happy.

And I had forgotten what that felt like.

Not that I would have considered myself *unhappy* before she arrived. I loved Bethany. We had fun together. I enjoyed working in the workshop. But the dull cloud of grief that had been hanging over me ever since Penelope left had lifted.

Life was good. And I wasn't ready to give it up. I wasn't ready to give Autumn up. Not yet. But being here tonight was bringing me face-to-face with the reality that I might have to.

I was pulled from my thoughts by Dexter and Hollie's front door swinging open.

"What are you doing out here?" Hollie said. "I saw you skulking from the window."

"Sorry," I replied. "Just finishing off a few messages." The lies had started already. "Am I late?"

"You're always late," she replied. "Come in and get warm. Thanks for letting Autumn get a sitter."

"No problem," I replied. "Sorry, I didn't bring anything. I meant to stop and buy—"

"Gabriel, don't even think about it. Having you here is all we want."

I'd liked Hollie since the first time I'd met her. Dexter had been an idiot, obviously, and nearly let her slip through his fingers, but he'd figured it out in the end. It was obvious to anyone who saw them together that they simply adored each other. I'd never asked but sometimes I wondered if anyone had suspected all wasn't well with my marriage. Had outsiders seen something I hadn't? I tortured myself enough without knowing the answer to that question.

Everyone chorused hello from where they were already seated around Dexter and Hollie's dining table. I swept my gaze across the room as I waved, trying not to catch Autumn's eye, nodding at Tristan, Beck, and Joshua. "Hey, Stella," I said, seeing Beck's wife and going to give her a brief kiss on the cheek. If Autumn hadn't been working for me—if we hadn't been living together—I probably would have greeted her the same way. Tonight, I'd have to avoid all contact in case someone saw a lingering or too-familiar touch that would give us away. I needed to stay out of her way. I had to remind myself that I couldn't just reach for her. Couldn't just slide my hand around her waist. Couldn't just smooth my thumb over her cheekbone and kiss her.

"You made it before the food came out, Gabriel. Are you slacking at work?" Joshua asked.

"Just because I have a responsible job and don't fuck around being *creative* all day . . . Whatever that means." I took an empty seat opposite Joshua who was sitting next to Autumn.

She smiled and I smiled back. Did she know how much I wanted to kiss her right then?

"I don't draw chalk pictures on Trafalgar square, Gabriel." Joshua turned to Autumn and rolled his eyes. "Did you forget I'm the CEO of the international marketing agency that I founded?"

"You never let us forget." It was a cheap shot, but if I hadn't thought he was trying to impress Autumn with his money and power, I wouldn't have said it. Joshua didn't brag. It wasn't him.

"Wow. Mr. Sunshine has arrived. Mike Green infected your mood again?" he asked. "You need to sack him as a client. I keep telling you."

"Let's not talk about my work. Not when we've got food to eat," I said, turning as Dexter approached the table carrying a board full of chateaubriand.

"This is why we come here so often," Tristan said.

"Don't forget the wine," Dexter said.

"It's the reason I'm marrying him," Hollie said, bringing in pots of vegetables. Friday night was a guaranteed feast in this house.

"Can we help?" I asked.

Dexter chuckled and a wave of laughter followed him as if everyone was having a joke at my expense. "Everyone pitched in before you arrived, Gabriel."

"We know it's why you're late. You just want to get out of chores," Tristan said. "I bet he doesn't lift a finger at home, does he, Autumn?"

All eyes turned to my housemate. Bethany's nanny. My lover.

"Of course he does," she said. "He can't do things if he's not physically there, though."

"And that's my theory proved," Tristan said. "He avoids places if there are chores to do."

I wasn't about to argue over something so petty. I glanced over at Autumn, who seemed to be avoiding looking at anything in particular. God, she looked beautiful—warm and relaxed. I just wanted the world to melt away until only the two of us remained. It was so much easier that way. She was wearing a necklace I hadn't seen before. Perhaps it was one of Hollie's designs. It rested delicately on her collarbone. I longed to trace it with my tongue.

Later.

"What's he like as a boss?" Joshua asked. "Bad tempered and so serious?"

"Oh, he's not so bad," she replied, scooping broccoli from the dish. "And Bethany makes up for anything negative."

I laughed. "Thank God for Bethany."

"She's the best."

"She still go to bed with Bear Bear?" Joshua asked.

"Sure does," Autumn replied. "Wouldn't be without him."

"Grotty little thing," I added.

"He's not grotty, Gabriel," Autumn said. "He's just well-loved." She said it in that same even-tempered, patient way she had with Bethany. But it worked. She was always utterly convincing.

Finally, Dexter and Hollie sat, and Beck filled my wine glass with a red that was bound to be good. Dexter had an incredible collection.

"So, Autumn, how are you finding the men in London?" Stella asked.

My throat constricted and the wine I'd just swallowed stuck in my gullet. I tried to choke as quietly as I could.

"You don't like that Barolo?" Dexter asked. "I can get you something else."

I managed to swallow. "It's good. Just . . . fruitier than I was expecting."

Dexter frowned but didn't say anything.

"I haven't started husband shopping quite yet," Autumn replied with a grin.

"I know a few single guys," Stella said. "What's your type?"

Oh, this was going to be interesting.

"I don't have one really," she replied.

"Not blond, six one, owns an ad agency?" Joshua asked and Autumn laughed.

I gritted my teeth and pretended I didn't want to grab him across the table and tell him to leave her alone.

"That's not true," Hollie interrupted with a sigh. "She likes losers."

I felt the corners of my mouth twitch.

"No one would be good enough as far as my sister's concerned," Autumn replied.

"Well, your sister loves me," Joshua said.

"So you think," Autumn said, gifting him one of her big, bright grins.

"Do I have to ask Hollie's permission to take you out to dinner?" Joshua asked.

I stared into my wine glass and tried to fix my expression in case anyone saw the rage inside me. Joshua could *not* take her out to dinner. *I* hadn't even done that. There was no way I would allow it. I didn't want her coming back, giddy from an evening with him. And what if he tried to kiss her?

"Joshua!" Dexter warned as he stood. "Drop it. And, Gabriel, can you help me with something?"

I snapped my head around. There was no way I wanted to leave the table while Joshua was on the prowl. He might come across as a nice guy, but I knew his history with women. And if Hollie knew what I did, there was no way she'd allow it.

Dexter nodded toward the doorway and reluctantly, I took my napkin from my lap and stood. Why the fuck wasn't he pulling Joshua to one side and having a word with him, rather than having me help him with God-knew-what?

I followed him out into the hallway. "I want to pick out a bottle you'd prefer to the Barolo," he said, leading me into a wine room with a glass door and low lighting. "Let's pick something."

"Can't this wait," I snapped. "Everyone's eating."

Dexter didn't say anything, so I gave in and stalked into the room. He closed the door behind.

"I don't care," I said. "This one." I pulled something off

the shelf without even looking at it. "Can I go back to my steak now?"

"What's going on, Gabriel?"

"I'm hungry. That's what's going on."

"I mean with Autumn."

My stomach sank through the concrete floor. Shit. Was it that obvious?

"What are you talking about?" I hadn't rehearsed what I would say if I was confronted. Autumn and I hadn't discussed it.

Dexter took a deep breath. "I've known you a long time. You've been the dad of the group even before you were an actual dad. Steam was practically coming out of your ears when Joshua was flirting with her."

I didn't know what to say because I wasn't quite sure what he was saying. I just nodded, trying to say nothing at all.

"Look, I can tell you there's no way Joshua's taking her out. You don't need to worry there. And I get that you're protective. She's your employee. You don't want her bringing Joshua back to the house and them doing . . . anything."

The idea was like curdled milk in my stomach. Autumn with anyone else was completely unthinkable.

"She's not going to be disrespectful. I know she cares about Bethany a lot."

"I know," I said, still wondering if he'd figured out there was something between Autumn and me.

"You don't need to worry about her," he said, patting me on the shoulder. "Anyway, Hollie said that guys flock to her. It's only a matter of time before she's dating someone who isn't Joshua."

"Right," I replied.

"And that you can't really do anything about. Remember she's only here until the end of July. And then she's gone."

I nodded. He didn't seem angry with me. And he wasn't telling me to keep away from Autumn. He thought I was looking out for her out of concern for my employee. Which was true. In a sense.

"I'm just wound up about work, Dexter."

"Look, mate, I know work is important. I respect that you don't want to live off your dad's money and you want to be a role model for Bethany, but it's good to have other things going on as well. Now that the divorce is going through, you might want to take a woman out to dinner. I'm not saying you need to get serious with anyone, but I think it would be good for you to have some balance in your life."

I nodded again. If only he knew that I'd taken his advice before he'd given it. I hated to lie to him and if Autumn was anyone but his soon-to-be sister-in-law and Bethany's nanny, I knew he'd be cheering me on. But I couldn't say anything. I'd not discussed it with Autumn and even if I had —what would I say? *I'm banging Autumn? I'm having some short-term, non-complicated sex with your sister-in-law?* He'd accuse me of using her to get over my divorce. Even if that was partly true, I liked Autumn. Cared about her. Enjoyed her company and her outlook on life.

"Can I let Hollie set you up with someone?" he asked.

"If you promise that we can go back to the table now, I promise to consider it. How about that?"

"Okay. I can live with that. For now."

I'd consider being set up. And I'd say no. I didn't want anyone but Autumn or anything but what we already had.

SEVENTEEN

Autumn

I almost couldn't breathe, the view was so spectacular. Gabriel had us in the penthouse suite, enjoying what must have been the best view in Italy. We could see for miles from up here. I took in the domed churches and higgledy-piggledy buildings from the doorway of the balcony, Bethany on my hip. "That must be St. Peter's," I said, pointing to the large grey dome. "I just can't believe I'm here with you guys."

"I can't believe it's bloody raining," Gabriel mumbled from behind me.

I tutted. "It's *California dew*. Not rain. I come from the Pacific Northwest, and California dew doesn't even get me wet. More importantly, we're in Rome. That's *Italy*, in case you didn't know. We brought raincoats and rainboots. We're all set." I wasn't about to let a bit of H_2O spoil this trip. "Bethany, Rome is the capital of Italy. It's on the river Tiber and it was founded in 753 BC."

Bethany nodded solemnly, squinting at the view as I lectured her.

"And did you know that it has the best ice cream in the world?"

"Really?" she asked. "Can we eat some?"

Gelato was definitely on our itinerary. "Sure. We have to make sure your dad tastes some too."

"And we can play hide-and-seek as well?"

As soon as we'd gotten into the hotel, Bethany's eyes had lit up with the idea of hiding in all the different nooks and crannies of the hotel. The thought terrified me.

"We gotta make a deal on this, Bethany," Gabriel said.

"Okay, I can deal," she replied.

"The deal is, when we come in that door, into our bit of the hotel, we can play hide-and-seek. You and me or you and Autumn. But outside that door, you need to be able to see Autumn or me all the time."

"Okay," she said, looking a little confused. "Deal."

"No playing hide-and-seek until we're in our suite. Okay?"

She nodded. "So, now we can?"

"Now is good. I'm going to count to twenty-five."

"Did you lock the suite door?" I said, concerned she wouldn't know which door led out into the hotel corridor.

"Yeah, and I put the chain on. She's not getting out of here."

"This balcony could be a problem," I said. Rome was going to be exciting, but I was going to worry about Bethany a hundred times more than I did at home.

"Not if your California dew keeps up. We'll have the doors shut."

"You have to learn how to dance in the rain, Gabriel.

Haven't you heard? You can't just wait for the storm to pass."

"I'm not dancing anywhere," he replied, his eyebrows furrowed together.

I spun around in the middle of the sitting area. "Well, you're going to miss out. And I refuse to let you. Let's go and find your daughter—who by the way, is hiding behind the door of the bathroom on the chair in there. Then let's go and get gelato."

"How do you know where's she's hiding?" he asked.

I shrugged. I wasn't about to confess that she'd started on again about playing her favorite game as soon as she'd seen that little seat. "If we find her there, you have empirical evidence that I know what I'm talking about, so you'll have to come out to eat gelato with us."

"Are you the second woman today that I find myself making a deal with?"

I grinned at him. "Absolutely."

He pulled me into his arms and pressed his lips against mine. Instantly I became boneless and forgot everything except the hot press of his skin on mine. It took all my willpower to place my palms on his chest and withdraw from his kiss. "We need to find your daughter."

"Okay," he said, before cupping his hands around his mouth. "Coming, ready or not." We headed to the bathroom to find Bethany. But she wasn't behind the bathroom door.

Gabriel beckoned me to follow him with a tilt of his head, and we wandered up the corridor toward the bedroom. "I have an idea."

As we entered the bedroom, I spotted Bethany lying on the bed, having tried to burrow under the pillows and cushions. "Where can she be, Autumn?" Gabriel asked, pretending he hadn't seen her and her socked feet poking out from the blankets. "Behind the curtains maybe." He went over and made a show of scooping up the drapes. "Nope. What about under the bed?"

Bethany giggled as he stepped closer to her, and then he pounced, grabbed her, and fell back onto the bed, his daughter in his arms.

They were beautiful together. They always were. They had a bond that seemed to be unbreakable. And I'd been proven wrong—Bethany hadn't been hiding where I thought she would.

"Looks like I lost our bet," I said.

"I had an advantage and didn't tell you." He tapped his nose. "Historic knowledge."

He was such a good father. Yes, he worked hard, but he paid attention and gave Bethany all his time at weekends. He was a wonderful man. No wonder Hollie hated all my loser boyfriends if there were men in the world like Gabriel.

He began to tickle Bethany and she giggled and squirmed before he set her on her feet and announced, "Ice cream in the rain is next on the agenda, I believe."

"But I lost," I said.

He shrugged and led Bethany out. "Apparently we can't wait for the storm to pass."

We headed out in our rainboots and slickers, with directions to the best gelato in Rome. Bethany insisted on walking between us, holding both our hands as we dodged puddles and pedestrians and navigated the narrow streets that led into open square after open square. We managed to squeeze past a moped coming in the opposite direction through a narrow path under some buildings, and then we were out in the open again. This time, surrounded by tourists. "Keep hold of her," Gabriel said, and I could tell by the dark tone of his voice he was in Sensible Dad mode. I tightened my grip on Bethany's hand. "We'll look but won't stay long."

"Look at what?" All I could see was people.

He lifted his head above the crowd and pointed. "The Trevi Fountain."

I followed his hand and looked up. It was the wildest thing I'd ever seen. We were in a tiny square but on one wall was a huge building that seemed to have a marble Triton bursting out of it in his chariot, bringing the crashing waves of the sea with him. "It's . . . wonderful," I said.

Gabriel grinned and then his face turned stern. "Keep close. I'm going to get us to the front."

He moved into the crowd with the confidence of a man who knew he would get to wherever he was headed. It must be why he was such a great lawyer.

Sure enough, we got to the front and it seemed even more majestic, more imposing from up close. "Can you see the horses?" I asked Bethany, pointing at the marble statues of the sea horses riding through the water. "It's like they freeze-framed an invasion," I said as I stared up at the onslaught of marble.

"Yes, it's very baroque."

"You hold tight to Daddy while I get some euros out." I rummaged in my purse and pulled out some change. "Here. You have to throw over your right shoulder," I said, tapping her gently to indicate the correct side. "Turn around." I handed her a coin in her right hand. "Throw it back over your shoulder and make a wish."

She did exactly what I'd said. "I wished for really good ice cream," she said, and I laughed.

"I hope that one comes true for all of us," Gabriel said.

"Now you," I said, pressing a coin into Gabriel's hand.

He rolled his eyes but turned around and threw the coin over his right shoulder just the same.

"What did you wish, Daddy?"

His gaze flitted between his daughter and me. "I wished to stay as happy as I am right now."

My stomach flipped and I reached for him, wiping the raindrops from his wet cheek.

"What about you?" he said, as he took Bethany's hand.

I turned around and tossed my coin over my shoulder.

"What did you wish?" Bethany asked.

"I cheated," I confessed. "I made two wishes in one. I want great ice cream and to stay this happy."

Gabriel held my gaze. When I'd left Oregon, I'd expected to come to London, start my job as a trainee executive, and have the time of my life. I had no idea that the time of my life would be had hanging out with the best man I'd ever met and his daughter. Unexpected as this was, nothing could have made me happier than I was right now.

EIGHTEEN

Gabriel

I couldn't remember when I'd had a better day. And now the skies had cleared and the view through the balcony doors was breathtaking. Autumn was putting Bethany to bed. She was sleeping in a rollaway in my room and Autumn had the second bedroom in the suite.

Autumn appeared in the doorway in her pajamas. "What did you do?" Her face broke into a grin as she took in the laid table.

I shrugged. "I made a few calls." Room service had delivered dinner, champagne, and flowers, and set it all out on the dining table that overlooked the floor-to-ceiling windows with a view of the city.

"I feel underdressed."

"I would argue the opposite," I said, pulling her toward me as I reached under her top, smoothing my hands around her waist.

"I had the best day," she said. "Rome is so much more than I expected. So . . ."

"Italian?" I offered and she laughed.

"So beautiful and over-the-top extravagant. It just feels full of life."

"Sounds a bit like you." I dropped a lingering kiss on her lips.

"You think I'm extravagant?" she asked.

"I think you're full of life." I kissed her again. "You breathe life into me."

Her hands slid around my neck. "I'm not sure your friends would believe how romantic you are." She stood on tiptoes and we kissed, our mouths meeting and tongues colliding, the lights of the city behind us. Everything just felt completely right. Completely perfect.

She pulled back and put her head on my chest as we looked out at the view.

"Speaking of my friends," I said. "We need to agree what we do if one of them asks straight out if there's anything going on between us." I shifted and started to pour out two glasses of champagne, my arm around Autumn while I did.

She shifted away slightly. "Did someone say something?"

"I thought Dexter was going to the other night, but he just talked about me being an overprotective employer. We need to be prepared."

"Okay," she said, frowning.

"I didn't mean to upset you."

She shook her head. "You didn't."

I passed her a glass of champagne. "Cheers to your first trip to Rome."

She clinked her glass to mine. "I'm so bummed you have to work this week."

"I know. But—" I almost said that we could come back

another time, but I stopped myself. There wouldn't be another time. Not for Autumn and me. "You get to enjoy it with Bethany."

"Let's not think about it and just enjoy dinner," she said, taking the cloche off a plate in front of her. "Pasta. If your kiss didn't make me giddy enough, this might push me over the edge."

I took a seat kitty corner to her so we could both see the view.

"I think we should be honest," Autumn said after she swallowed her first mouthful. "To your friends. Or Hollie."

"Okay," I said, not wanting to commit myself to anything. What did honest mean? What would we tell them?

"But only if they ask." She twirled her fork around, catching her spaghetti. "Hollie will be pissed whether or not I've been hiding it from her."

"I like the idea of being honest," I said and took a forkful of pasta. It didn't sit well with me that Autumn was keeping things from a sister she was so close to. And that I was keeping something from Dexter that I knew he'd feel strongly about. But honesty was more than just responding to a question. It was offering up information if you knew someone would want to know. Wasn't it?

"And if they ask, we say . . .?" I took a sip of champagne and waited for Autumn to reply. My feelings for Autumn had grown the more time I spent with her, but I understood that going forward wouldn't be easy. She wasn't going to be Bethany's nanny beyond July, and she was planning out the rest of her life. I couldn't demand to be included.

Autumn was never shy, but the way she looked at me from under her eyelashes suggested she didn't want to be the first to offer an answer.

"I guess we say that we enjoy each other's company," I suggested.

She nodded as she chewed then swallowed. "Exactly. We like spending time together. And we're hanging out and having fun."

I chuckled. "I'm not sure Dexter will believe that. 'Fun' isn't the first thing my friends associate me with."

"Well Dexter hasn't slept with you, so he would have no idea how fun you can be." Her eyes widened and she grinned as if to say, *Yes, I really said that.* "What else would we say?" she asked, lowering her voice, almost like she didn't want to ask the question. But it was a question she was going to have to answer. I didn't want her to give anything up by being with me.

"I think your suggestion is good," I replied. "We're having fun."

"And we're using condoms and I'm still on the pill."

I tried not to choke. "Do we have to get into that much detail?"

"Hollie is terrified I'll get pregnant before I 'fulfil my potential.' I used to get lectures about it all the time back in Oregon. And to be fair it's not like she didn't have reason. There were so many girls back home who you'd think were going places before bam, they'd get knocked up by their boyfriends. Before you knew it, they'd be behind the registers at Trader Bob's, working night shifts so they could look after their eleven kids during the day."

"Wow. That's an image."

"Maybe not eleven, but you get the picture."

"I do," I replied. "But we're not in Oregon. And—" I stopped myself before I said I didn't want eleven kids. We couldn't have that conversation. Because that was about the future. And we didn't have one. We were having fun. We enjoyed each other's company.

"Okay, so we have birth control covered," I said.

"And I'll just tell her that Bethany doesn't know. We're not hurting anyone."

"Right," I replied.

She exhaled what seemed like a long-held breath. "Right," she said. "Ultimately, it's no one's business except ours."

"Except that Dexter is one of my oldest friends. And I like Hollie and would hate to upset her."

"I'll handle her," she said with a sigh.

"We'll handle them both," I said and took her hand. "And in the meantime, we'll have fun. And enjoy each other's company."

She laughed. "Well that's a guarantee coming from you, Gabriel Chase."

I smiled despite the kernel of unease settling in my chest. I didn't know what it was about Autumn, but despite me doing my best to stay in the here and now, when I was with her, my mind couldn't help wandering to the future.

NINETEEN

Autumn

We looked up at the ceiling of the huge ballroom and tried to count the number of lightbulbs in the ornate glass chandelier. It must have been at least three hundred. "Just the name *Dorchester* sounds fancy," I said.

I'd never stepped inside a fancy hotel before I came to London, and not only had I stayed in one in Rome that was at least a thousand times bigger than the trailer I'd left behind in Oregon, I was now checking out all the best ones in London. Not to stay in, but for Hollie's wedding venue.

"This is almost overwhelming," Hollie said. "It's just so big." She sighed as if she was sizing up the prison cell she was going to call home for the next twenty-five to life, rather than her wedding venue.

"We're just looking though, right? It's not like anyone is going to force you to have a big wedding," I said, trying to reassure her.

"Right. Can you do me a favor and take photographs?"

she asked. "I'm bound to forget. I can barely think straight. And you have such a good eye for detail."

"Sure," I replied, pulling out my phone. I tipped my head back to see if I could get the entire chandelier in one shot. In the end, it took three.

The room was all huge mirrors and silk wallpaper and baby blue drapes that looked so full, they might be able to cover all of London if they were straightened out. The entire room was like being on the *Bridgerton* set. I took a handful of shots, trying to make sure I captured the scale of the room. "It's beautiful," I said, turning a full three hundred and sixty degrees to make sure I hadn't missed anything.

"So it seats up to five hundred and ten people," Beatrice, the woman from the hotel who had shown us in, said. She came up behind us out of nowhere, making me jump like I'd been caught stealing candy from Trader Bob's.

"But the huge advantage is the private entrance from Park Lane."

I recognized that name from the Monopoly board—it was smack next to Mayfair, the second-most expensive property on the board.

"You said you had smaller rooms as well," Hollie said. "Can we see those?"

"Absolutely," Beatrice replied. "If you follow me to the lifts, I can show you our penthouse, which can seat up to thirty-four guests."

Hollie nodded. "Yes, that sounds like a more manageable number." The green tinge to her face began to fade and she smiled.

"So where is Dexter?" I asked as we got into the elevator, which had walls covered in green silk. I wasn't sure if fabric on the walls was a British thing or just a rich-person thing. But I took a picture just in case we needed to remember the elevators. "Shouldn't he be here today rather than me?"

She sighed. "He had some crisis at the store in New York. A security incident, whatever that means. He said if I narrowed it down, we could come back together and look at the rooms I liked best. But we don't even know how big to go. He knows far more people in London than I do. Although he's said he'll charter a plane to bring people over from Oregon."

"A plane? But who would you invite from there?"

She shrugged. "Exactly. I just don't know. Mom and Dad obviously. Anything else feels uncomfortable. Like I'm trying to show off or something."

It was typical of my sister not to make a fuss, even when she was going to be a bride. "Well, like it or not, you're going to be the center of attention on the big day."

Beatrice guided us out of the elevator and through the door of what looked like a bedroom. Hollie froze as soon as she stepped into the room. "Oh wow. That view."

I followed her eyeline and couldn't repress a soft gasp. We were high enough up to see the London skyline stretched out in front of us, a jumble of buildings, big and small, with splashes of green breaking up the offices, palaces, shops, and homes. "You can see for miles. I completely love it."

"If the weather's nice, we could do pre-wedding breakfast drinks on the terrace," Beatrice said. "Obviously, it's difficult to imagine on a day like today. We've even held some ceremonies out here, but it's a little stressful being so weather dependent."

"Yes, that would be worrying." Hollie stepped toward the windows, following the view, and I trailed after her, taking pictures of everything that caught my attention. "But inside you still get the view." She turned around to take it all in. "It's less intimidating than the ballroom but still beautiful."

"This room is so much fun," I said, lowering my phone. "The dramatic red drapes and the cherubs in the fountain—it's all very baroque," I said. "Like a glamorous fairytale."

My sister glanced at me. "Baroque?" she asked as if she couldn't believe that I would have even heard of the word.

"Yes," I said. "I've been to Rome now, didn't you know?"

Her face lit up with a smile as if moments like these were all she could have wanted for me. Me going to Rome with Gabriel and Bethany wasn't exactly how she thought I'd get to travel, but I knew she was pleased I was spreading my wings.

"I can show you the Orchid room next if you want to follow me?" Beatrice said. "It's very pretty for weddings."

"How's the view?" I asked. Beatrice winced slightly.

"Sorry, there isn't a view in that one."

"Then I don't think we need to see it," Hollie said. "I'm feeling a baroque vibe for this wedding."

I laughed and linked my arm through my sister's.

She shrugged. "London brought Dexter and me together. It only seems fitting that it should be a guest at our wedding."

Even though I'd only been in London a couple of months, I understood the pull the city had. The energy, the vibrancy. It was a hive of possibility, and it was where my sister's dreams had come true. This city would be the jumping-off point from where I was going to fulfil my ambitions. "I think that's a lovely idea."

We thanked Beatrice before clambering into a cab and heading to the next hotel.

"At least I know I want a room with a view—I think. Show me the pictures from the ballroom again," she said, peering over to my phone.

I opened my photos and began to scroll backward. "Those red drapes were amazing. And did you notice the windows on the side? You get one hundred and eighty degrees of London in that room."

"I want to see the ballroom again," she said. "I don't know if I'm being ridiculous writing it off so quickly."

I kept swiping and eventually we came to the ballroom. "It's really pretty," I said. "The wallpaper is everything."

Hollie nodded. "Do you have a wide shot?" She leaned over as if she were trying to swipe to the next photo herself.

"Let me see . . ." I kept swiping until I got to pictures of the chandelier that I'd taken first. "No, sorry, but I bet we can find something online or get Beatrice to send us something."

"Keep going," she said, pointing at my screen. "Maybe there was one before the chandelier."

"There wasn't," I said, swiping again to reveal a picture of Gabriel and me in Rome. I quickly snapped the image back to the pictures of the ballroom, hoping she hadn't noticed. "It's a beautiful chandelier." My heart clanked against my ribcage. She hadn't seen that, had she? I'd only seen a flash of something before I'd changed tack. Hollie couldn't possibly have made out what was on that last picture. It had been Gabriel and me on the balcony of the hotel. I'd been trying to get a selfie of the two of us with St. Peter's in the background, but Gabriel was more focused on kissing me than posing for the camera.

"What was that?" she asked.

"That's the last one," I said, nodding at the image on my screen. "The chandelier was the first picture I took."

"No, the one after that. It was a picture of you with a man."

My heart plummeted to the ground like a skydiver without a parachute.

I started scrolling through to the pictures of the penthouse, pretending I hadn't heard her and hoping to distract her with thoughts of her wedding. "I really prefer a room with a view," I said, showing her the screen of my phone.

In a flash, she grabbed my phone out of my hand and tried to scroll through the pictures. "Hollie!" I said, trying to take the phone back, but she turned her back to me. I tried to climb on top of her, but she twisted out of the way. "Give it back."

"Jiminy Cricket, it locked," she said, as she turned back to face the front and pushed my phone into my hand.

"You're insane. What are you doing, stealing my phone?"

"Tell me who that man was."

"In. Sane," I snapped, and I shoved my cell into my purse where Hollie couldn't reach it. I folded my arms, fuming.

We sat in silence as the cab stopped and started along Piccadilly. She was going to have to apologize. How dare she just take my phone like I was a teenager she'd caught doing something wrong.

Out of the corner of my eye I could see her glancing over at me. I turned my head so I was focused on what was going on outside on the street.

More silence.

"I'm sorry," she said, finally.

"How would you feel if I'd done that to you?" I snapped.

"I don't have anything private on my phone," Hollie replied.

She was so annoying. She knew that it was the principle that mattered. "Not the point. If you want to see something, ask me. I'm not a child."

"I know," she replied. "I'm losing my mind. Can I blame the wedding planning?"

I shrugged. I didn't want to ruin her day, but she was way out of line. "Fine. Just don't do it again."

"I promise," she said. I could hear the *but* before it was even out of her mouth. "But are you going to tell me who it was?"

I sighed. This was it. I was in store for a mammoth lecture. But I couldn't lie. We didn't do that to each other. I turned to face her. "I'll tell you if you promise not to lose your goddamned mind any more than you already have."

She slumped back on her seat, shaking her head. "It's Gabriel." She said it with certainty, as if I'd already confessed. "I knew it."

"I don't understand what your objection is. The guys I dated before were losers. I get why you didn't like them. Gabriel isn't anything like them."

"No, he's serious and a father and very settled. None of those things describe you or where you are in your life."

"But it doesn't mean I don't like him or *can't* like him. That we don't or can't like each other. I don't get it."

"You're both at different stages of your life. You want to travel and see the world. He's got different priorities."

"Well, first off, let me remind you who's responsible for me going to Rome. I got to go to a wonderful city and see amazing things that I could only ever dream about, all because of Gabriel. So don't act like he's stopping me from fulfilling my dreams. In fact, he's actively supporting me in them."

Hollie shifted around so she was facing me. "But that's one trip. What happens if you want to go to Bali for three months? He's hardly going to strap Bethany on his back and stay in some hostel with you and a bunch of other twentysomethings."

"You'll be happy to know I've realized that five-star hotels make a much nicer base than hostels when travelling." I laughed, hoping to lighten the atmosphere. "Also, I've never mentioned Bali. I'll start a job in September, which means I won't get a chance to spend three months anywhere but London."

"But you're in their *international* program. What happens if they assign you outside London?"

"You're thinking too far ahead, Hollie. It's not venues for *my* wedding we're looking at today." I didn't want to think too far in the future. Things would get complicated that way, and I liked how things were now. Easy. Simple. Right.

"So you're not serious about him?" she asked.

I didn't allow myself to think about the answer to that question. It kept popping up in my own head, but each time I simply dunked it under the surface like the boys used to do to each other in the pool.

"We're having fun," I replied, giving the pre-arranged answer Gabriel and I had agreed on.

"Gabriel doesn't do 'just fun.' He's a serious man with serious responsibilities."

"Trust me, he knows how to have fun, Hollie." I raised my eyebrows at her.

"Oh God, tell me you're using birth control."

"Yes. Condoms and I'm still on the pill."

"Well, that's one thing at least. But seriously, he's been hurt before. His wife leaving devastated him, from what Dexter has said. If you're just having fun and he's serious about you—"

"I didn't say that." The last thing I wanted to do was hurt Gabriel. I wasn't sure what had happened with his wife, but I couldn't imagine what would make a woman walk out on a man as truly good and kind and sexy-as-hell as Gabriel. Or a daughter as fun and vibrant and wonderful as Bethany.

"So, you're saying you're serious about him?"

Whatever I said, Hollie wouldn't be happy. If I was serious about Gabriel, I'd be compromising my future. If I wasn't serious about him, I'd be bound to hurt him. I was in a lose-lose situation.

"Look, if I'm being completely honest with you, I've never felt like this about anyone." She looked like I'd just told her I wasn't going to attend her wedding, but she needed to understand. "He's kind and funny and caring. He loves his daughter. He's thoughtful and a great listener. I enjoy being with him."

"Oh, Autumn. But you're so young and—"

"Just listen for a second. We know that whatever there is between us is . . . There are external factors that . . . You know, it's difficult. So we've agreed not to look too far ahead and just enjoy each day."

But in the moments after Bethany fell asleep and before Gabriel came home, I couldn't help thinking about *what if*. I liked Gabriel. Really liked him. And I suspected I wouldn't want to give him up when it came time for me to leave.

"I know you better than you know yourself," Hollie started. Her voice was quiet and gentle—no trace of the

Sensible Sister tone I'd expected. "And to most people you might come across as some kind of free spirit who's drifted along, happy to be pushed in one direction or another by your sister. But we both know that's not true. I didn't *make* you work your ass off at school and college. You had your sights set on a better life just as much as I did. You're focused and determined and you've always got one eye on the future. Those boys you dated back in Oregon were always going to get left behind by you. You've said it yourself. But what about Gabriel? Is he just another that you'll leave in your rear-view mirror, or are you going to compromise what you want to stay by his side?"

"Maybe there's a way for us to be together without making any compromises," I said. I'd never run through options because there were too many moving parts, and I didn't want to know it was hopeless. "I don't think we need to play this out to the end and decide that it's not going to work. If you did that, then on paper, most relationships would be doomed to fail." I wasn't sure which one of us I was trying to convince. "You and Dexter shouldn't work, but you do."

"But we're not talking small issues. Are you saying you're prepared to take on another woman's child at twenty-three? You don't think that's a compromise too far?"

Hollie didn't often shock me, but her question was like a punch to the gut. "Bethany's not another woman's child. She's Gabriel's daughter. Describing it as *taking her on* makes it sound like she's a virus or something. She's sweet and loving and I adore her."

"I'm sorry." She had the decency to look embarrassed by what she'd said. I was grateful that Hollie was always there to fight in my corner, but she didn't always know what was best for me. "Children are a big responsibility. That's all I'm trying to say."

"I know. And there's a lot that would need to be worked out. I'm not saying we will work it out or that we'd even want to." But the more time I spent with Gabriel, the more time I wanted to spend with him and the less I looked forward to leaving at the end of the summer. "I'm just saying that we don't need to think about that now. And if in the future we do want to think about it, we can deal with it then."

"I want you to be happy. But more than that, I want you to know what's possible."

"What do you mean?" I asked.

"Tammy Greenfield's the perfect example. She's the happiest woman at the Sunshine Trailer Park, am I right?"

"Absolutely." Tammy was a cheerleader in high school. She married the quarterback. They had three children. They both had jobs and their trailer was the nicest one on the street. "She's got reasons to be happy."

"She does," Hollie agreed. "But you can bet she's not going to feel the way you did when you went into the Pantheon or when you saw Big Ben. Tammy has made lemonade out of lemons, but I don't want you to have lemons to begin with. I want you to know what's out there and then choose what will make you happy. You've always been so good at making the best of what we had. You were always the one who could get me to look on the bright side. But I don't want you to have to. I don't want you to *make do* when it comes to your future."

I could accuse Hollie of being an interfering, overprotective big sister, but when she said stuff like that, I couldn't do anything but love her for all of it. "I'm so lucky to have you as a sister."

"Not as lucky as me."

"I don't want you to think I don't get it. I understand what you're saying. But we're not in Oregon anymore. You coming to London showed me that anything is possible. And we got out. Both of us. I'm not going to end up like Tammy Greenfield. It's already way too late for that. I promise you."

"Well, if you ever dare to dye your hair that circus red, I'm going to disown you."

"If I make you a promise that my hair is never going to be anything like Tammy's, can you try to be just a little supportive of me sleeping with my married, single father, much-older-than-me boss?" I started to chuckle as my description of Gabriel laid bare so many of the obstacles to us having a future together.

"Oh my God, Autumn. Nothing's ever straightforward, is it?"

"That's the way life is. And look how it turned out for you," I said, peering out the window as we pulled up in front of the Savoy.

"I could never have even dared dream that someone like Dexter would love me, or that I would love anyone as much as I love him. I want that for you too, Autumn."

"Same, sis." I didn't dare let myself think about loving Gabriel. For now, I was happy to be happy. Happy to be with him. Happy to feel as good as I did when we were together. Before today, I'd only had a trickle of thoughts about my feelings for Gabriel and what the future might hold. Talking about it with Hollie had made it clear that deep down, in the bottom of my heart, I was holding back a tidal wave.

TWENTY

Gabriel

I padded downstairs to the smell of Autumn's cooking, having just put Bethany to bed. Weekends, when I got to see my daughter from the moment she woke up to the moment she went to bed, were what I lived for.

"I poured you a glass of wine," Autumn said as I entered the kitchen.

"That rounds off a great day. Thanks." I took the glass from the counter beside the hob and took a sip. "Bethany passed out before I finished *Zog and the Flying Doctors.*"

"Best book ever," Autumn said with a wide grin. "Chicken pasanda tonight, if that's okay."

"More than okay. Can I help?"

She shrugged. "Nothing to do for dinner, but you could look at those résumés I left out for you. I've arranged interviews for all four this week because there's only a month before I leave. They look amazing."

I groaned. I didn't want to think about another nanny because that meant Autumn was leaving, which didn't bear thinking about. There wasn't going to be anyone like Autumn. Apart from the fact that I was sleeping with her, she was wonderful with Bethany and I trusted her completely. Anyone else was going to be a step down.

"Look at that top one." She nodded to the stack of papers on the island. "She's a Norland nanny like the royal family always have, and she's got years of experience. Plus she has a lifeguard qualification."

Just like Autumn to think of everything. "She's not you," I huffed.

"We'll find someone better than me. Your mail is in that pile of papers as well. It's building up."

I pulled the stack of envelopes from underneath the CVs and started to flick through them to see if there was anything other than water bills and bank statements. "There's one for you here." I pulled out an envelope and handed it to Autumn.

She set down her wine and grabbed it from the side and set about opening it. "I never get mail."

After looking at them, I set the envelopes down. There was nothing in my post that I wanted to open. I'd rather chat and pretend to help with cooking dinner.

I glanced up to find Autumn's face frozen in a grin that even I could tell was forced. "You okay?" I asked.

"Yes," she said, resolutely. "Absolutely fine."

She didn't look fine.

I glanced down at the letter. "Does it say anything interesting?"

She folded the letter and stuffed it back in the envelope, tossing it onto the counter before heading back to the hob and stirring the chicken vigorously. "They're cancelling my trainee-executive position. Fifty percent of our year has been cut. I'm out."

"They did what?" I asked, wondering why she was so calm when the role she'd moved across an ocean for had just gone up in smoke.

"It's fine. Better this way probably. I wouldn't have had enough money to see much of Europe in August anyway. I can get a bar job or even stay on with you and Bethany if you like." She picked up her wine and took a gulp. I slid my arm around her waist, and she froze. "I'm fine. It's better this way. And it's not like I really want to be in an international program anyway. I want a job in London because this is where Hollie is. This is for the best."

I turned off the hob and took the wooden spoon from her hand. "It's awful news, Autumn. I'm so sorry."

"Don't be," she said through gritted teeth. "Like I said, it's fine. If you don't want me to stay on, that's fine too I can find something else. I can—" She pulled in a breath. "I can even go back to Oregon for a while. I'll get to spend some time with my mom and dad."

How was she just shrugging this off? I knew the last thing she wanted to do was go back to Oregon.

"You're right. I don't want you staying on as Bethany's nanny," I said, holding her by the shoulders. "I want you to be doing what you've had your heart set on for months."

"Well, that option is no longer on the table. You have to deal with what you've got, not what you'd like. Let's look on the bright side—"

"No, Autumn. Let's not look at the bright side. Let's get drunk and send those arseholes who just fired you a letter telling them you're going to sue them. They can't just string people along like that."

"Don't be ridiculous," she said, picking up the wooden spoon and stirring the cooling curry. "That's not going to help. I just need a few days to make a plan. Things will work out for the best. They always do."

"Autumn!" I snapped. "What the hell is the matter with you?"

She turned, shock flashing behind her eyes. "What?"

"You're being ridiculous. You can't tell me you're not upset about this."

She shrugged. "There's no point in putting my energy into being upset." She stopped and winced. "Don't say anything to Dexter. He'll tell Hollie and she'll start freaking out and it will be a mess."

"Freaking out would be the right response," I said. She was behaving like a robot. I loved the fact that she was sunny and positive all the time, but she was taking it to an extreme. "You don't need to look on the bright side tonight. Maybe not ever. Maybe this is just a shit thing that's going to happen and you can be pissed off and angry and sad and—"

She shoved the wooden spoon into the curry and pushed past me. "Worse things have happened to me, Gabriel," she said, her voice lifting slightly as if she were on the verge of actually expressing how she felt. "I can't break down when I have a setback. If I did, I'd never pull myself together. And I'd certainly never be able to help Hollie if I was constantly getting angry and pissed off about how life was unfair. These things happen."

"Just because worse things have happened—just because bad things happen—doesn't mean you can't feel things. It doesn't mean you have to put on a smile and pretend everything's okay. You can shout and cry and stamp your feet."

"That's not what I do," she said, her eyes beginning to

water. "If I give in to it and collapse, I don't know if I can get back up."

My heart squeezed. Here she was, trying to keep her chin up, when anyone else would have given in to devastation.

"Of course, you will. You're strong and capable and independent. But you don't have to be all those things *all the time*. And I'm here to give you a hand up, if you need it." I pulled her into my arms, and she sank into me, boneless.

"I don't know how to give in to it. I just . . . want to be happy."

I wanted that for her too. "Even the sun brings shadows," I said. "Nothing is all good, all the time. It's in the shades of grey that we learn who we are."

"I've always been the happy one. The one who pulls Hollie and me up and makes us believe we can get through."

I'd always loved how sunny and positive Autumn was. How she always saw the silver lining in every cloud. I hadn't realized until tonight that she'd cultivated that disposition because she'd faced so many impossible situations. It was a coping mechanism as much as it was a personality trait.

"Not all the time," I said. "You can take turns."

Her sobs were almost unnoticeable, but I held her tightly as she let out everything she'd been holding on to. I wanted to make it better for her—perhaps that was the example she set me—but there was nothing that could make it better. Not tonight. This evening was just going to be terrible. All I could do was hold her.

"I need wine," she said eventually.

"That I can do," I said, not letting her go as I shuffled us both toward her glass.

"I don't know what to do," she said, her voice wobbling. "Hollie is going to be so disappointed in me."

"No," I said, pulling her tighter. "She's going to be disappointed *for* you. Not *in* you. You don't need to concern yourself about that."

"She's going to worry."

"She knows you better than that. There's no need to worry."

"There are always a thousand reasons to worry, Gabriel. And I don't need to be one more."

Thoughts started to slot into my brain and make sense, like the final pieces of a jigsaw. She was always so happy and upbeat because she didn't want to be a burden. She didn't want to be another item on anyone's list of worries, especially not Hollie's.

"Your sister loves you. She's bound to worry sometimes. That's natural and it's okay. But that doesn't mean you're a burden."

"She was the reason I had food in my belly and a roof over my head growing up."

"But not anymore. You got your executive training position yourself. You'll get another. And you know what? You are a capable, independent, creative woman. I would bet money that you took a chunk of the burden growing up. I've seen the way you organize this house. And Bethany—you saved her life, for goodness' sake. And you even organize me." I nodded to the candidates for the new nanny she'd shortlisted. "I can't imagine you ever being a burden. You might have been younger, and you might have supported each other in different ways, but you were both in a very difficult situation. You both fought hard to survive.

"It's okay for things not to be okay sometimes," I said. "It's okay to need help and it's okay for people to give you help." I kissed the top of her head. "I'm here to help where I can. Even if it's to pour your wine. You will figure this out. I have no doubt."

Her bottom lip wobbled, and she rested her head on my chest. "How do you know exactly the right thing to say?"

"Believe me, I learned what it is to need help and what it is to get it from five of the best friends a man can have."

"Even Tristan?" she asked.

"Even him. There's nothing he wouldn't do for any one of us. And vice versa. You have that with Hollie. It's a two-way street."

"Thank you," she said as she looked up at me. "I'm so disappointed. I thought I was about to make this final move away from my past. And without that job . . . I just don't know where to go from here."

I nodded. "I understand. But you don't need to know where to go right away. You have time to figure it out."

As I held her, I realized that the more I knew about Autumn, the more I liked her. Yes, I loved that she was sunny and positive and always looked for the silver lining. But I liked her even more as I understood why she was built like that. Most of all, I felt honored to be the man who got to pour her wine and hold her when the sky clouded over, not a sliver of sunshine in sight.

TWENTY-ONE

Gabriel

I squeezed Autumn's hand as she sat beside me in the cab on the way to the restaurant, trying to give her some wordless reassurance about tonight. So far, nothing I said had stopped her chewing her lip and digging her nails into my hand.

I hadn't seen Dexter since Autumn told her sister about our relationship, and Autumn hadn't seen Hollie since she'd told her about losing her job just over a week ago.

"I'm not sure I'm cut out for these fancy London restaurants, even though it's my birthday," she said. "I'm happy with meatloaf and a bottle of wine."

"We don't have to go if you don't want to." It would be much easier for me to stay at home with Autumn. Dexter was going to be pissed. His anger wouldn't change anything —I wasn't going to give up Autumn.

"Of course I have to go, are you kidding? Hollie has been planning this for weeks. And it will be nice," she said as if she was convincing herself. "It's good to get out and do things, and Hollie said the restaurant was amazing. Have you been before?"

"Maybe," I replied. The name sounded familiar, but a restaurant was a restaurant as far as I was concerned.

"Apparently the bathrooms are eggs that open up or something."

"Eggs?" Jesus, couldn't London restaurants just have good food and good wine and leave the rest up to the people who were dining?

"Sounds weird. Anyway, it will give everyone something to talk about so hopefully they won't focus on gossip." Autumn wasn't in her normally sunny mood tonight.

"These are very old friends, Autumn. They won't be gossiping. Well, not about me or you, anyway. Dexter messaged me and said he wanted a word and so no doubt, we'll have to speak but everything's going to be fine."

"It's usually me telling you things will work out."

"Right? What happened?"

"I just don't want Dexter giving you a hard time. You and me . . . I'm a consenting adult."

"You're also Hollie's sister. He's got a right to be protective. If I had a little more self-control around you then it would have been easier."

"Easier? It would be easier not to be with me?" Autumn's clouds were out in force tonight, but I took it as a compliment that she was showing me what was going on inside her. I wasn't sure there was anyone else in the world who got to see that.

"That's not what I said." She thought I had regrets, but I didn't. Not one. "But I breached Dexter's trust. And he deserves an apology and some reassurance from me."

"Reassurance?"

"You know, that I'm not going to dick you around."

"Have you ever dicked anyone around your whole life?" she asked.

"No one's perfect."

"If you say so." She leaned against my shoulder and I pressed a kiss on the top of her head, thanking her for the compliment, despite it being far from true.

We lived together. She knew my flaws. She understood how demanding my job was and how most of the time, I liked to escape into my workshop rather than talk about what was going on. I was closed off and wary of letting anyone in. But here I was, holding this woman's hand. This person who was almost all sunshine but was finally letting me see her clouds.

We pulled up in front of the restaurant and climbed the steps, where Dexter and Hollie stood waiting for us.

"It's the birthday girl," Dexter said as he greeted Autumn with a kiss. "And my one-time best friend."

I sighed. "Are we going to have to duel?" I asked, shaking his hand.

He cocked his head, indicating a bar across the hall. He turned to Hollie. "Order us something and we'll be there in a minute, will you?"

I pulled off my coat and unwrapped the scarf from my neck, and Dexter leaned against the bar.

"Don't fuck her around," Dexter said.

I nodded. "I won't."

"And she's young, Gabriel. I don't want either of you to get hurt because you're not heading in the same direction." He paused. "But relationships are messy and if you end up with your heart splattered on the wall, I'm here for you, mate."

"I appreciate it. We're not fast-forwarding anything. Just enjoying the moment."

He patted me on the shoulder. "Good. Shall we join the others?"

"Is that it?"

He shrugged. "What do you want me to say? I'm fucking happy you have someone. Autumn's a great girl. You've said you won't fuck her around and I believe you. What did I miss?"

I was lucky to have a friend like Dexter. And the rest of them. Dexter knew my heart and trusted me. There really wasn't anything more to say. "You're a good man, Dexter Daniels."

"You too, Gabriel. I'm happy if you're happy."

We headed back out to the lobby and got directed into the restaurant, where I could see Autumn and Hollie at the bar. She was laughing at something and then her hands were in the air and she was scrunching up her face.

"What are you two laughing about?" Dexter said.

"Autumn was just telling me about her bad mood today and I told her that it never lasts long."

"Right," I said. "Ten minutes tops before she's found a positive angle on the worst situation."

Someone called Autumn's name and when we turned, Tristan and Joshua were heading toward us.

"You look stunning," Tristan said to Autumn, kissing her on the cheek. "So do you, Hollie. Great necklace."

"The beautiful birthday girl," Joshua said, pulling her into a hug.

I wanted my friends to like Autumn. I just didn't want them to like her too much.

"Right." I had something to say. There was no point in hiding it from my friends any longer. "Joshua, and maybe you need to hear this too, Tristan. You should both know that Autumn and I are together. You can flirt all you like with her, but at the end of the night, she's coming home with me."

Tristan's eyebrows looked like they were going to disappear over the top of his head. "Fucking hell, I knew that face of yours would come in handy one day."

"What has my face got to do with it?" I asked, completely confused.

"Don't pretend you don't know you're a handsome devil," he replied and nudged me.

I shook my head. "I have no response to that."

"Can we eat now?" Autumn asked, sliding her hand into mine. It was the first time we'd held hands in public. Even in Rome, we'd had Bethany with us and hadn't crossed that line. "I'm *famished,* as the Brits would say, and I need a drink so I can see these eggs everyone keeps talking about."

"Follow me," said Dexter, leading us all over to the hostess. "Andrew, Beck, and Stella will have to catch up with us."

"Speak of the devil," Joshua said. "The three most beautiful women in London and none of them on my arm. I need to figure out my priorities in life."

"You said it," I said, slapping Joshua on the back as we made our way to the table. "I keep telling you, you work too hard."

"Right," he said, offering me a half smile. "Maybe that's it."

I made a mental note to take him to lunch in the next couple of weeks. Something was up but now wasn't the time to get into it. I wanted tonight to be all about Autumn.

Dinner was more enjoyable for me than for Autumn. These had been my friends for as long as I cared to remember, but I could tell Autumn wasn't entirely herself. Like she said, she'd have been just as happy at home with meatloaf.

I cleared my throat to get the table's attention. "Can I suggest we finish up here? I've organized a little afterparty."

I could see Autumn looking at me out of the corner of my eyes, her eyebrows pinched together.

"Afterparty?" Stella asked. "That sounds exciting."

I smiled. I was about to announce a trip to my own personal hell. But it would be worth it, because Autumn would have the time of her life. I hoped.

"What do you have planned?" Dexter asked.

I pulled out my phone. "I've hired this place out for our group." I showed them a picture of the Theatre Café, which I'd found out was a little café on St. Martins Lane in the West End that was dedicated to musicals and regularly had cast members from current musicals in to perform. "I've invited some of the cast of *Mamma Mia* and *Wicked* along to sing some songs, and we all get to join in."

"Really?" Autumn asked me, clearly thinking I was joking. "Honestly?"

"Wow," Hollie said from across the table.

"Unfortunately, Idina Menzel wasn't available, but the stars from the current productions are coming," I said. "I thought you'd like it."

Autumn shook her head, a grin spreading across her face like butter. "But you hate my singing."

"That's true," I replied. "But I want you to have a fantastic birthday more than I value my eardrums."

Autumn laughed. "You are the best of men, Gabriel Chase. I can't imagine a better birthday gift."

Seeing Autumn happy would be worth enduring whatever was to come.

TWENTY-TWO

Autumn

I wasn't sure I'd ever been attracted to a man more than I was to Gabriel when he told Joshua and Tristan they could flirt all they liked, but I was going home with him. It encapsulated one of the things I liked best about him—he didn't say much, but when he did, every word counted. He was all strong, brooding confidence that didn't need to shout. Some guys were possessive or territorial, but it was all about their ego. When Gabriel said what he did, it was a statement of fact to stop his friends wasting their energy.

And then he told us about the Theatre Café, and I didn't know if I should kiss him into next week or faint from all the swooning.

It was just past one in the morning when we got home, which meant we had six hours until Bethany got up.

We could get a lot done in six hours.

Gabriel put his key in the door, and I placed my hand on his, making him stop and turn to me.

"You okay?"

I nodded. "You need to get rid of the sitter as soon as possible," I said, and reached around to the crotch of his pants. I let out a small moan as I found him hard as rock in my hand. "I have plans for this."

"Believe me, I have plans too," he said and opened the door, gesturing for me to go in first.

The sitter was gone in less than sixty seconds. As Gabriel shut the door, I slid my hands around his waist.

"Did you have a good time tonight?"

"Of course," I replied. "I was with all my favorite people. *And* I got to sing. Anyway, the night's not over yet."

He tilted his head to one side, and I don't know if it was the way his eyes seemed to narrow ever so slightly, or the way he seemed to tower even taller over me than he did normally, but I felt like he was getting ready to devour me. And I was looking forward to being his prey. The starting pistol had been fired on my heartbeat, which set off at a sprint. "I think you've been a little wound up for me all night."

He slid his hands over my ass and yanked the bottom of my dress up. Jesus, how could this man be so polite in public? So taciturn and suave when he was in company? Then a switch flipped as soon as we were alone, and he turned dirty and provocative and knee-weakening sexy.

His hands slid into my panties, his fingers into my folds, and I sighed with relief that finally, I was right where I wanted to be.

"Shit," he spat and spun me around so I was pressed up against the door. "Have you been this wet for me all night?"

I nodded as he lifted my leg over his hip and slid his fingers inside me.

"You're soaked," he said, pushing his fingers inside, his thumb finding my clit. "I'm surprised you lasted this long without an orgasm." He coaxed my g-spot awake with his fingers and I couldn't stop myself from twisting my hips to get more. I needed relief from this built-up need I had for him. "I'm shocked you weren't begging for me in the cab. If you'd have said, I would have been more than happy to have reached up your skirt into your hot, tight pussy and made you come."

I tried to keep control over my breath as he spoke, but it was no easy feat. He was right. I'd been so wound up all evening. So desperate for him. Now that he was touching me, I was already so close to the orgasm I'd been imagining getting all evening.

In a flash he let go of me, took his hand away, and stepped back, shoving his hands in his pockets. I stayed pinned against the door, unable to function. My disappointment at his lost touch felt like a chasm opening in my chest.

He pulled out a foil square and in record time, had his pants open, the condom on, and my leg around his waist. "This what you need?" he asked as he thrust into me.

It was exactly what I needed, and I exhaled with relief at having him inside me finally. "Yes," I choked out. "It's all I need." I held onto him, clinging to his thick, muscular arms as he pounded into me, just as I'd hoped he would.

He fucked me with hard, deliberate, achingly deep movements, and I could do nothing but let him. Nothing but give myself up to him. I'd spent the evening wondering how I was going to seduce him, but I should have known that seduction wasn't necessary when it came to Gabriel. He knew what he wanted and he took it, and I was happy to let him.

"I've been thinking about this all night. I've been imagining all the ways I'm going to fuck you," he said between heavy breaths. "First it's going to be like this up against the door. Then I'm going to go down on you and make you scream. Then I'm going to fuck your mouth. And you're going to come and come and come."

It was too much. His words. The friction. The feeling of being impaled on him, my back against the hard wood of the door. "Gabriel," I cried out.

"That's right," he said, his voice softening, his pace slowing but not stopping as I shuddered against him.

He lifted me up as I floated down from my climax, and I pulled him closer. I wanted to stay like this for as long as possible—him and me, joined. Connected. Together. In every way.

"You okay?" he asked as he sat me on the kitchen table and began to undress me and then himself. His cock stood thick and upright against his belly, and my eyes trailed up to its crown, to his flat stomach, his hard chest, his wide shoulders, and that oh-so-beautiful face.

I nodded.

"You seem . . . a little sad."

I shook my head. "I'm not sad at all." I paused. My instinct was to hold back. To keep things sunny and light. But the fact was, he seemed to like to hear everything about me. The good *and* the bad. And I wanted him to know how I felt about him. I wanted to be real with him. "I *really* like you, Gabriel," I said. It was important he knew that. Important that he understood this wasn't just about the sexual chemistry. It wasn't just about the way he was wise and caring. It wasn't any one thing. It was everything.

He paused and looked at me as I sat naked on the table in front of him and cupped my face. "I *really* like you too." He stroked his thumb over my cheekbone. "More and more."

I tilted my head into his hand, and he bent to press his

lips against mine. If whatever we had was growing stronger as time went on, then how was I going to feel when August arrived, fresh with its invitation to travel? Would my wanderlust fade, burrow itself beneath my feelings for Gabriel? We had just over a month before I'd be gone. And then what?

Before I could drown in what-ifs, Gabriel's insistent tongue and urgent lips worked their way down my neck, between my breasts and over my belly. Roughly, he pulled my legs apart and kneeled before he buried his head between my thighs. He was impatient and greedy, and he made me feel as if I were the most valuable prize he could ever wish for.

His tongue soothed me at first, long, languid, slow strokes that calmed my pulsing clitoris and gave me a chance to revel in his desire for me. I sighed and his tongue grew firmer and more insistent, ratcheting up my yearning for more of him. He knew, and began to circle and flick his tongue in a circuitous release of pleasure that climbed up my body.

My body had surrendered and my orgasm galloped toward me, unrelenting and urgent. Just as I began to fall, he took away his tongue and his fingers and stood.

My eyes widened as I waited for him to explain himself. But he said nothing and simply lay me down on the table as if I were the main course at his one-man banquet. He stood at one end of the table and I shifted, understanding Gabriel was a man who always kept his word.

He was going to fuck my mouth.

He guided my head off the end of the table and tilted it back. "I'm going to get so deep—right at the back of your throat."

I groaned and opened my legs so he could see what his

words did to me. What his tongue and his cock had already done to me. I was red and swollen and so, so wet.

He slid against my tongue with a groan and swept his hands through my hair, holding my head as he pulled back and rammed his cock into my throat.

Any other man and I would have said no, but I wanted this just as much as he did. I wanted him to fuck me exactly how he wanted to fuck me. I wanted him to take everything I had to give. I wanted everything with him.

He slid his hands over my breasts, twisting my nipples, causing me to moan at the sparks of pleasure it set up as he kept fucking me where I lay.

"Autumn, you're so gorgeous," he growled. He dipped his hand between my legs. "And so fucking wet."

I came as soon as he touched me. Shuddering as he withdrew from my mouth. "Oh baby. You're still so wound up."

Two orgasms and I still wanted more.

"I should have cut this evening short. Made some sort of excuse and come home to fill you up."

He walked around the table and scooped me up, this time placing me at the edge of the oak. "I think you just need a good, hard fuck again, don't you?"

He grabbed a condom from where he'd left the packet from the first time, but I didn't want him to use it.

"I'm taking contraceptives," I said. "And I was tested before I left the U.S."

He stalked back from where he'd left me with my legs open, waiting for him. "You want me inside you, skin to skin," he said as a flat statement. "I was tested after my ex-wife left and there's been no one since."

"Yes, Gabriel," I said, clawing at his chest.

He stood between my legs and positioned himself at my entrance. "You want it?"

I nodded.

He pushed in so slowly, our eyes locked on each other as if we were stepping over some kind of line in the sand.

"It's so good, Gabriel." He felt so perfect. As if my body had been waiting for him my entire life.

"Because you're amazing."

"With you," I replied. I was amazing with him. There were no reservations about the strength of my feelings, about what kind of man he was or how he cared for me. And he cared for the whole me, not just the piece of me that I chose to show the world. He liked my shade as well as my light. I didn't think that was possible. The only obstacles between us were external, and the longer I knew him, and the deeper my feelings grew, the more the issues that once looked unsurmountable seemed to diminish in size and importance.

Was that what love was? Something that could conquer all?

TWENTY-THREE

Gabriel

I loved fucking Autumn. So much so that I wondered if I'd ever be able to exist without having her naked beneath me. I certainly didn't want to find out. But more than fucking her, I loved being with her afterward and before and all the times in between. It felt so natural and right. And she was so funny and interesting—I was becoming completely captivated by her.

"It's late," she said as she took her legs from where they laid over my lap as we recovered on the sofa. I'd managed to pull on some boxers and trousers. Autumn was wearing my shirt, which made her almost unbearably tempting, and we'd just been sitting together, chatting about nothing and everything. "You have to be up early for work."

She was right. It would be dawn soon, but I wasn't ready for her to go to bed alone. I wanted more time with her before I had to give her up. "I haven't given you your birthday gift yet."

"I think you gave me your gift already," she said. "Four times, if I'm counting correctly."

I grinned as I stood and held out my hand. "Well, I know nothing can top *that*, but I do have an actual gift for you."

"Honestly, Gabriel, I've had a more than enjoyable evening. Eaten out at a fancy restaurant. Been eaten out by a fancy guy. And of course, there was the singing. What more can I ask for?"

I chuckled and led her to my workshop. "It's only a small gift, so don't get your hopes up." Since Autumn and I had started sleeping together, I'd spent less and less time in my sanctuary. But when I had been in here, I'd been working on Autumn's gift. I flicked on the light and looked over at the bench where I'd wrapped what I'd made with a red velvet bow.

"My hopes are always high," she said. It was true—despite her clouds, she was relentlessly optimistic about everything.

"Here," I said, indicating the box on the bench. "Usually I refinish, restore, and bring something back to life. This is the first thing I've made from scratch."

Her wide, innocent eyes peered at the box. "Gabriel," she said softly. I wasn't sure I'd heard the catch in her voice before. I could tell she was surprised, but was she trying to save her feelings by masking her disappointment? "This is beautiful." No, Autumn's truth always shone through. She stroked her hand across the waxed walnut lid of the square jewelry box.

"I could have bought you something but—"

"This is the best present you could have ever given me. I can't believe you made this for me." With one hand still on the box, she slid the other up my chest. I grabbed her hand and kissed her knuckles.

"It's a jewelry box. I know Hollie gives you her designs and I know how important your sister is to you . . ."

Her eyes went glassy and she looked away, dipping to examine the box in more detail.

"It opens," I said, chuckling at her awe and pulling at the bow.

She glanced at me with a smile and then lifted the lid.

"American walnut outside. And English sycamore inside." I hadn't realized it until now, but it was like the box represented us. American and English, bound together as one.

"It's amazing. I've never owned anything so beautiful. You made this for me?"

"Yes, of course for you. I wasn't sure how it was going to work out because, like I said, I don't normally make things from scratch. But it didn't turn out too badly." It had taken a while to make but I'd gotten up early for the last month or so and stolen a few hours here and there when Autumn had gone to bed.

She ran her fingers around the internal squares that would separate each piece of jewelry. "It's just so pretty."

"There's two layers there. The top is a tray that lifts out." I showed her, pulling out the tray and replacing it once she'd peered into the space underneath.

She put her arms around my waist and just seemed to stare at it.

"I don't think I've ever had a gift that I love more than this." She looked up at me. "'Thank you' doesn't seem to be enough."

I wanted to tell her that it was me who should thank her. Thank her for coming into my world and sprinkling her sunshine onto my dark soul. Thank her for warming me with her light. Thank her for being just what I needed. "You don't even need to say thank you. I wanted to do it."

I wanted to give her something of me. I wanted her to have something special. She deserved it all.

"How am I ever going to let you go if you keep doing stuff like this for me?"

What she said was like a knife piercing my armor. I realized I didn't want her to picture a future without me. "Maybe it's all part of my plan to keep you," I said, trying to use the same breezy intonation she had but meaning every word. Maybe that was why I'd given up sleep to make this box. Subconsciously, perhaps it was my invitation to her to stay in my life. To stay in Bethany's life. Neither of us wanted to lose her.

She looked at me with forlorn eyes, her smile having faded, and wrapped her arms around my waist. "I'm serious," she said. "I really like you and when I move out—"

"I'm serious too," I interrupted, not wanting her to finish her thought.

"Can we figure something out?" she asked. "I know I like to see the bright side of things, but I'm not sure there's an upside to not being with you."

I exhaled, grateful that she'd verbalized what I'd been feeling. Of course it would be Autumn, the bravest woman I knew. "I'm sure we can figure something out." I wasn't sure. I knew I wouldn't hold her back if what she wanted to do was travel the world or move back to America. I knew she was young enough that a lot could change in a few months. But I had started to wonder whether or not Autumn was someone I could accept a promise from.

TWENTY-FOUR

Gabriel

Mike's very grey office suited him. I just didn't know why I was sitting here first thing this morning. We'd gone over a few strategy points on the Rome deal, but nothing that couldn't have been discussed over the phone.

He narrowed his eyes at me. "What's the matter with you?"

"Nothing." *Other than the fact that you called me across town for no reason.* "Why do you ask?"

"You don't normally look so happy."

I chuckled. "Sorry to disappoint you, Mike. I'm going to leave you to it. I've got a busy day." I stood and headed out, still laughing to myself. Mike wasn't the first person to mention my mood today. This morning my secretary had said I sounded like I'd caught up on my sleep. Little did she know that I'd had little more than an hour on Saturday night.

But I'd choose a naked Autumn over sleep any day of the week.

And apparently naked time with Autumn had created my good mood. Perhaps it would be a permanent shift over time.

As I got out into the street, my phone buzzed in my hand. It was my solicitor—perfect, she was due to call when the divorce papers finalized. At this rate my positivity would at least last the day.

"Gillian," I said as I answered the phone. "I'm actually not too far from your offices. You want me to call in and sign the papers?"

"Actually no." She cleared her throat. "I've not had the papers yet, but her solicitor has called this morning with a request from her."

The blood in my veins stilled and I stopped in my tracks. All I could see was Bethany. Happy, laughing, mine.

I put my finger in my free ear because I didn't want to mishear anything. "What does she want?" It could only be Bethany. What else?

"A meeting."

There was no way that woman was going anywhere near my child. She'd proven just how unreliable and untrustworthy she was by walking out. She didn't have Bethany's best interests at heart at all and I didn't want anyone near my daughter who was focused on anything other than what was best for Bethany.

"I'll see her but I'm not taking Bethany. She's not going to lay eyes on my child." A whoosh of noise from the street filled my ears as if I'd been brought back to life. I'd crawl from the grave to protect my daughter.

"If it makes you feel any better, there was no mention of Bethany. She wants a one-on-one conversation with you."

I took a couple of deep breaths and tried to think. What

was she up to? After all these years she suddenly wanted a meeting? It didn't make sense.

Unless it was about money. Her family had money but perhaps they'd cut her off? Maybe she just thought she was owed. Whatever the reason, my ex had changed her mind and had decided she wanted some of my fortune after all.

"I don't want to see her. Can't you just get a number? Find out how much she wants."

"I've tried that," Gillian said. "She's assured me she doesn't want money."

Irritation prickled at the back of my neck. She might be saying that. But she'd also said *'til death do us part*. And that she loved Bethany. And me. I'd never believe another word that came out of her mouth.

"Right. And *I* don't want to see *her*. I'm not interested."

"Gabriel, I understand how you feel but we need to find out what she wants. We're in touching distance of getting this divorce, and if that's something you want to pursue, you should probably just agree to a meeting."

I wondered if this was how my clients felt when I advised them to do something they didn't want to do. The difference was this was personal. Not business. I didn't want to sit in the same room as the woman who'd left our baby. Who'd left me. Who'd broken every promise she'd ever made.

"A meeting about what?"

"Maybe she wants to explain. She did leave in rather a rush."

I wasn't sure it had been a rush. She'd taken every single item of clothing she owned. And over the months after she'd left, when I'd come out of the initial fog of grief at losing my wife, I'd realized there was nothing in our home that had been hers before we'd married. Her graduation photos. The pictures of her and her sister. Even the chair that had been her grandmother's had mysteriously disappeared. She hadn't just taken off on impulse. She'd planned it. Every time I thought about it, it was like her leaving for the first time, and a fresh wave of anger engulfed me. She hadn't wanted to talk then. She hadn't wanted to discuss anything as she was removing every trace of her life from our house. She'd done that in complete secret.

"Maybe you'll find out why she left," Gillian said.

"I don't care why she left." Of course, I'd tortured myself in the aftermath. How had I driven away my daughter's mother? Why hadn't she come to me? What had I missed? And then answers started to drip through. Alternatives that came to me in the middle of the night.

She'd met someone else.

She'd been having an affair all along.

She'd only been after my money.

She didn't like being a mother.

But none of the answers mattered because there was one thing I knew for certain—she'd lied to me. She'd lied when she'd said she loved me. She'd lied when she'd said she loved my daughter.

"If you don't want answers, then think practically," Gillian said. "What we want to avoid is her turning up on your doorstep out of the blue."

The thought crawled over my skin like a cockroach.

"This way you get to control the situation. You'll know exactly where you're going to see her, when, and for how long."

She had a point. If she was determined to speak to me, she'd find a way. She knew where I worked. Where I lived. And if she came to the house and Bethany was there, with Autumn . . .

"Okay, I'll meet her. But I want it to happen soon. Your offices."

"Her solicitor suggested the two of you could have lunch."

Her solicitor could fuck right off. Lunch was never going to happen. "If she wants a meeting, tell her it will be at your offices Monday at four. I'm not negotiating on this."

"Very well. I'll go back and see what they say."

"Tell them it's a binary choice. Meeting at your offices or no meeting."

I shut off the call and headed back to the office. I had a job to do. A daughter to provide for. I wasn't going to waste time thinking about my past. I was going to focus on my future.

TWENTY-FIVE

Autumn

Hollie and I sat at a table that looked like something out of a magazine—glinting flatware, cream orchid head in a tiny vase, and a crisp white linen tablecloth. I bet burgers weren't on the menu here. We were by the window and could see the Thames peeking through the bright green leaves of the trees. Even now I was constantly surprised at the amount of green in London—far more than I'd been expecting. I was forever stumbling on a square or a park I'd never heard of and no one had ever mentioned, and I loved to explore.

"How did you talk Dexter into bringing me here today? Doesn't he want to taste all the food for the wedding?" I asked as I glanced around, trying to take everything in from the deep pile carpets to the ornate gold and frosted glass light fixtures over the bar.

"I guess he's used to this kind of thing. Going to lunch at the Savoy is no big deal to him."

I could have lunch at the Savoy every day for the rest of

my life and I still wouldn't get used to it. "But it's his wedding."

I was pretty sure I'd be able to be a wedding organizer by the time Hollie and Dexter were married. I'd been happy to discuss every detail with Hollie and support her in her choices so she didn't feel guilty or awkward. The money, the glamour, and the people she now mixed with changed the rules for her, and I knew it still made her a little uncomfortable. Even I found it intimidating at times and I wasn't living with it every day. But, as always, if we did things together, nothing was unsurmountable.

The waitress poured two glasses of champagne and Hollie and I clinked as if champagne at lunchtime was just one of those things that the Lumen sisters did.

"He saw the menu and said he liked the sound of everything. And he's not coming back from Dubai until this afternoon."

I took the cream card from the center of the table and scanned down the list of food. The bits I recognized sounded amazing. The more I ate at these kinds of restaurants, the more I realized that I liked most things. "I'm happy to be his stand-in. I feel like I'm enjoying Dexter's lifestyle on his behalf, which is fine by me. Do you feel like you're missing out doing this stuff with him?"

"Not really. He's busy. I'm busy. The wedding is no big deal, or so I keep telling myself. If it makes you feel better, he's figuring out the wine by himself and he came to a dress fitting last week."

"He saw your dress?" I asked.

"He has a great eye for design, and I want him to like whatever I wear." She shrugged. "You think that's a problem? It's only a small wedding. It's not like we're following all the traditions."

"I think you should make your own traditions and it's true, he has a great eye."

"Also, he's going to make some jewelry for me. He needed pictures so Primrose can design something."

I laughed. "Wow. Bespoke jewelry. It might be a small wedding but it won't be cheap."

A waitress interrupted to put something involving shrimp in front of us. "This is the first of the three starters."

"We're eating every option?" I asked, wondering if I should have dug out something to wear that had an elasticized waist. I'm sure I'd like the food, but I didn't need three of everything.

"*Tasting it.* You don't have to finish every plate but we have to know what it's like. How else would we choose?"

"If you say so." I wasn't sure I'd be able to resist finishing every plate.

"So, how goes the job hunt?" Hollie asked. "Anything I can do?"

I shook my head as I tried to ignore the swirl of dread in my gut. "I've applied for lots of different things. There aren't many management training programs starting in September that still have vacancies, but there are a few. And then I've applied for some entry-level positions at banks and insurers. I have a couple of interviews next week." I'd rather focus on the food than have the inevitable conversation hurtling toward me. I didn't want to think about the future, all the *buts* and *what-ifs*. I took a forkful of the shrimp and as I suspected, it tasted heavenly.

"So, you're definitely going to stay in London?" she asked, bringing me back down to reality.

I wanted to be here with Hollie but realistically, I wasn't sure that was possible. I was going to try. For now I didn't need to mention the jobs I'd applied for in Portland,

New York, and Tampa. Hopefully, I'd find something here. "I'm not sure. If I don't get something by the beginning of August, then nothing will happen until September. The new nanny starts in a month and—"

"So, you come to live with me and Dexter. I told you that I can use you as an assistant."

I was grateful to Hollie but I didn't want to be her assistant. I wanted my own thing. I wanted to be independent and not have my big sister look after me for the rest of my life. "I know but—"

"And when I say assistant, I mean business partner really. You could really help on the marketing side—you're creative and clever and organized. I'd be lucky to have you."

"I agree, you would be lucky," I said, grinning at her. "But I'm way too expensive for you. And seriously, Hollie, I appreciate the offer, but I need to figure this out and get something on my own."

She didn't say it, but the question hung in the air like expensive perfume: *What if you don't find another job?*

"But you'll come live with us when the new nanny arrives? Just until you work it out?"

I nodded. It was that or go back to Oregon. "I'm travelling in August. I thought about cancelling my trip, but nobody is holding interviews in August. It's now or September. And I have the money saved up . . . I won't spend all of it." Six months of being paid as a London nanny with no living expenses had been good for my savings, but the idea of spending so much when I didn't have a job to come back to pinched at me. There was a part of me that wondered if I should just get another nanny job. Just until I found something more permanent. I really didn't want to go back to Oregon. I didn't want to leave Hollie. And Gabriel. And Bethany.

Gabriel and I hadn't talked about what happened next. And although I knew the things he whispered into my ear when we lay naked, breathless with our limbs tangled together—knew the way he looked at me when we played Monopoly or cooked or I made him watch musicals—I just didn't know how things would work when the new nanny arrived. When I moved out. I should ask him. But it seemed pointless until I knew something more about my future—at the very least, what continent I'd be living on.

"You've wanted to go for so long, Autumn. You should definitely still go and see the rest of Europe."

"You never know, I might get one of the jobs I'm interviewing for next week."

Hollie nodded enthusiastically. "You're sure to. You went to a great college and I bet you give a great interview."

"Anyway," I said, wanting to change topic. "You think Mom and Dad will cope with all this?" I said, scanning the well-heeled diners and ever-attentive wait staff.

"They'll figure it out. They don't pay rent since Dexter bought the trailer park, so they're used to having a bit more cash and . . . I've had Mom send me their measurements. They've picked out outfits online that I'm having made for them."

I laughed out of shock. "They're going to have bespoke clothes?"

"Honestly, it's a bit of an excuse. If I organize their outfits, I know they'll actually have something to wear and not turn around the night before and realize they need to go shopping."

"You've thought of everything."

"Apart from you. What are you wearing?"

I rolled my eyes. "You're not buying me something."

She winced, wrinkling up her nose. "I know you're

going to think I'm controlling and that's true. But I saw this, and I just loved it and so I went ahead and bought it." She pulled out one of those fancy cardboard bags with *Alexander McQueen* emblazoned across the front in a font that just screamed expensive.

"Are you serious?" I asked, half mad at her and half super-excited to see what was inside.

"Wait until you see it. It's *so* good." She swiped on her phone. "I took a screenshot from the website. Look, see."

I took in the picture of a white, ruched bustier with black pants. She knew me too well. It was far too amazing to say no to. It was the kind of elegantly chic thing I'd see in magazines and wonder what kind of woman I'd feel like if I wore an outfit like that.

"It's a jumpsuit even though it looks like a top, and that sweetheart neckline is going to look amazing on you."

"It's gorgeous," I agreed, feeling a little conflicted. "But I've come to London to be independent. I don't need you to buy me—" The fact was I was in a very different position now than when I'd landed here. I no longer had a job to look forward to.

"I know you can stand on your own two feet now, but I'm still your sister. And since I'm not having bridesmaids, I think it's only fair that you let me buy your outfit. If you don't like this one, then something else, your choice."

"You're insane," I said, holding the bag to my chest as if she was going to grab it from me. "As if I'd let you take this back now. It's mine."

She grinned, happy for me and happy she'd gotten her way. "It should fit. Let me know if it doesn't."

The waitress came and delivered the next starter, which seemed to be the vegetarian option. It tasted divine whether it was cabbage or cardboard.

"You're too good to me," I said. "But that's been true forever."

"You're just as good back to me. It's so amazing to have you in London. I still can't believe we're both here."

"I can't believe how much I like it here. Oregon is familiar but it doesn't feel like home anymore." I wasn't sure that London felt like home either, but it was getting that way. Having Hollie here helped. And Gabriel.

She nodded her head as if she knew exactly what I was saying. "How is Gabriel doing?"

"He's good. Busy at work but no change there. The guy is a workaholic. But he's so kind and easy to talk to and you've seen him with Bethany. He's taking her to paint pottery today; can you believe it? He's such a good dad."

"Not to mention hot. How's he coping with the divorce and everything? I can't believe that wife of his wants to talk to him after all these years."

I paused, a forkful of who-knows-what suspended mid-air while I repeated what she'd said in my head to make sure I hadn't heard her wrong. "His wife what?" I asked, just to be sure.

Hollie's eyes widened as she realized I didn't know what she was talking about. I tried to keep my breathing steady despite my tightening jaw and the uptick in my pulse. "I thought he would have told you."

That makes two of us. "What's going on, Hollie?" There was no way she was going to clam up now.

"Maybe I have it wrong, but I think Gabriel told Dexter that his ex-wife wanted a meeting before she agreed to a divorce."

My stomach roiled. I put down my fork and leaned back as if to get as far away from what she was saying as possible.

"He hasn't told me that." I tried to file through the reasons why he wouldn't have said anything to me.

It was no big deal and he'd forgotten.

He'd told her he wouldn't meet her.

He didn't want me to know. He didn't want me to know. He didn't want me to know.

"I'm sure he'll tell you. He's probably just trying to process it."

I nodded, trying to swallow down the sharp pangs of insecurity that stuck in my throat. This couldn't be as bad as it seemed. I just wouldn't allow it to be. "It's probably because it's no big deal. Or he's said he won't meet her."

She sighed. "I think he's agreed to meet her. I'm sorry. I'm sure it's just to sign the papers. Or maybe she wants to explain herself or something."

I focused on keeping my breath steady. This was a private thing between Gabriel and his wife. It was okay that he'd not told me he was meeting her. "It's very personal," I said, trying to convince myself this was fine—I was fine. "And nothing to do with me if you think about it."

"I'm not sure about that," Hollie said. "I mean, you're a couple now, aren't you?"

It felt like we were a couple, but no words had been exchanged. I knew he wasn't sleeping with anyone else. Not only because we shared the same home but because of the way he touched me, the way he looked at me. But we didn't wake up in the same bed. We weren't together in front of Bethany. Perhaps he wasn't part of a couple in his mind.

"He certainly cares about you," Hollie said, trying to be reassuring. "There's no way he would have risked upsetting Dexter if he didn't."

That was true. I knew how much Gabriel cared about his friends. And I was certain he cared about me. I knew he did. I just didn't know what that meant. The strength of our bond hadn't been tested and I had no idea whether it would last an argument about pineapple on pizza, let alone the stress of a divorce or a wife who might want him back. I knew what I felt for him was nothing I'd felt for anyone. But even I didn't know what that meant for Gabriel or for our future as a couple.

"I think he just wants to get it over with," Hollie said. "The meeting, that is."

"He hasn't seen her since she left." Perhaps when they met, she'd realize she was still madly in love with him and want him back. I swallowed, trying to keep my breathing steady. "What if she wants him back?"

"I'm sure it won't come to that," Hollie said. "She caused way too much damage."

Was it damage that could be repaired? They were still married after all. She'd been Gabriel's family not so long ago and she was still Bethany's mother. It would be naïve to think that wasn't a strong bond. Perhaps it was a bond that was bent but not broken.

"I guess this is good in a way," I said, pulling back my shoulders. "He'll get the closure he needs or—" I didn't want to think about the alternative.

I wasn't ready to give him up. I'd never be ready to give him up. Gabriel was the best man I'd ever known. But if I understood that, then maybe his wife had come to her senses and realized that too.

TWENTY-SIX

Gabriel

This meeting would be utterly pointless. When I'd pressed my lawyer for more detail on what my ex-wife wanted to discuss, I'd simply been told that she wanted to talk about what happened. Well, I wasn't interested. But I'd treat this like our monthly partners meeting: I wasn't interested in most of those but I sat through them anyway. Usually, I spent the time figuring out the answer to some complex tax issue that was stalling my current acquisition, or a real estate problem that had affected price on my latest disposal. This would be no different. I would sit there, but I wouldn't engage.

I'd insisted the meeting would be at my lawyers' offices and in front of our respective representation. I didn't want her to think this meeting was personal.

It was business, nothing more.

I caught the lift before the doors closed and went to press the button to the eighth floor, but it was already illuminated. I straightened and faced the doors, wondering whether a preemptive bid on the tech deal I was working on was the way to go.

The lift stopped at every floor and I stepped aside, letting people from behind me exit. On the third floor, I looked up as the doors closed and there she was.

The woman I'd stood at the altar with and vowed to love the rest of my life.

The woman I'd brought a child into the world with.

The woman who'd walked out on our family with no explanation.

"Gabriel," she said in a whisper.

I turned back to face the doors and she stepped closer.

"You look good, Gabe."

No one called me Gabe except her.

I hated it. When we were married, I'd thought it was intimate. Special. But all of it had just been fake. All the times she'd said she loved me. All the plans we'd made for the future. Nothing about her had been real.

"How's Bethany?" she asked.

I wasn't sure I could endure this meeting without burning the place to the ground. How dare she ask about *my* daughter? I ignored her and focused on the numbers above the doors as they flashed four, five, six, seven—the doors opened, and I waited for her to step out. When she didn't, I went first and headed straight to the reception desk without looking back. The receptionist showed me to the meeting room and my lawyer met me at the door.

We sat and waited. Gillian knew me better than to try to make small talk.

Someone knocked on the door and I stood, my eyes fixed on the blank wall in front of me as my ex and her lawyer were shown into the meeting room. I sat, not wanting to greet either of them.

"Thank you for coming, Gabriel," Penelope said. I'd forgotten the timbre of her voice and how sweet she sounded. It was one of the first things that had attracted me to her. But she was anything but sweet.

I looked her right in the eye. "I have twenty minutes and then I have to get to another meeting."

"Always so busy," she said with a smile.

I didn't reply. This wasn't a conversation as far as I was concerned. It was a means to an end. If I sat here for twenty minutes, I'd get the divorce papers signed. It was as simple as that.

"Well, I appreciate you making time in your day for me," she said when she realized I wasn't going to respond.

Without warning, she stood and moved her chair around the table so we weren't across from each other but kitty corner. What was she doing?

"I want to say I'm sorry," she said. "I'm sorry for not talking to you. I'm sorry for leaving and I'm sorry for not being in contact since. I know it must be impossible to forgive me, but I wanted you to understand that I know I was wrong, and I take full responsibility." She took a deep breath when she finished, seeming relieved to have it all out.

It took all my strength not to laugh. She said it as if she was expecting me to be grateful. That I would tell her that as long as she knew it was wrong, it was fine—she could do anything she liked if only she accepted responsibility. But I didn't laugh. I didn't say or do anything. I just focused on the clock overhead and how I only had eighteen more minutes of this to endure.

"I don't want you to think I didn't love you," she continued. As if I cared. "I did. And . . . still do."

This time I couldn't hold back my laugh. What she was saying was so ludicrous. So utterly ridiculous.

"It's true, Gabe. I never stopped loving you. I was just scared that my life was all planned out. I was young. And bored. And tired. And I wanted to explore what else life had to offer."

I glanced at my solicitor, wondering if we could wrap this up early. I didn't need Penelope's explanations. What was done was done. It didn't matter how we had gotten to this place—we were here.

"I left because I would have turned into someone else if I'd stayed."

I didn't respond. But part of me wanted to. The lawyer in me wanted to rebut her arguments. We all change and grow as the years go by. I'd thought we were going to do that together. As a couple—as a family.

I glanced at the clock again. There was too much time left.

"I made a lot of mistakes," she continued. "And I understand I hurt you. And I hurt our daughter."

She hadn't hurt Bethany. When Penelope left, Bethany had been too young to remember having a mother. She and I had been fine, and were still. We were a team.

"But everyone deserves a second chance. And I'm asking you to give me mine."

My gut twisted like it was an old towel being wrung out by a heavyweight boxer. She couldn't be serious. "You're asking me what?" I said, almost hissing the words.

"I want my family back." Her voice hitched at the end of the sentence. A ghost of a memory made me flinch.

I'd heard apologies like these a long time ago. Over and over, I'd heard my father ask for one more chance. And another one. And another one. Infinite fresh starts hadn't been enough for him.

"Your family doesn't exist," I said simply. What did she

think? That she was going to meet me after three years and I was going to be so grateful that she'd come back, I'd welcome her with open arms? Did she really think I was that desperate? What could she possibly think she had to offer Bethany or me? Nothing except disorder and broken promises. Nothing except a cloud of expectation that it would happen again. I didn't want to exist in a world where every day I remembered that Bethany and I weren't enough to make Penelope stay the first time, and that we probably wouldn't be able to keep her from leaving again.

I wouldn't put up with that for me, and certainly not for Bethany. My daughter deserved better. She deserved to be brought up by a parent who kept their promises and loved her enough to stay even when life got difficult.

"I know you're a good man, Gabe. I knew Bethany was safe in your hands."

I tried not to roll my eyes as she spoke.

"I needed to leave," she continued. "I needed to go to understand how much I had at home."

She had no home with me or Bethany.

"And now, I'm back and I want to be part of your lives."

The buzzer went off on my phone and I stood. "Twenty minutes is up. I have a meeting."

I swept out of the office, knowing that by the time I reached the lobby, Gillian would be calling.

She rang before the lift doors opened.

"She wants to see Bethany," she said before I had a chance to say anything. "She said that if you won't take her back, then she wants a custody arrangement."

My lungs filled with concrete and I sucked in a breath, trying to find air. Custody? "She's a stranger to my daughter," I choked out. "She can't do that, can she?"

I staggered to the door, desperate to steady my breath.

"She's the biological mother. Of course she won't get fifty-fifty custody at this point, but the court will allow visitation."

After all this time, she could just waltz back into our lives and try to pick up where she left off? And just expect that we could all go back to how it was before?

"No," I said.

"We can fight," she replied. "But given her position, we might be better off trying to come to an agreement. You might end up with more that way, Gabriel."

"No," I repeated. There was no way I was letting her anywhere near Bethany.

"Think about it. We want to avoid a court battle. It's expensive and will take you away from your daughter. In the end, you'll have to give her something."

I hung up. I couldn't listen to it any longer. I needed to get home. I had to protect what was mine.

TWENTY-SEVEN

Autumn

I put on Bethany's nightlight and folded back her bed covers. She hopped in without me having to ask twice.

"Sleep tight," I said, smoothing back her hair. "Don't let the bed bugs bite." I kissed her on the forehead and headed out, leaving her alone with her dad. I watched from the doorway as Gabriel bent and told his daughter he loved her.

"Can you stay home tomorrow, Daddy?"

"I don't know, darling. But I'll try to come home early more."

"Margaret likes to have dinner with you," she said, referring to her dolly. "And Bear Bear."

"I like having dinner with them as well."

Something bad had happened. He never came home from work early but this afternoon, he'd returned, changed, and spent the rest of the afternoon with us. Baking animal cookies and decorating them before having a doll's carpet picnic, during which Bethany licked the icing off at least three quarters of everyone else's cookies.

I didn't question him being home. I asked him if he wanted me to leave him and Bethany together and he'd answered with a squeeze of my hand.

It was nice having him spend the afternoon with us unexpectedly, but I couldn't shake the feeling that tonight, once Bethany was in bed, he was going to tell me about his wife wanting to see him.

I padded downstairs and fixed myself a soda. "You want anything?" I asked as he arrived in the kitchen. "Seems like maybe you need a beer to take the edge off."

"Yeah. I'll get a beer. You want one?"

I shook my head, raising the can of soda in my hand. No, I wanted to keep a clear head. I needed to be calm and rational without alcohol putting its two cents into the mix.

"Bad day?" I asked as we headed into the TV room.

"Yeah," he replied. The dark circles under his eyes made him look older than he was. I was sure he hadn't had those when he left this morning. When we sat, he shifted me closer to him and put my legs over his.

"Wanna talk about it?" I asked.

"Not really," he said with a sigh. "But I need to."

"Whatever it is, there's always a silver lining," I said. I believed it was true. Whatever life brought, there were always lessons to be learned, maybe even laughter to be had along the way.

"I wish that were true."

I slipped my hand into his, wanting to reassure him that everything would work out.

"I saw Penelope today."

Even though I knew she'd wanted to see him—had known for days that it was a possibility—it was still a shock to hear him say her name and to know that they'd been together today.

"I'm sorry," he said. "I should have told you that it was going to happen, but I thought it would just be a formality. I assumed she just wanted closure and then she'd disappear again, like she did before."

So she wasn't going to disappear. She was back. It had always been a possibility; I just thought I could wish it away.

"But it's not a formality?" What was he trying to say? Were they getting back together?

"You don't seem shocked," he said. "I thought you might be upset with me because I'd not told you."

I wasn't going to lie to him. "Actually, Hollie told me by accident when I met her for lunch. She assumed I'd know."

He closed his eyes as if disappointed. "I'm sorry. I should have told you. Why didn't you say something?"

"I figured you'd tell me if you thought it would affect . . ." I wanted to say *us,* but I wasn't sure what *us* meant. "If you thought I needed to know."

"I wanted to but . . ." We were both holding back. We were both not saying things and I wasn't sure if that was because Gabriel was unsure of what to say or because he thought I wouldn't want to hear it. "Anyway, for whatever reason, I thought I'd handle it and she'd sign the papers and that would be it."

"But instead?"

He groaned and tipped his head back to rest on the couch. "Instead, she wants my forgiveness and she wants to see Bethany. She's threatening a custody battle."

A shiver of shock rushed up my body. I pulled my legs from his and sat up. "She can't do that, can she?"

"Apparently she can."

"But she left. And Bethany wouldn't know her if she met her."

"I know," he said. "I said all this to my solicitor, but it doesn't matter apparently."

"You're a great lawyer. You'll fight it."

He paused, a look of concentration on his face. Running through the options, I guessed.

"I don't know what I'm going to do. Maybe I'll let her see Bethany, she'll get spooked again, and will disappear for another three years."

"Spooked?" I asked. We'd never discussed why his wife left and Hollie said no one knew. Not even Gabriel. "Is that why she left before?"

He pushed a hand through his hair. "She'd never offered an explanation until today. She said something about how she was young and bored and wanted to see what life had to offer."

"And now what?" I asked. "Now she's decided the grass isn't greener after all?" I was angry for Gabriel. Angry for Bethany. Angry that someone could be that selfish. "Maybe she should have thought about that before getting married and having a child." As soon as the words were out of my mouth, I regretted them. She was Bethany's mother. Gabriel's wife. He'd loved her once.

Gabriel took a swig of his beer. "Right." He sighed and shook his head as if everything was hopeless. "I don't want to spend more time away from my daughter because I'm fighting a custody case that I'm going to end up losing."

"Why would you lose?" That didn't make any sense to me. Sometimes it felt like the three of us were in our own bubble of happiness. I didn't want it to burst.

"Gillian says without some concrete reason like abuse or addiction, the court will award her something. I suppose the courts believe in redemption."

I let his words sink in. The courts believed in giving

second chances. And really . . . wasn't that the right thing to do? Weren't people allowed to make mistakes? God knows, everyone made them. If Hollie hadn't given my parents a thousand chances, they would probably be homeless by now. If she hadn't put up with me being an asshole at times, I would have never been able to finish college. Families gave each other second chances—and third and fourth and infinity chances, didn't they? But walking out on your infant daughter and husband for three years was more than a mistake. Maybe there was no way of righting that kind of wrong.

I stayed silent, aware that whatever I said might not be helpful. I liked to look at the bright side, but Gabriel had taught me that sometimes it was important to sit under the cloud for a while. And he likely wasn't ready to hear how it might be better for Bethany to have her mother in her life.

"So what's next?" I asked, trying to stay neutral.

"Gillian is trying to find out what Penelope's endgame is. God forbid she wants full custody."

"She didn't say at the meeting?"

"No, she was too busy trying to convince me we were a family and that she wanted to try again."

My heart burned in my chest. Penelope didn't *just* want to be back in Bethany's life. She wanted Gabriel back, too.

I placed my hand on his stomach. I needed to feel him. I wasn't sure if I was looking for him to reassure me, but he just stayed silent and placed his hand over mine.

Right in that moment, I wanted to tell him that I'd never felt for anyone what I felt for him. I wanted to say that I couldn't be excited about travelling or the future in general because thoughts of tomorrow meant that whatever we had today would shift, and I'd never been so happy. I wanted him to turn to me, clasp my face in his hands, and say he felt exactly the same. I wanted him to reassure me that he didn't want his wife back. That he wanted me—only me. That he saw Bethany, me, and him existing in this bubble forever.

But silence stretched between us and I couldn't help thinking that this was the beginning of the end. We were about to be over before we had even begun.

TWENTY-EIGHT

Autumn

Today was about Bethany. I was just her nanny. Her care-
giver. Her protector. I should remain professional and bury
the nerves swirling about in my stomach.

The doorbell rang and I wanted to throw up.

"Postman?" Bethany asked as I stood from where we
were bandaging up Bear Bear's arm.

I didn't want to lie to her, but I didn't know how to
explain who was at the door. Gabriel was at work—everyone
agreed that it would be better if he wasn't here when Penelope came around. There had been lots of rules put in place
before Gabriel had agreed to today. The first meeting
between Penelope and Bethany would be an hour long. It
would take place in this house. Penelope wouldn't bring
gifts. Penelope had to be accompanied by an independent
psychologist. There were other things Gabriel had told me
about, but they had gelled into a hard ball in my gut. I just
knew I wasn't going to leave the room. Not for a second.

Gabriel had hired a security guard who would be stationed outside the house all morning. It was clear he didn't trust Penelope with his daughter. And who knew what her game plan was? The more I thought about it, the less I understood her explanation for leaving. Even if she'd felt trapped and bored—why be gone for so long? Why come back now? Why hadn't she stayed in touch? Sent Christmas presents? Something.

I took a deep breath and opened the door.

"Hello," a very glamourous, blonde woman said. "You must be the nanny."

Irritation crawled up my skin. *Yes, I'm the woman who spends all day with your daughter. I'm the one she kisses goodnight and hugs when she's fallen over. I'm the one who's here every day. Who the hell are you?* But I didn't say any of that. I just smiled and gestured that she and the woman behind her should come in.

"Who's the guy outside?" she asked me, nodding toward the security guard on the door.

I just shrugged. I wasn't about to get dragged into anything. "Bethany, this is Penelope," I said pointing at her mother. "And this lady is . . ."

"Jade," the psychologist said.

Bethany waved and said hi without even looking up. Penelope tried to catch her eye but Bethany was too caught up in Bear Bear's injuries.

"They've come to visit," I explained. Gabriel had been clear that no one was to refer to Penelope as Bethany's mother. He thought it would be far too confusing for Bethany.

"Please have a seat," I said. This might not be my house to invite people to sit down in, but it sure as hell wasn't

Penelope's either. "Can I get either of you something to drink?"

Penelope shook her head, her eyes fixed on Bethany. It struck me like a blow to the head: Penelope was Bethany's doppelganger. They looked exactly alike. The long blonde hair. The bright blue eyes.

They were both beautiful.

Penelope sat on the floor next to Bear Bear and tapped his nose. "Hi, Bear Bear."

She knew him. Of course she did. There was history here that couldn't be erased.

"He's hurt his leg," Bethany explained. "I'm making him better with ban-ges."

"That's kind," Penelope said carefully. "How did he hurt it?"

"He fell," Bethany said.

I sat the other side of Bethany, making sure I was in touching distance.

"Autumn," Bethany said, tugging at the elastic fastener that fixed the end of the bandage. "Please, may you help?"

"I can help you," Penelope said with a glance to me, checking it was okay.

It was no big deal, right? She was just helping Bethany fix a bandage on her bear. Something I would have done if she hadn't been here.

Penelope took the small section of elastic with the metal ends and placed it on Bear Bear's leg, holding the bandage in place.

"Thank you," Bethany said and looked up at Penelope. "Are you Autumn's friend?"

Penelope glanced at me again as if I had the answer to that question. "I'd like to be your friend," she said.

I had to give it to her, it was the perfect answer. For

now. First, she wanted to be Bethany's friend and then she'd want to be her mother. I wanted to ask her questions. Did she regret leaving? Did she know how much she'd missed? Even in the short time I'd been Bethany's nanny, there'd been so many changes. The questions she asked, the different toys she played with, her bravery on the monkey bars at the park. Everything was different. But Penelope left Bethany before she could walk. Before she could talk or blow a kiss. She'd never get any of that back.

It wasn't anger for Bethany that I felt. She had a father who loved her, and Gabriel's inner circle had adored Bethany since the day she was born. Instead, pure sadness rushed through my heart like a swollen river after rainfall. I was sad Penelope had missed so much of Bethany's life. She had to live with that decision forever—had to come to terms with the fact that she'd never know her daughter in the way a parent should.

"He's going to sleep now. That way he'll get better," Bethany announced as she stood and pulled a cushion from the couch. "Please get a blanket from over there," she asked Penelope. Bethany wasn't a shy child, but she was very accepting of Penelope and I wondered if there was a bond between them from before. Maybe Bethany saw herself when she looked at Penelope. Maybe it was a pheromone Penelope gave off, or just something Bethany found familiar about her. Whatever it was, Bethany was comfortable with Penelope.

And that was good, wasn't it?

I wasn't sure Gabriel would think so.

Penelope and Bethany played for the rest of the hour as if they were old friends. I didn't interfere. Jade didn't say anything, other than to ask me a couple of questions about how long I'd worked for Gabriel.

"I think our time is up," Jade said as she stood.

A sheet of disappointment crossed Penelope's face, but she kissed Bear Bear on his hurt leg and stood. "Get better, Bear Bear."

"He'll be okay," Bethany said, reassuring Penelope. God, that kid made my heart melt.

"Thank you for playing with me, Bethany," Penelope said.

"We've got lunch to make," I said, hoping Bethany wouldn't think it was weird that these two women had turned up, played with her, and then left.

"Can I have happy cow cheese?" she asked, referring to her favorite snack and completely unfazed by the two women leaving. She was oblivious to the tears I could see Penelope holding back.

"We can make that happen," I said. "Let's say goodbye to Penelope and Jade."

We moved out into the hallway and opened the door, Bethany clutching a bandaged Bear Bear. "Bye-bye," Bethany said, moving her bear's arm so he was waving.

"Bye-bye, Bear Bear. Bye-bye, Bethany," Jade said.

"Bye-bye—" Penelope's voice cracked, and she covered her mouth with her hand. Jade guided her out and I shut the door.

"Cheese, please, Louise," Bethany sang.

I smiled as she slipped her hand into mine and half skipped, half hopped as we headed to the kitchen. "What about an omelet with a triangle of happy cow on the side?"

"Yum," she said.

The most important thing in all of this was that Bethany was happy. Despite my concerns, seeing Penelope hadn't upset her. Penelope hadn't pushed too hard, hadn't broken any of the agreed-upon rules. It had been a good reintroduction for both of them. It would be the start of a road back to a relationship. When Bethany was older, she'd barely remember her mother ever not being in her life. Gabriel might not want to admit it to himself, but Penelope being back was almost certainly what was best for Bethany. I just couldn't figure out where that left me.

TWENTY-NINE

Gabriel

After the rough morning, I'd needed the afternoon with my daughter. And the night with Autumn. I slid my arms around her waist as she stood at the kitchen island.

There had been no point being at work. I'd done nothing productive in the office. I'd just watched the clock until it hit midday. After I texted Autumn to make sure Penelope had left on time, I'd raced back home.

The three of us played tea party, painted pictures of rainbows, and plaited Autumn's hair. And I'd done my best not to think about how Penelope had been in the house just hours before.

"She's zonked," I said, and kissed Autumn's neck.

"It's been a big day," Autumn replied.

I knew I should ask how it went but I wanted to forget about it. To pretend it hadn't happened.

"I think it went well," Autumn said as she turned in my arms. "Penelope was very respectful. And Bethany didn't question anything. Just one time she asked Penelope if she was my friend, and Penelope just said she'd like to be Bethany's friend."

I wasn't sure if Autumn was telling me this because she thought I'd want to know or if she thought she should. But I didn't want to hear it.

"Bethany's fine. That's all I need to know," I said as I bent to place a kiss on her neck. She smelled like almonds and rainfall and I wanted to dive into her scent and lie in it for a while.

"Yes, I think it was good. When's the next visit?" she asked.

I groaned. "I don't know. Do we have to talk about this?"

"But you must be pleased it went well?" she asked, and I stepped back, dropping my arms to my sides and heading to the fridge to get a beer.

"Like I said, as long as Bethany's okay. I wish it didn't have to happen at all." I twisted the lid off my beer and took a swig.

"But she's her mother. And in a few years, Bethany won't even remember that she left."

She was so naïve. "In a few years, Penelope will be long gone. Believe me, Autumn."

I glanced at Autumn, who was frowning at me, confused. "You think she'll leave again? What makes you say that?"

"She did it once. It's bound to happen again." I'd seen it a thousand times with my father. If they left once, they'd keep on leaving. It was how people were made. I'd been broken when she left. Devastated for me and for Bethany. But I'd built myself back, piece by piece. I was happy now. Why couldn't she have just stayed away? Bethany didn't need her. I certainly didn't. Our meeting that Penelope had insisted on had been ludicrous. Why would she think I would be prepared to take her back? After all these years, she really thought I was the desperate fool who would just fall to my knees in relief and beg her to come back into our lives.

She was delusional. I wanted nothing to do with her and I never would. If I didn't think it would hurt Bethany, I would have fought her every step on custody. I'd prefer her to slink off back to wherever she'd gone and never come back.

"But she's older now," Autumn said. "She said she felt too young." Autumn followed me over to the sofa. "Presumably if she's back, she's over that now."

I wanted to get naked. Have incredible sex. Sleep. In that order, preferably. But Autumn was like a dog with a bone. "Don't be naïve. She'll be off again next time she's bored and if she's bonded with Bethany, I'll be left to pick up the pieces. Again." Bethany hadn't noticed when her mother left the first time. She'd been too young but this time she could cause real damage. "She should understand the potential to cause harm at this age. She's just being selfish." I'd have to limit the amount of time Bethany saw Penelope over the next few months, until she left again. That way I could minimize the damage.

"You don't think she'll stick around? Maybe she's changed."

I rolled my eyes. "People don't change. I'm just entering some kind of cycle where I have to protect Bethany as best as I can and prepare her for when Penelope takes off again."

Autumn tucked her knees under her chin as we sat together in silence. "How can you be so certain? I know she left before, but people make mistakes."

"And are destined to repeat them," I replied. It was nice that Autumn saw the best in people, but she was being ridiculously naïve. She'd not experienced the reality of the world which presented the evidence very clearly: people didn't change and second chances were always wasted. "I've seen it all before." I tipped my head back on the sofa. I'd lived this cycle once already.

"I thought she just left once? Did she walk out before?"

"Not her," I said, remembering the arguments. The flowers. The door banging. The late-night pounding on the doors.

Autumn slid her hand into mine and squeezed. I was taking my bad mood out on her. It wasn't her fault. She didn't know people like I did.

"My father cheated on my mother. A lot. She'd make him leave and then he'd come back. Say he'd ended it. Apologize. Assure her that it would never happen again. She'd take him back. Then a few months later the cycle would start all over again. Each time he convinced her that he'd changed, that he deserved a second chance. But he was always the same weak, pathetic liar. And she always fell for it."

I wouldn't make the same mistake. My mother had been frightened to divorce my father. She hadn't wanted the social stigma, the money worries, the loneliness. But she'd paid a very high price for staying married. And as her son, so had I.

I wouldn't put Bethany through that. I wouldn't put myself through that. Not again.

"Did Penelope leave for someone else?" Autumn asked. "Was she cheating?"

"I don't know and I don't care." It didn't matter why she'd left. I'd heard every excuse under the sun for letting your family down. Not a one of them was excuse enough.

"But if the problem wasn't cheating, then maybe she

just had a hump to get over and now she's over it and ready to be a mother and a wife?"

It sounded like Autumn wanted me to take Penelope back, wanted me to give her a second chance. It was the last thing I wanted to hear. Especially from Autumn, who I cared deeply about, who I raced home from work to see, who I'd just begun to see a future with.

"I should go into the workshop," I said, standing. I needed some space and I wanted to get away from this conversation. I'd said all I had to say about Penelope. There was no need to rehash it. "I've bought an old desk that I'm going to polish up and put in the bedroom next to yours. I'm going to work from home more. That way I can be home for bedtime more often."

Autumn stood and smoothed her hand over my cheek. "You're a great father. A good man." And she shrugged. "And hot as hell. You need an apprentice to help buff your wood?"

I chuckled at her ridiculousness. I wanted to be angry and sullen about my situation, but Autumn made it impossible. But she couldn't shine her light and make *everything* perfect. She needed to see there was no future where Penelope was part of my life. I'd gotten over her leaving and I wasn't going to step back onto that roller coaster again.

THIRTY

Autumn

I was officially pissed off on my sister's behalf.

"Are you mad at him?" I asked her as we stood in front of the store that had fresh pink and blue flowers draped around the storefront like some kind of magical fairyland. Hollie had called me this morning and begged me to come to the florist with her. Dexter had had some kind of issue with a client not being happy with her ginormous diamond and had to go sort it out, and Hollie didn't want to choose their wedding flowers by herself.

"He was really upset that he couldn't be here. We tried to rearrange but this woman is booked up for like, five years and a day. I'm sorry I had to drag you here."

"It's fine," I said.

"I thought you might be busy with Gabriel," she said, stepping forward to smell one of the hanging lilacs that drooped over the door.

"We didn't have particular plans. And I always like hanging out with you. I'm just a little concerned with

Dexter's lack of participation in your wedding. I mean, I know he offered to take your name and everything, but it feels a little sexist."

"It looks that way. But there's so much to do and I think he's actually done more than me. The guest list, the invitations, the seating plan. All Dex. He's not intentionally missing meetings."

I supposed I didn't know what went into planning a wedding, but if Hollie thought it was okay then I supposed it was. She was usually right.

She peered into the window and rang the pink old-fashioned bell that sat on the pink doorframe.

"Who has a doorbell on a store? Aren't they supposed to be encouraging people to go inside?"

"People don't need encouragement. This flower store is so sought after it's like an urban myth. Dexter had to get one of his clients to pull in a favor to get us an appointment here."

Rich people were crazy. Roses were roses. What could be so special about the ones here?

A small lady with a short blonde bob appeared at the door, peering over her old-fashioned semi-circle glasses perched on the end of her nose like I'd only ever seen in the books I read to Bethany.

"Welcome to our world," she said in a hushed voice. "Come through."

Inside was like a fairytale come to life. I wished Bethany was here. She would have loved it. There were different types of flowers everywhere I looked. Some falling from the ceiling, some hanging from the walls, covering tables and desks. I could see nothing but petals and color wherever I looked. Even the floor was completely covered, other than a path that wound around to a door leading to a room in the back. It was like some kind of Disney experience, only better because the scent of every flower in the world surrounded us.

"This is amazing," Hollie said.

"A floral experience," the lady said. "That's what we aim to create."

Could I move in? "It's beautiful," I said, turning a full three hundred and sixty degrees to make sure I hadn't missed anything. I pulled out my phone so I could grab a picture.

"Sorry, no photographs please." She gave no explanations and I put my phone back in my bag. "Come through and we can discuss the experience we will create for you."

The next hour was surreal. I saw examples of every type of flower I'd ever imagined. I could tell Hollie was getting overwhelmed because she clearly loved it, but she was also trying to keep the wedding simple.

"Why don't you focus on the tables and go from there," I suggested. "I like these, where the flowers are high and trickle down to the tabletop." I pointed to one of the table displays in front of us.

Hollie nodded. "I do like the orchid combined with the lily of the valley. But then I really like the roses and the wisteria as well. What do you think?" she asked the self-styled *floral designer*.

"I think," she replied in hushed tones, "that you need to just *be* in the flowers. And the decision will come to you. I will leave you and return and you will have the answer."

"Did we just land in California?" I whispered once the woman had left.

"I just have to *be* in the flowers. So . . . let's sit." We took a seat on the tiny silk sofa, the only surface not covered in flowers.

"You think we should close our eyes?" I asked.

"No, I think you should tell me how the visit with Penelope went."

I groaned but gave her the highlights. "I've never seen Gabriel like this. He's adamant that she's going to leave again and furious that this time, Bethany will know more and be disappointed."

"That's an understandable concern though, isn't it?"

"It is, but he's so adamant that it's going to happen. It might not. This could be good for Bethany. It could be good for him." The more I thought about it, the more I thought that perhaps Gabriel was fighting the inevitable. "Apparently, she'll get some kind of visitation, because she hasn't been abusive and isn't an addict or whatever. But Gabriel is fighting it so hard, and I wonder if . . ." I'd barely been able to let myself think about the reasons for Gabriel being angry. "He has such strong feelings; I can't help but wonder if it's covering up the fact that deep down, he wants her back. He wants his family back." I wasn't expecting it, but from somewhere, my eyes began to water. I had to swallow down sobs. "I can't blame him."

Hollie sat forward and grabbed my hand. "Autumn, are you in love with Gabriel?"

I shook my head. "I can't allow myself to think about it. I'll be off in a few weeks anyway. I'm going to lose him, whatever happens. It's just . . . I think back to all those guys in Oregon that I used to date . . . They were just interim guys. I don't mean that I didn't like them, but they were for the moment. And Gabriel started off like that but now . . . Now I'm *his* interim girl. You know? The one he picks up as he's passing through life from one serious relationship to another."

Hollie squeezed my hand and I just tried to focus on not crying. God forbid, I stained this beautiful silk couch.

"And for once," I continued. "I don't think he was my interim guy, you know?"

Hollie's face was full of sorrow. "I do know. It was what I was afraid of."

"Usually, I can put a spin on things. Look to the positive. But now I'm in that house, with him, and I'm so happy." My voice cracked and I took a breath. "I'm really, properly happy, Hollie. And I've been pretending to myself that it can go on like this. That I can be happy without having to spin anything for once in my life. That the present would last forever. And now I try to think of the positives of not living with Gabriel and Bethany. I try to think about how I'll be better off when I go travelling and start a new job but when I do, I'm utterly miserable. There doesn't seem to be a bright side without Gabriel."

"You'll find one," Hollie said. "It's what you do. You'll find out how to make this work and how to move forward. I promise you." She shifted closer and pulled me in for a hug, putting her chin on my head like she used to when I was a child. "In the meantime, we're going to get out of here and I'm taking you day drinking."

"Don't be crazy. We need to pick your flowers."

At that moment, the blonde lady was back.

"I've decided," Hollie said, standing. "I want that one but with wisteria and cream roses."

"As you wish," she said.

"Are you sure?" I asked. "Is that even an option?"

"She's sure," the blonde lady said and gestured for the door. Apparently, we were leaving.

"I need you to do something for me," Hollie said as we

stepped out onto the sidewalk. She turned me to face her and put her arms on my shoulders. "I know I've spent our entire lives telling you to think about your future but now, I need you to focus on this moment. I want you to enjoy each day you spend with Gabriel and Bethany. I want you to take each new experience in London and squeeze everything you can from it. Forget about what might happen with Penelope or what Gabriel could be thinking. Stop worrying about what's going to change when you start a new job or travel. Just enjoy. Just live. Just be."

I exhaled as I thought about what she'd said. "Did you inhale too many flower fumes or something?"

"Maybe," she said. "But it's good advice all the same. Don't ruin today thinking about tomorrow." She linked her arm into mine and leaned into the road to hail a cab.

"Where are we going?" I asked as a taxi pulled over.

"We're two American girls in London looking for a place to day drink. And we have a black Amex. We're off to the American Bar at the Savoy, of course." She ducked and climbed in. "They tell me there's a slice of bright side with every cocktail."

Thank God for my sister. She was always there to pick me up when I fell. And sometimes, like now, just as I was about to.

THIRTY-ONE

Gabriel

That feeling I got the first time I laid eyes on Autumn—like my lungs had malfunctioned or my heart might need a nudge to restart—resurfaced every time she walked into a room. Even after four months of living together.

"You look so pretty, Autumn," Bethany said.

"Beautiful," I added as Autumn twirled around, the ruffles on her very short dress lifting as she moved.

"You promise to be good going to bed tonight," Autumn said. She bent and kissed Bethany goodnight.

"And when I wake up, pancakes?" she asked.

"Pancakes for sure," I replied.

"But Autumn will make them with blueberries."

"Yes, I'll make them," Autumn replied, shooting me a glance that said *Your daughter understands your lack of skill in the kitchen.*

I gave the sitter my number again and headed out, taking Autumn's hand as I did.

"She didn't seem to mind," Autumn said as we climbed in the cab. "That we were going out together."

"Why would Bethany mind? She loves you."

"I just wondered if she thought it was weird. What did you say when you told her?"

"I just said that you and I were going out to dinner." Autumn and I had been careful not to show any obvious affection for each other when we were both with Bethany. We hadn't had a conversation about it—it had just been an unspoken agreement. We never slept in each other's bed. We never kissed each other good morning.

It was time that changed.

I wanted to take Autumn out to dinner—not to her sister's house but dinner, just the two of us. I didn't want to fuck her on the kitchen table anymore. I wanted her bent over a bed or naked in the shower. I still had a daughter I didn't want to confuse. But I also had Autumn, who I wanted to spend time with. I slid my hand up her bare leg. "You're stunning."

"It's a little short," she said. "But I'll take Hollie's hand-me-down Balmain any chance I can get."

"It's gorgeous on you. You heard it from Bethany."

"Then it must be true." She sighed and tightened her grip on her bag.

"You nervous?" I asked.

"Not exactly. I just was worried how Bethany would be. And it's a relief she's not weird about it."

"She was never going to be weird."

She shrugged. "Anyway, where are we going?"

I put my hand on her thigh, pulling her closer to me. "The Savoy," I said.

"Oh, I like it there. How weird is it that I've been to the

Savoy before?" She shook her head. "I'm getting a little too used to the good life."

"You deserve regular trips to fine hotels. You deserve everything good in life."

She looked at me and tilted her head. "You're wonderful."

Her words filled me up. I hadn't realized the size of the hole inside me until Autumn had come along. She'd filled it and I was overflowing. I wanted to lock in what we had now. Freeze time and spend the rest of my life like this, with Bethany and Autumn.

But tonight, I'd settle for the Savoy. I had an entire evening planned. And dinner was just one part of it.

When we pulled up, one of the doormen opened the cab and helped Autumn out.

"Mr. Chase," one of the staff said as we entered the hotel. "Let me show you to your suite."

"What's this?" Autumn said. "I thought we were going to dinner."

"We are," I said as we headed to the lifts. "A private dinner."

When we arrived on the top floor, the butler assigned to us opened the door to the royal suite and began to show us around. There were various seating areas, a bedroom, a dining room, and a bar. The table had already been laid, ready for our meal.

"When would you like to eat, sir?" the butler asked as he opened the bottle of champagne on the bar.

"Give us thirty minutes," Gabriel said.

"Make that an hour," Autumn added. "I want to enjoy this view before we eat." She looked directly at me, not taking in the London skyline at all.

I knew that feeling. As much as the city lights were beautiful, nothing matched watching Autumn.

The butler left and Autumn looped her hands around my neck. "You got this entire suite just for dinner?" she asked.

"Well not just dinner," I said. "I just wanted to be with you. I love my daughter, but I wanted to have some time with you that wasn't stolen or hidden or tucked away."

That unintended pout of hers parted. "I like that idea." She dropped her hands and stepped back. She reached under her dress and shifted her hips, pulling down her underwear. The black lace landed on the thick carpet and she stepped out of it, tilting her head before she said, "Wanna take in the view from the balcony?" She held out her hand.

Instantly I was straining in my trousers, desperate to be inside her.

I slid the balcony doors open and stepped toward the edge of the terrace. The wall separating us from the city was waist height, and I wrapped my arms around Autumn as we looked out onto the city. Impatiently, she ground her arse back into my crotch.

"Out here?" I asked. She turned around and looked me in the eye as she nodded. "You want me to fuck you in front of eight million people?"

She reached for my fly, but I turned her back around.

"Hands on the wall."

She groaned, turned on by my words as she always was. "I know you're so wet that my cock is going to slide so deep into you," I whispered into her ear as I unzipped my trousers. "And I barely have to lift up this dress to get inside you. It's so short. Is that what you were hoping?" I nudged at her entrance and she pushed back.

"So impatient for me." I pushed her hips back a little and pressed her forward from the waist before sliding my hand onto her shoulder to keep her in place. I thrust in hard and deep. Wanting to give her what she wanted and wanting to have her as quickly as I could.

It wasn't New Year's Eve, but I swear fireworks burst into the sky at the perfect pressure of her pussy around me.

"Gabriel," she cried out.

She was right. It was so good. So fucking amazing. Her heat, her breath, that scent of almonds was all exactly how it should be. I pulled out deliciously slowly, before thrusting up hard and fast. And again. And again. And again. Jesus, I wanted to do this forever. I wanted to fuck this woman until I was ninety and barely able to stand.

"All those people out there in the city. You think anyone can see us? You think anyone knows how wet you are? How my cock is driving into you over and over and over?" I wanted everyone to know. I wanted to take a full-page ad out in the *Times*. Write it in the sky for the entire city to see. I reached around to her clit and slid my fingers between her folds. Her legs buckled. This is how I loved Autumn—weak with need for me.

"I love fucking you," I whispered into her ear. "I love making you tremble, making you weak, making you scream." I loved being with her. Seeing her with Bethany. I loved sitting with her and talking. I loved . . .

"I love you fucking me too," Autumn said breathlessly. She turned her head, looking up at me as if I were everything to her. And I wanted to give everything I had to her. She should have everything she ever wanted. And more.

I groaned, shoving deeper, clamping my hands over her hips to hold her still so I could get closer. She reached back, at nothing in particular—she wanted more. I grunted, trying to hold my orgasm off and give Autumn what she needed. I fucked harder, deeper, faster. On and on I drove into her, ignoring the clamoring of my climax rattling my bones, wanting to be let out. She froze as she reached the precipice and then began to shake as she fell over the edge, falling into my arms as she collapsed. I stilled and bent over and held her. We just stood there, London as our backdrop as our heavy breaths evened out.

I wasn't ready for it to be over. I wanted her to know how I felt. I wanted her to know how I wished I'd met her before. Before I'd been married. I wanted to have shared our entire lives. I wanted her history. Since the instant sizzle of our first meeting, it had felt as if we were destined. As if resistance was futile, because she'd been made for me. And I existed just for her.

I straightened and she turned in my arms. I lifted a leg and pushed into her again. I started to fuck, just small, intense movements, claiming her in front of the entire city. In a weird kind of way, I hoped people could see. Everyone should know we were together.

"You're so beautiful," I said, slowing. "Gorgeous."

She looked at me, her face turning serious for a second as she pushed her fingers into my hair. "So are you. Inside and out."

She tipped her head back and I clamped my mouth down on her delicious skin, wanting to consume her. I trailed my teeth down to her collarbone and sucked and bit every exposed inch, like I needed to make up for the time we'd not been together. How had I lived without her for all the years that came before her? I wasn't sure I could even remember my life clearly without her. Wasn't sure what it was like before I had something to come home to at night when I'd missed my daughter's bedtime.

She tightened around my cock as my teeth sank into her throat again. And I slipped my hands over her silk-covered breasts, squeezing her hard nipples. She shuddered against me and this time the pressure on my cock, the friction, the drag of her perfect heat was too much, and I exploded inside her with a groan.

I held her against my chest as we recovered our breath.

"Gabriel," she sighed, her voice so soft it faded in the noise of the city. "My Gabriel."

I was glad she knew it. I was hers.

THIRTY-TWO

Autumn

I pushed the dollhouse back to where it lived by the window. I'd pulled it out to the middle of Bethany's bedroom for her to play with it more easily during Penelope's visit. Directing everyone's focus seemed like a good idea, since it helped avoid strained silences or Bethany getting whiny. So far, we'd dodged any awkward questions such as *Why do you want to be my friend?* and *Why does Jade always sit back and never play?* and *Why do you always cry when you leave?* Long may it continue. I'd have to remember to tell the new nanny when she arrived. She'd be here in less than two weeks.

"Is it time for lunch yet?" Bethany asked.

"Yes, let's just tidy up from you and Penelope playing and then I can fix you something."

The second visit had gone without a hitch. And Penelope had made Bethany laugh as she made up voices for the dolls that occupied the very grand house Bethany had stuffed full of furniture. Everyone was happy. Especially me. I swear the Savoy had put something in the water that made my soul float. Or maybe it was just being with Gabriel. Whatever it was, I'd been walking on cotton candy since the weekend. Even being forced to wear a turtleneck on a hot day to cover the marks Gabriel had left on my neck didn't worry me. It was worth it to be reminded of Gabriel's mouth on my skin.

The doorbell rang from downstairs.

"I'll get it!" Bethany cried.

"I don't think so," I said. It would only be a courier delivering something, but Bethany wasn't about to start answering the door at four years old, even if she could reach the locks standing on her step stool. "It might be those new pens I ordered yesterday," I said. "If you want, we can draw your daddy a new picture for his office. They have glitter in them, and you know he's sure to like that." I held out my hand and we went downstairs to get the door.

"Glitter? He loves glitter."

"Right?"

"Shall I draw his favorite dinner?" she asked, making me laugh.

"That's a good idea."

"He really likes peas."

Where did this kid come up with this stuff?

I opened the door and my heart dropped to my stomach when I came face-to-face with Penelope.

What was she doing back here? And where was Jade? I flicked through the possibilities in my mind. Was she going to force her way in and snatch Bethany? I'd persuaded Gabriel to ditch the security guard. Maybe that had been a mistake. I took a breath. Perhaps she'd just forgotten something?

"Sorry to disturb you," she said, looking at Bethany. "Hi, Bethany."

"Hi," she replied and cocked her head. "Have you come to play again?"

Before Bethany could invite Penelope in, I interrupted. "Bethany, can you go and get your paper out for the pictures? I'll be there in a second." I put on my calmest voice and a fake smile. She'd know, but hopefully she wouldn't cause a fuss. She shrugged and headed back down the hallway.

I turned back to Penelope. What could she possibly want?

"I just wanted to say how much I appreciate you making our play dates so relaxed," she said.

"Okay," I replied, bracing myself for the real reason she was here. She could have said that in front of Jade.

"Bethany is obviously well looked after by you. And it's nice that she's got someone to care for her until . . ." Something behind her eyes stopped her from finishing her sentence. "I've missed so much of her growing up," she said. She clasped her hands together, her fingers jittering like she was either nervous or in rehab. "I've only realized how much I've missed since I started seeing her. I have so many questions. There's so much I want to know about her."

It was hard not to feel sorry for her. Bethany was a lovely child and three years was a lot to miss of anyone's life, let alone someone as young as her daughter. "I understand," I said.

"I'd like to make up for it," she said. "I just want a fair shot at a second chance."

I pulled in a breath. From what I could see, Gabriel wasn't giving out second chances to anyone.

"You must understand this. As another woman." She

looked up at me, desperate for me to do something that would help.

I nodded. "I don't make any of the decisions around Bethany. That's all up to Gabriel. I'm just the nanny."

"The thing is, I'd be happy to look after her while Gabriel's at work."

I wasn't sure how she wanted me to respond. She couldn't think I was going to hand Bethany over and go to the spa for the day, did she?

"If you think about it, Bethany doesn't really need a nanny now I'm back."

Oh God, was she trying to push me out of the job? She didn't know I was leaving anyway in a couple of weeks but even so, there was no way Gabriel would just let Penelope take over. "I don't know what to say. You need to talk to Gabriel."

She thrust her hands into her coat pockets. "You're fucking my husband." She said it so matter-of-factly. Like it was as obvious as the sun rising in the morning.

"I think you need to leave." I went to close the door and her arm snapped out to stop me.

"I don't want to cause trouble," she said. "But from what I can see, it's you standing in the way of me and my daughter. Me and my family. Do you see that?" she asked. "We're still married, and that means something. He never asked for a divorce. Not in all these years. I know he would take me back if . . ."

She didn't need to finish the sentence. I could fill in the gaps. She meant that if I wasn't around, she would be able to fit back into her old life with Gabriel.

Gabriel would deny it. But maybe it was true.

Had he really not asked for a divorce for all these years? He'd been adamant about not giving Penelope a second chance, but if that was really true, why hadn't he cut legal ties sooner? Why was the man I was sleeping with still married to a woman who left him three years ago?

It didn't make sense.

I stayed silent, the unanswered questions chipping away at my defenses.

"Gabriel's a good man," she continued. "I'm not sure if it's serious between you or just convenient."

Convenient? I might live under his roof, but I was his best friend's future sister-in-law. And his employee. There was nothing convenient about me as far as Gabriel was concerned.

"But he's my *husband*." She emphasized the word as if I couldn't possibly understand what she was trying to say. "I'm Bethany's mother. And you seem like a nice girl. Do you want to live the rest of your life knowing you broke up a family?"

"You need to leave," I said, as calmly as I could manage. There was no point in having this conversation. I needed to shut the door, get away from this woman, and organize my thoughts.

"If you weren't on the scene, we'd all have a chance at being together," she said. "You're ruining Bethany's chance of having her mother and father together. Of spending time with her mother, rather than the hired help."

"I'm going to shut the door," I said, my jaw clenched and my shoulder poised to ram closed the black door. I wasn't the one who walked out on my family three years ago. She was trying to push the blame of what she'd done onto me. And I knew it wasn't my fault.

"Do you really want to live your life as a homewrecker?" she asked. Her manner wasn't menacing or threatening, but the implication was. She was telling me I was the problem. She was telling me I was ruining her life, Gabriel's life, and Bethany's life. Part of me knew it was manipulative, but was it possible for her words to be manipulative *and* true?

"I'm sorry," she said, stepping back. "Like I said, I don't want to cause any trouble. I know I've made mistakes and bad decisions. I just want my family back. I don't want to miss any more of Bethany's life." Her voice faltered at the end of the sentence. She looked desperate. Like she was really remorseful.

It was hard not to feel sorry for her. Yes, she'd walked out three years ago and not been back before now. Yes, it was her choice. But now she was here, and she was trying to right her wrongs. She was trying not to compound her mistake. She was fighting for what was hers. How could I blame her?

"Penelope, this is a conversation you should be having with Gabriel."

Her gaze dropped to her feet like she knew that wasn't the answer. "That's the theory," she mumbled. "Like I said, he's a good man, but he doesn't forgive so easily."

"He's trying to protect Bethany." And himself.

"Sometimes people don't make the right decisions," she said. "I didn't when I walked away. But if Gabriel doesn't let me make it right, won't that be a bad decision too?"

Would he be more forgiving of Penelope in different circumstances? If he hadn't watched his mother forgive his father over and over and over, only to be let down and betrayed every time, wouldn't he think Penelope deserved forgiveness?

And if I wasn't living here. If I wasn't sleeping with him. What if?

"I think you should talk to him. Like you said, he's a good man."

"Are you a good woman?" she asked. She put her hand up to stop me answering. "I'm going, don't worry. But ask yourself whether or not you can sleep at night, knowing you ruined Bethany's chance of having a mother and Gabriel's chance of having his wife back." She turned and walked up the street. I watched her, fingering the neck of my sweater.

Had I taken her place? And if I walked away, would it leave a vacancy she would fill? Would my absence force Gabriel to finally, at long last, give someone a second chance?

THIRTY-THREE

Autumn

How didn't I know until now how awesome libraries were?
They were particularly awesome if you wanted to know
everything there was to know about travelling in Europe.

I glanced around to find nothing had changed in the
hours since I'd last looked up. There were still a couple of
librarians behind the main desk, none of whom ever seemed
to speak to each other. There was a man on the computer on
the far side, behind the thriller hardbacks. And the desk in
front of me was still covered in piles of travel books.

All I knew was that I was definitely starting in Paris.
Nope. A flight to Amsterdam. That would be better. And
then on to Copenhagen and Stockholm. The pictures of
Stockholm looked so different from London. That would be
good. I would need distance by the time I left.

"You going travelling?" A bearded guy with a weird
accent asked as he approached my desk.

I nodded. "Can you tell?"

"Make sure you've got Oz on the itinerary."

"Because I want to see the wizard?"

"Not that Oz." He chuckled. "Australia."

"Oh wow, no. I'm staying closer to home." London did feel like home to me now. Maybe it was because Hollie was here. Maybe it was because I was so pleased to be out of Oregon. Maybe it was because of Gabriel. But I couldn't think about him right now. "Just around Europe this summer," I said. "I take it that's where you're from—Oz, I mean."

"Absolutely. You can't tell from the accent?" he asked. "But if you've not been down under, then make sure you put it on your list," he said, pointing at the notebook I had open. "And don't leave out the west coast. Shark Bay, mate. Best place on earth."

"Okay," I said. "I'll make a note of that."

He saluted and carried on walking, taking his books to the circulation desk.

Shark Bay? I'd never even heard of it. And I hadn't even considered going to Australia. Europe had always been the plan. It was still. I had two weeks left before I was due to fly out, and I'd been putting off the planning for too long.

The conversation with Penelope had brought with it a lot of questions. I still didn't have answers. But burying myself in travel books was a good distraction until I decided I wanted to figure out what was next.

My phone flashed with a message from Hollie. *What am I doing outside the Shoe Lane Library?*

I scampered to gather up my things. I'd lost track of time and forgotten I was supposed to be meeting her.

I emerged from the basement level to find Hollie outside, looking up at the sky.

"You okay?" I asked.

She snapped her head straight. "Fine. I didn't even know this place existed."

That was one of my favorite things about London. There was just so much of it. And it came in layers. The touristy sites—the Tower of London, Buckingham Palace, St. Paul's Cathedral—would take a couple of weeks if you did nothing else. Then there were the lesser-known things to see, like Portobello market, the Inns of Court, and Banqueting House, that would take months to do. Then there was everything else. The web of interesting things that bound the city together. Thousands of places that would stay hidden unless you tripped over them. One of the few buildings to withstand the Great Fire, the house Benjamin Franklin lived in, the street Dickens based Fagin's lodgings on. I loved it all.

"London's old but there are always new things to discover," I said.

"I'm so hungry. Where are we going?" she asked, linking her arm through mine. "I don't come over this way a lot, so I have no idea where to eat."

"Up here," I said as we headed up the hill. "We're going toward Smithfield Market."

"Eww, isn't that a meat market?"

"It should be gross but it's really beautiful. Look," I said, pointing at the huge building ahead that looked like one of London's Victorian railway stations, rather than a working meat market. "It's beautiful." The building was trimmed in ironwork that had been painted in purples and reds and greens. Statues kept watch from the roof.

"It's like a meat palace," Hollie said. "London is a strange place at times."

"I'm pretty sure anyone who came to the Sunshine Trailer Park would say the same thing."

We couldn't have been further away from Oregon if we'd tried. And we'd tried.

"So, how come you've been in the library? You studying for something?"

"Planning my trip. It's coming up soon," I said. Sooner than I'd imagined it would.

We arrived at the restaurant and pushed through the dark red door before settling into a table toward the back.

"I came here once with Gabriel. Make sure you check out the back of the stalls. It's a little shocking to my delicate sensibilities." There were pictures—subtle ones—of women's vaginas hung on the back of each door. The British were quirky.

"How intriguing. I think. As is your trip to the library. Tell me more."

"Nothing to tell. Just planning my trip."

Hollie scanned the menu, but I could tell she wasn't taking it in. "I thought you might not end up going."

"I know you did." I pulled the napkin from the table and put it in my lap.

"Does this mean you definitely are?" she asked.

The waiter came over and took our order. When he left, Hollie looked at me expectantly.

"I guess. I'm just so confused about everything. I really care about Gabriel and Bethany. And honestly, if it was just that simple, I probably wouldn't go."

"But you have to think about your goals in life," she said. "You don't want to regret not travelling."

"There's that." I'd be crazy to turn away from the opportunity to fulfil my dreams. Unless those dreams had changed, and something had shifted. When I fantasized about travelling around Europe and seeing the gigantic world outside of Oregon, it was because I wished for more.

It wasn't because now I didn't want to go to all those places and see all the wonderful things Europe had to offer. I did. But being in London faded the desire to spread my wings further. A little at least. And being with Gabriel—well, it showed me what else there was to want.

"What else is there?" Hollie asked.

"I got a visit from Gabriel's . . . What do we call her? Wife? Soon-to-be ex-wife?"

"Let's just stick with Penelope. What did she have to say?"

I gave Hollie the highlights.

"She's insane if she thinks you're standing in the way of her and her perfect life," Hollie said.

"I know. But at the same time, there's part of me that thinks she deserves a second chance."

"You think if you weren't around, Gabriel would just say, no problem, y'all, just move all your things back in and let's pick up where we left off?"

I knew it was more than just me standing between Penelope and her second chance. It was Gabriel's past as well. But I was concerned that with me in the picture, he'd never make the effort to face his demons and give the mother of his child a chance she deserved. "No, but maybe there would be a chance for things to be different. I guess we'll find out soon enough . . ." I laughed but it was hollow. Like a cough in an empty theatre. "Maybe it would be better to have a clean break."

"I thought you were serious about him."

I'd hoped I could have Gabriel and all these new experiences too, but maybe that was just greedy. I should be more than happy with an opportunity to travel to a dozen different countries. That had been my ultimate dream at one point.

"I know I wasn't all that supportive of you being with Gabriel at first, but over these last few weeks, I've seen how happy you are. How happy you both are. I was beginning to believe that it might be serious between you—serious enough that you'd both be willing to sacrifice things to make each other's dreams come true."

"You're talking in fairytales," I said. "We both know life doesn't work like that. We have to figure things out and work around obstacles."

Hollie groaned. "Not always. I'm living proof that the fairytale is real. You were the one who convinced me not to give up wanting it."

"I'm not giving up," I said. I wasn't sure that was true. This morning, I'd woken up before the sun and gone downstairs to find coffee. On the way, I'd watched Bethany asleep in bed. She was the most beautiful little girl, and she deserved the best of everything. "I just want what's best."

"For who?" Hollie asked.

"For everyone. I'm just considering whether I should take a step back. Can you imagine if Bethany turned around to me in fifteen years and said, if you hadn't been sleeping with my dad, my parents would never have divorced."

"You're talking like you're the reason Penelope left."

"No, I'm talking like I don't want to be the reason she doesn't stay." The more I talked about it, the more I realized I had to go. Not because I wanted to see the world. Not because I wanted to be sure that I wouldn't resent Gabriel in twenty years because I hadn't left. But because he needed me to leave so he could reach out and give his family a second chance.

"Is your guest room still available? I think I'm going to need a place to stay before I start my trip."

Hollie grabbed my hand. "Are you serious? Of course. Always. But, Autumn, are you sure?"

I nodded. It was clear to me now that I couldn't stay, and more than that, I had to leave with my whole heart. If I went with the promise of returning, Gabriel would never confront his past. He'd never give Penelope a chance.

I needed to help him. I needed to show him—show us both—that he needed me to leave. I just hoped I was strong enough to walk away.

THIRTY-FOUR

Gabriel

I closed the door behind me and sniffed the air, taking in the smell of cooking spices. Friday nights had fallen into a routine where Autumn cooked us a curry and I brought home some great wine to have with it. She'd been busy helping Hollie with the wedding recently, and I'd missed her.

"I'm home," I called, dropping my coat onto the rack and parking my documents case by the hall chair.

Autumn came down the stairs, her smile a little less enthusiastic than usual. "Good day?" I asked, smiling at her. She looked so beautiful when she had her hair up like that. Or down. Or with a hat. Or without.

She nodded and I pulled her into my arms as she got to the bottom of the stairs. She didn't mold against me as she usually did, instead pressing her hands on my chest. "I need to get our chicken out of the oven."

"Can I help?" I asked as I toed off my shoes and padded after her.

"It's all done," she said.

Was it me or was she avoiding my gaze? "What did you do today?"

She sighed as she slid the hot dish onto a trivet. "Usual thing. Nursery, then we went for a walk around Lincoln's Inn Fields."

Something was definitely up. On any normal day, Autumn would be bubbling over about Lincoln's Inn. About the "quaint" buildings and hidden walkways. It was the kind of place she loved. But today there was no enthusiasm in the way she spoke. Perhaps she was worried about the new nanny starting, although I'd offered the job to the woman Autumn had recommended and raved about. Maybe she'd had some bad news about the interviews she'd been going on.

"You hear anything about the analyst job at the investment bank?" I asked.

She shook her head as she pulled out another dish from the oven and set it on the side. "Nope. They won't be making a decision for weeks yet. Said they'll let me know."

"And Bethany's okay, because you would have told me if she wasn't."

"Yes, she's happy as usual, although Bear Bear is in need of a few stitches under his arm. I have to do it before I go."

Hearing her talking about leaving was like a dull punch to my gut. I hated the idea that she was going to be away for an entire month.

"I'm going to miss you," I said, circling my hands around her waist as she stood at the kitchen side. "How will I cope?" This time she leaned against me, letting her body relax against mine. "I shouldn't be so selfish. You'll be back in just a few weeks. And you'll have a job by then and—"

She spun in my arms. "I don't know if I'll have a job. I

don't know if I'm going to be in London. And I've been thinking . . ." She trailed her fingers down the buttons of my shirt.

"Sounds ominous." I was desperate to lift the heaviness that had settled in the air tonight.

"We haven't talked about it and I don't exactly know what you were thinking would happen with us after I left . . . but I think it might be better if we . . . went our separate ways." She spoke to the collar of my shirt, refusing to meet my eyes. The veins in my neck pulsed like the ticking of a clock.

"What are you talking about?" My face went numb. I dropped my arms and stepped back.

"I think you need to spend some time with Penelope." She exhaled as if she'd just unloaded a lead cloak from her shoulders.

"Has she been here again? What has she said this time? That you're responsible for terrorist activity in Iran and her shitty school grades?" I'd told my solicitor that Penelope had been trying to intimidate Bethany's nanny into leaving. She reassured me that it would count against her in any trial. But of course, no one wanted a trial.

"No, she hasn't been back," Autumn said, stepping toward me and cupping my face in her hands. "But I've been thinking about a few things."

Bloody hell. Penelope had got inside her head. Anger revved in my chest like the engine of a racecar before its first lap. "You need to ignore what she said. She's manipulative and refuses to take responsibility for anything. She needs to remind herself that she walked out on us three years ago. I didn't even know you then."

"I know," Autumn said. "This isn't about me. Well, not entirely about me."

"So why are you talking about going our separate ways? Granted, you need to figure out a new job, but I'm here to support you in that. I know you're young and I'm really trying to hold back because I don't want to push you too hard too soon, but bloody hell, Autumn. I'd accepted you might not want to live with us, but walking away? Where's this coming from?"

She dropped her hands and closed her eyes as if she were trying to blink away reality. "I think it's for the best."

The blood in my veins sped up and gained force. "This isn't what's best for me. So, what you mean is, this is what you want." I fought against my instinct to leave her there and disappear into my workshop. I needed to stay and convince her she was wrong.

"I want what's best. *For you.*"

"That's you. I want *you.*" Perhaps I should have been clearer earlier, but I'd thought it was understood between us that what we had wasn't just a passing affair or some kind of transitory romance. It was more than that. It was . . . like she'd been made for me.

"You've said how you thought you and Penelope and Bethany were a perfect family—just what you'd always wanted after the childhood you had. And then Penelope blindsided you. You were devastated."

My family had been less than perfect. I'd accepted that there was no such thing. "Things happen, Autumn. I thought our marriage was something it clearly wasn't. I'm trying to move on."

"Penelope isn't a bad person," she said as if she hadn't heard me. "And she's desperate to try to make things right again."

"She doesn't have a time machine. So there's no making things right." It was almost as if people didn't understand what had happened. My lawyer was the same: Penelope was sorry. Penelope wanted to be in Bethany's life. Penelope *wanted*. She'd given up her right to want anything the day she left.

"Everyone deserves a second chance, Gabriel."

"Says who?" It was such a ridiculous saying. "If you murder someone, you don't get a talking-to and told not to do it again or there'll be trouble. You go to prison—partly so you *can't* do it again."

Autumn looked up at me. "Penelope didn't murder anyone. And I'm not saying you should give her a second chance just because she deserves it. I'm asking you to do it for *you*. She's Bethany's mother and your wife. You need to give yourself a second chance at having the family you've always dreamed of. I don't want to be the person who stands in the way of that."

I tried to let her words soak in. Didn't she understand that it wasn't Penelope I wanted, wasn't Penelope I saw completing the family in my dreams? "But I love you."

I'd not said it before, but I'd felt it from the moment I saw her at Dexter and Hollie's place. The feeling hadn't been small. It hadn't been subtle. It didn't start as some seed and grow tall—it smacked me around the head and left bruises. I'd tried to ignore it. Deny it oxygen. Beat it back. But it refused to give up.

I didn't want Penelope. I didn't want anyone else. I loved *Autumn*.

Autumn put her head in her hands, covering her face so I couldn't see her reaction. Silence thundered between us, stretching the few centimeters between us into a valley.

She didn't say it back.

I knew she felt it. But she didn't say it back.

She dragged her fingers from her face and exhaled.

"You owe it to yourself to give her another chance," she said after what seemed like hours. "And I can't be the person who stands between you and your opportunity at having a life you always dreamed about, Gabriel. I can't be the person that stops Bethany's mother from being with her."

"You're not," I said.

"I don't want to be an excuse."

"An excuse? What, you think I'm getting an itch scratched with you, so I don't need to take my wife back?"

I hated the way she winced when I spoke. I'd never seen the expression on her face before—like she was in pain and didn't know how to heal.

"I don't want to be the reason you don't try to make it work. The reason you don't give your wife and the mother of your child a second chance."

"Even if you weren't here, I wouldn't take Penelope back." I'd made that decision the day she left. I wasn't going to subject Bethany to the merry-go-round of Penelope coming in and out of our lives. She left; she'd have to live with that decision.

She looked me in the eye. "You said you loved me." She said it like a question.

"Yes. I love you. I think I've loved you since we met, though I wouldn't admit it to myself."

She blinked again and again and again. "Then do it for me. Do it because I asked you to. Try again with Penelope."

"This is insane. I'm not going to take Penelope back. Us not being together won't change that."

"Prove it," she said.

"You want me to call her and tell her?" She was shaking her head before I got the words out. "Then what? Tell me what I need to do to prove it to you and I'll do it."

"Try to make it work. Spend time with her. Take her to

dinner. On a date. Remember why you married her. Try to picture that family you had in your imagination when you were a child and do your best to recreate that."

"You can't be serious." I didn't understand what she was saying. Why would giving Penelope a second chance be for her? It didn't make any sense.

"I have faith in you, Gabriel. You think you saw second chances go horribly wrong when you were a kid, but you've been breathing second chances into every piece of furniture you restore. Every time you strip the varnish off an old desk or replace the hinges on a bookcase, you give that piece of furniture a second chance. It's inside you." She reached out and placed her hand on my cheek. I knew in that moment that there was nothing I could do to change her mind.

I wanted to sink into that feeling of her soft skin against mine, wanted to drink it in and commit it to memory. I'd do anything to make her stay.

"If I try and it doesn't work, then what? I spend the rest of my life wishing for you?"

"I'm away for a month, Gabriel. Not even in the same country as you. Give it time. You all deserve some time to get to know each other again."

"And then?" I knew I'd miss her as soon as she closed the door.

"Don't think about the then. Just be in the present this summer. I'll see you at Hollie and Dexter's wedding."

"What? That's weeks away."

"It's really not long at all."

"But we can talk and—"

"Please, Gabriel. Don't think about me. Focus on your family. Give it these few weeks and see how you feel then. Do it for me," she said. "For Bethany. For you. Put your anger aside. See that Penelope isn't your father and taking her back doesn't mean you've become your mother. It's not just Penelope that deserves another chance. Or Bethany. It's you, too. You deserve that perfect family you always wanted."

Penelope wasn't my family. Not anymore. "And what if you're my perfect family? Are you really going to walk away?"

She shook her head and for a moment, I thought she might stay. "What if I'm not, Gabriel? What if you're meant to be with Penelope?"

She closed her eyes as if she were saying a silent prayer. A shiver passed through me and ice crawled up my spine, paralyzing every movement, every breath, every beat of my heart. And I didn't know if I'd ever feel warm again.

THIRTY-FIVE

Autumn

I'd been paralyzed by indecision since I opened my laptop last night. I hadn't slept at all and despite it being five after seven with the light bleeding around the edges of the curtains, I still hadn't decided whether I should cancel my Eurostar ticket to Paris the day after tomorrow. Maybe I should fly somewhere else. Some place less romantic.

Every click of the mouse and tap of the keyboard was an effort. Someone had opened the tap and drained all my energy. Then they'd come back and frozen any decision-making power.

I'd barely seen Gabriel since our conversation. It was better this way. He had a second chance this way. And I didn't have to live with the knowledge that I might have been the reason a family didn't reconcile. I'd spent the week focused on Bethany and settling the new nanny into the role. Last night, when the week was over and the new nanny was settled, I'd loaded my things into Dexter's car and come to stay with Hollie. I'd left Gabriel a letter, but whatever there was to say had already been said. I wanted him to be happy. More than anything.

There was a flight this afternoon to Madrid. Another tomorrow. There was even one on Thursday to Perth, Australia, and from there it was only a trip up the coast to see Shark Bay. I'd planned to spend the summer in Europe, but nothing about my life was going to plan at the moment.

I struggled into a sitting position and went through my flight options again. Would leaving today be running away? Or simply avoiding the temptation of running back to Gabriel?

The man who loved me. The man I loved so much I'd asked him to try to make it work with his wife.

I hadn't wanted to go. Leaving had been the most difficult thing I'd ever done. But more than I wanted to stay, I wanted Gabriel to have the life he dreamed of. And whether or not I liked it, that life wasn't with me.

I wanted him to have what he didn't growing up—have the dream become a reality. He'd fought me on it. I knew he would. But he'd soften over the next few months. He'd adjust. He'd remember what he'd had with Penelope.

"Is she okay?" I heard Dexter ask Hollie from outside my bedroom door. "I can't get Gabriel to pick up."

It would be better to get away soon. Then I wouldn't be able to waver or weaken or give in to the almost-overwhelming need to run back and tell him that it had all been a terrible mistake, and I loved him so much it caused physical pain to leave.

It would probably be too late anyway. I had no idea if he'd take Penelope back. I hoped he'd try at least. But I was almost certain that he'd never forgive me.

I booked the flight to Madrid. There was no point in staying here. I didn't want to spend the next few weeks miserable, with Hollie and Dexter whispering their concerns on the other side of closed doors. The weeks leading up to their wedding should be a special time for them. They should enjoy it without worrying about me.

I'd just confirmed my booking when there was a faint knock on the door. "Come in," I said.

Hollie poked her head in. "I thought you might be sleeping."

I shook my head. "Not much chance of that. But I'm feeling more positive now," I lied. "I just booked a flight to Spain. I'm going to be able to spend an entire week there now."

"Always looking on the bright side," Hollie said as she came in, her words sounding flat.

"What other choice do I have?" I asked.

"I thought we could go out for brunch," she said. "Somewhere nice like the Savoy."

My stomach curdled and I pushed away the memories from the night Gabriel and I had spent there. "Actually, I've got a flight to catch. My plane leaves at five."

"Today?" she said. "We haven't had a chance to talk or anything. You can't just leave."

I nodded. "It will take my mind off of things. And it will be good to go. The weather's amazing there." I remembered the advice Gabriel had given—I needed to make sure I put the Thyssen on my itinerary. "I should start packing. You're okay with me leaving things here?"

Hollie rolled her eyes. "Of course. Do you want me to come with you for a few days? I'm sure Dexter wouldn't mind, and it might be nice for us to have some time together."

I smiled at her, grateful for the offer, but she couldn't solve this for me. She couldn't salve this wound. I wasn't sure anything could. Maybe time. Maybe distance. The first was out of my hands, but I could jump on an airplane and try to get some miles between me and the man I loved. Try to take the edge off this hot ache I carried in every muscle and bone. "No, honestly, I'm looking forward to it. It will be an adventure."

"Why Spain? I thought you were going to start in Paris."

"Too romantic," I said, standing and pulling out the case I hadn't even unpacked yet.

"Maybe I can come out one weekend? Dexter could come too . . . or not." Hollie's voice wobbled.

"I don't want you to worry," I said, kissing the top of her head. "I'm going to be fine. Us Lumen sisters always land on our feet. And I'm going to attend any weddingy stuff via video call. It won't be a problem."

"I don't care about the wedding. I just hate to see you sad."

"I know," I said. Usually, I'd deny it. Plaster a smile on my face. But Gabriel would tell me that it's okay for things not to be okay sometimes. And now was one of those times. "But you know what? I get to see you marry Dexter. That's more than enough happiness for both of us."

"You'll definitely be back for it?"

My eyes widened. "Of course. As if I'd miss it. And I've got to come back and deal with my job situation. Or my lack of one."

"So you're for sure not leaving London?"

I couldn't promise anything. Frankly, I'd go wherever I got a decent job. But I didn't need to tell Hollie that. "How could I?" I asked. "You're here." I needed to leave for now. I needed space to breathe, and for time to do whatever it was time was supposed to do.

"Wherever you are, I'll be there for you. You know that, don't you?"

"I've never been in any doubt," I said, plunking down in her lap and pulling my arms around her. Maybe that's why I could always see the bright side? Because however murky things got, my sister was always out in front, finding a way through the darkness.

THIRTY-SIX

Gabriel

From where I was sitting on the sofa, I sorted through emails and watched Penelope play with Bethany out of the corner of my eye. The irony was bordering on comical. Penelope had picked out the wallpaper in this living room. She'd said she liked the green, as it reminded her of springtime. She'd probably forgotten. Now, she was just an unwanted houseguest.

The new nanny had said I didn't need to work from home today and that she'd had experience with supervised visits from parents in our situation before. But there was no way I'd leave Bethany alone with a stranger who'd been working for us for just a few days. So I was here. With my ex-wife and my daughter in a corrupted version of what my life was supposed to have been. And on top of that, I was trying to forget that it had probably been Penelope's unscheduled visit that led to Autumn leaving. I was trying not to hate Penelope even more than I did.

My soon-to-be ex-wife was sitting cross-legged on the

rug, playing a memory game with Bethany. The new nanny was hovering beside them and Jade sat and observed.

Bethany was giggling at the game in front of her. "Daddy, look," she said, holding up one of the small cards. "The monkey is wearing lipstick."

"It looks like your mouth when you've eaten an ice lolly," I said. "Find the other matching one."

She knew exactly where it was. "Here," she said, picking up one of the cards lying face down on the floor. She didn't even check it was the monkey before she held it up to me. She was smart and confident. Yes, definitely my daughter.

"Clever girl," I said.

She shrugged and allowed Penelope to take her turn. She didn't make a pair and I couldn't work out whether or not her mistake was deliberate.

"I'm bored," Bethany said. "Daddy, please can we go to the swings?"

"You don't have to come," Penelope said before I could respond. "I can take her. Jade will be there."

I wasn't about to leave Bethany alone with her mother. And some time away from my laptop would be good. "Come on then," I said to Bethany. "Get your jacket."

Bethany had her coat and shoes on in record time. I grabbed my keys from the kitchen drawer and herded everyone out.

"Did you pick up your phone?" Penelope asked.

I'd forgotten it but I wasn't going to let Penelope think she'd helped me remember. "Don't need it," I said.

Penelope chuckled. "How times have changed."

I ignored her. I had no desire to share laughs about old times with her. I didn't want to be reminded about how it had all been a lie.

Bethany's hand slipped into mine as we took the familiar route around the back of the house to the park, Jade and Penelope following behind us. "Can you push me a thousand times?" Bethany tugged on my hand.

"My arms will fall off if I do that."

Bethany laughed. "No, they won't. Please, Daddy."

"I'll push you ten times," I countered.

"Twenty," she said.

"Deal." If I could successfully negotiate with a four-year-old, my current transaction—a one-point-two billion tech acquisition—would be child's play.

We entered the playground and found it almost empty. "Penpee, will you push me twenty times same as Daddy?" Bethany asked, racing toward her favorite swing.

I glanced over at Penelope and wondered how it felt that her daughter didn't call her Mummy. Not that she was a mother. She'd resigned her position three years ago. But at least Penelope hadn't pushed it—hadn't demanded to tell her that she was her mother. I had to give her some credit for putting Bethany first, because that didn't happen when she left. There was no way I'd let Bethany know that Penelope was her mother, only for Penelope to disappear again. Bethany would start to question if she was the problem and worse, might wonder if I'd leave her too. Up until now, I'd always explained to Bethany that her mother lived far away and that she and I were a small, special family together. She'd known nothing else, so she'd simply accepted it.

"Absolutely," she said. "You need a hand getting on?" Bethany held her arms up and Penelope lifted her onto the seat of the swing and started to push.

"Higher," Bethany demanded. "High. High. High."

"Now you can do it on your own," I called out. When

she got going, I stopped pushing her. Penelope wouldn't know this particular trick.

Autumn would. We'd laughed about it one evening just after we'd kissed for the first time.

I closed my eyes, trying to erase the memory of her from my head but knowing any time *not* thinking about her would be temporary. She lived permanently in my mind, if not my house.

Bethany brought me back to the moment. "Daddy, see how high I am?"

"That's really high. Be careful," I said.

Bethany spent ten times longer on the swing than I had patience for, and I wished I had my phone. Finally, when I'd pushed her double the times we'd agreed, she moved to the slide. There was nothing for Penelope to do other than stand aside and watch.

"Would you mind if I took a photograph?" she asked me, glancing at Jade.

I shrugged. "Go ahead."

Now she wanted to capture memories? She'd missed out on three years' worth of pictures.

"Thank you," she said after she snapped a couple. "It means a lot to me."

"Have you dropped this issue of getting custody?" I snapped as Bethany climbed the stairs to the slide again.

Penelope didn't respond as we both watched her get to the top of the stairs and slide to the bottom, then race around to start the process again.

"I know that I've hurt you," she said in a small, low voice. "And Bethany—"

"You can see she's completely fine."

She paused while Bethany came down the slide again only to race around to the steps. "I know that I've made choices that I regret, and I know they have consequences. But I'd like to try to not have the mistakes I've made last forever."

"You can't undo leaving," I said. "You can't suddenly expect those three years to disappear."

"I know," she said, pushing her hands into her pockets and pausing again until Bethany was out of earshot. "But I left for three years. I don't want to let that turn into sixteen. Or a lifetime."

I tried to think back to my earliest memory. When I was Bethany's age, I spent a lot of time hiding in the small cupboard in my bedroom. I'd climb in there when my parents argued. Every time my mother shut herself in her bedroom to sob. When I first became aware of her crying, I would try to comfort her—I wanted to somehow turn off her pain. But she'd tell me she was fine and would send me away to play. So I'd go to the cupboard where I wouldn't hear and I could pretend it wasn't happening.

I didn't want Bethany's childhood memories to be of her hiding anywhere.

At the same time, I didn't want to create a new problem. I didn't want Bethany to come to me one day and ask me why I hadn't let her see her mother.

"I'm not trying to take her away from you, Gabriel. I would never. You're a good man and a wonderful father. Bethany is very lucky to have you. I don't want to ruin any of that."

Didn't she see that she already had? "There are no second chances," I said. "Not when it comes to me. Not when it comes to my daughter."

Penelope sighed. "I know, Gabriel," she said in a resigned tone. "I know."

Bethany moved on to the roundabout and Penelope

rode on with her as she spun them both around. Then onto the monkey bars. Bethany had been trying for a while now to cross them without falling.

"Go as quickly as you can," I said as she ran over to me to hand me her jacket. She nodded, determination in her eyes.

She got halfway across and dropped to the ground.

"You okay?" I asked, as Penelope rushed to her.

Bethany sprang up and went right back to where she'd started. "I'm going to try again," she said.

"Good girl." *Never give up.*

Penelope backed away. "See. If she gave up when she failed the first time, she'd never learn to master anything," she said.

I huffed out a breath. I could see right through her. There was no way she could equate the two circumstances and I wouldn't allow her to manipulate me. "But you did give up, Penelope. You gave up for three years."

Bethany passed the tricky halfway point and was almost across. "Keep going," I called. "You're nearly there."

Just before she hit the last rung, her hand slipped and she fell to the ground—just thirty centimeters or so. She'd been so close.

"How are your hands?" I asked.

She held up her palms. "Sore."

"Maybe take a break and try again next time. You were so close."

She nodded and skipped over to me to collect her jacket. I helped her into the sleeves so her top didn't ruche up on the arms in the way she hated.

"My palms were sore, Gabriel. I needed a break," Penelope said. "But I don't want to give up. Not on my daughter. And not on my marriage."

I didn't reply. I didn't have anything to say. Marriage and a child weren't trying to cross the monkey bars. Sometimes you just needed to push through—do what was being asked of you by the people who loved you.

Bethany raced back to me and slipped her hand into mine and we headed home, Penelope and Jade following. My mind started replaying my conversation with Autumn, as it had a hundred times since she left. I had no desire to try again with Penelope. But I wanted Autumn. More than anything, I wanted her to come back. If I was following my own advice, I needed to do what was being asked of me. Perhaps I just had to push through.

"What are your plans for tomorrow?" I called over my shoulder.

"Me?" Penelope asked. "Nothing. Why?"

"Meet me at Primitivo's at one," I said, referring to a restaurant around the corner from my office. We'd met a couple of times there before Bethany had been born. Lunch with Penelope would be the start of what Autumn had asked of me. I'd spend time with Penelope. I'd hear her out. But only because that's what it would take to get Autumn back.

THIRTY-SEVEN

Autumn

So much for the amazing weather. It was raining. And not just in a gentle drip. This rain consisted of large, violent splashes of water my umbrella was almost useless against. My sneakers squelched when I walked, and my pants stuck to my legs as if I'd put them on straight from the washer.

But I was dry from my waist up thanks to the water-proof coat I'd brought from Oregon, and I wasn't cold. I was invigorated. It was as if the rain was determinedly washing away anything bad. I thought about Gabriel constantly. But I needed to focus on the positive—the man I loved got to have the family he'd always wanted. I had to be happy for him. My devastation at having to give him up would pass. At some point the sharp edges of loss would soften and I would start to feel whole again. In the meantime, I would distract myself. If that took getting soaked to my skin in Madrid, then so be it.

I saw some large white columns to my left, which must

belong to the Prado. I raced toward them, desperate for shelter. I darted under cover and shut down my umbrella, stamping my feet in the vain hope that it would shake some of the water from my pants.

"I thought it was supposed to be sunny in Spain," an American, male voice said from behind me. I spun around and found a tall, handsome guy, trying to dry his face with his sweater.

"You're American." It was funny to hear that accent in such a faraway place. Perhaps it was a sign that right here was where I was meant to be.

"SoCal," he replied.

I laughed. No wonder he looked so butthurt. "The rain isn't personally directed at you. And anyway, look at how green it is, even in the middle of the city. Trees need the rain. It's a tradeoff. You can't have the greenery without the water. Breathe it in." I faced the torrents and opened my arms in welcome. "It cleans everything away so we can start fresh." I had to believe that Madrid was the beginning of my future and not just a stop I was making while I ran from my pain.

"I'm Jackson," he said, and I turned to look at him. "And whoever you are, you just made me feel a lot better."

I grinned. "I'm glad. I'm from Oregon, so I guess I'm a little more used to the rain."

He shook his head and huffed a chuckle. "So, Oregon, want to go grab a cup of something hot before taking in the Goya?"

I shrugged. I was just thinking how I needed distracting. "Sure," I said. "As long as you don't spend the whole time complaining that Europe isn't just like California."

"I promise," he replied. A corner of his mouth turned

up as he smiled, creating a dimple in his cheek that I wanted to poke with my index finger.

The Prado was waiting. My future was waiting. I just needed to keep taking it one step at a time.

THIRTY-EIGHT

Gabriel

Penelope was always late but that didn't mean I had to be, so I got to the restaurant exactly on time. I reached the hostess's podium and saw Penelope waving from a table by the window. As much as I hated to admit it, every time I'd expected Penelope to stumble since she'd been back, she surprised me. She'd not missed a single play session with Bethany. She hadn't tried to push me to tell Bethany that she was her mother. She hadn't been underhanded and told her anyway. When I'd asked her to lunch, I hadn't had to negotiate on day, time, or place. And she was on time.

"Please can I get some water?" I said to the hostess. "You want anything?" I asked Penelope.

"Water's great." She grinned at me. "Did you come from the office?"

I sat down and my phone buzzed in my pocket. "Excuse me." I pulled out my mobile to see who had messaged me. Unsurprisingly, it was Mike. He seemed to get worse rather than better, constantly checking up on me—like I'd ever dropped the ball—and second-guessing my decisions.

"You need to make a call?" she asked. "It's fine."

I shook my head and picked up the menu. Mike would have to wait.

"I can't believe you're still doing it. Well," she said, shrugging, "I never understood why you did the job in the first place. It's not like you need the money."

There was no need to dust off this dance that we'd done a thousand times before. My job wasn't any of her concern. "You know I think it's important that Bethany has a good role model. It's good for her to see that everyone has to go out into the world and earn a living." Working, and working hard, wasn't a bad thing. "I don't want to be just another trust fund kid."

"I know," she said. "But I don't think that's the only reason you do it." I didn't ask her to elaborate. I wasn't sure I wanted to know. "You're never going to end up as your father. You have far too much character for that."

It was the kind of thing she would have said to me when we were married. At the heart of our relationship, there had always been mutual respect. It was what had always puzzled me about Penelope's leaving. We didn't argue. We bickered over little things but there had never been a fundamental disagreement. Or so I'd always thought. Her departure had come out of the blue. I'd been completely blindsided.

"Going to work keeps me honest."

She paused and looked at me. "Really? Going to work and doing something you hate keeps you honest? Why not choose something you love?"

I wasn't interested in a come-to-Jesus moment for

myself. I wanted to hear about hers. "So, Penelope, why are you back?" I asked. "Why now?"

"I suppose I figured out what was important."

"And that took three years?"

"There were reasons I left. And there were reasons why I didn't come back. They weren't necessarily the same. I don't know how to explain it to you."

"Try," I said. I wanted to hear this. I *deserved* to hear this. "All I've gotten so far is some messed-up analogy about monkey bars."

She smiled and shifted her fringe out of her eyes. The fringe was new. It suited her.

"I always loved Bethany, but over that first year of her life, it felt like the walls were closing in. It felt like my life wasn't my own and that my choices had been taken away from me." She looked sad but she didn't look beaten or tired, and it occurred to me that before she'd left, that was how she'd looked—as if the color had drained from her face and someone had switched her into slow motion. The woman who sat before me was much more like the woman I'd married compared to the one who'd left.

"All I could see was a future being an unpaid servant to this squirming human, and I knew you wanted more than one child," she said. "I felt as if my entire future was laid out for me. I didn't like it."

I kept my expression neutral. I wasn't sure if Penelope was telling me she'd been depressed, and if that's what she was saying, I didn't want to be insensitive. "You didn't say anything at the time."

"I don't think I could have articulated it at the time. I just had this sense of panic, needing to run, needing to escape. I didn't see that I wasn't coping. I just felt this urge to leave. It didn't help that I was clearly terrible at caring for Bethany."

I frowned. "What do you mean?"

"I was so impatient with her. Remember when I screamed at her for crying? Like that was going to help." She shook her head while she worried the edge of the menu with her nail. "When you were around, you were so patient with her, so calming. You only had to pick her up and she settled. It emphasized the way I didn't feel any of those things. I was the opposite of calm. The opposite of patient. I just felt like a failure. Like she'd be better off with you and without me. I could get out of the way and let the two of you be."

As much as I'd like Penelope to have turned into a monster, she was still the same woman I'd married. The woman who set her standards way too high and beat herself up far too much when she didn't meet them. "I should have paid more attention. I had no idea you felt any of this."

She reached over and grabbed my hand. "This is not your fault," she said. "We were trying to navigate not killing a tiny human. That is quite the distraction."

I smiled, remembering how we used to hover over her cot to check she was breathing, how we baby-proofed our entire house before Penelope had given birth, even though Bethany wouldn't crawl for months. We'd been so cautious and careful about everything. Everything except our own relationship. That had been left to wither and die.

"After I left, over the following few months, I sort of emerged from a fog only to be enveloped in shame and guilt for leaving," she continued. "I wanted to come back a thousand times. But what would I say? How would I explain myself?" she said. "I'd left my child. It's the ultimate crime for a mother." She pulled her hand from mine and took a sip of the water that had appeared on our table without our noticing. I waited as she swallowed and took a deep breath, trying to push away the obvious upset. "I loved you both, yet I abandoned you." She shook her head. "I have to live with myself for doing that."

She glanced down at the menu, clearly not trying to decide on her order. "Every time I thought about it, I ran further away in the hope that my shame would be left behind, but of course it followed me around and just got bigger. I figured out that the only way it wouldn't just continue to grow and eventually eat me alive, was to turn around and face what I'd done."

"You're back to face the shame of leaving?" I asked. Was she asking me for absolution? She couldn't know me very well if she was.

She shook her head. "No, I had a lot of therapy to handle the shame. I'm back because I don't want to compound the mistakes I've made by staying away. I did a terrible thing to you both, but I don't want that to be the end. I don't want to walk away and never return. I want to move forward. Be Bethany's mother. And map out a new relationship with you."

I shook my head. Autumn would want me to agree and that would be that. But she didn't understand the scar Penelope's leaving had created.

She put up her hand to stop me from speaking. "Before you say anything, I know we can't go backward. That's not what I'm asking. Whatever happens in the future—whatever relationship we manage to salvage—I understand that it won't be what we had."

Whatever we'd had hadn't been enough. It hadn't stopped our family from falling apart.

"I know I'm asking a lot. And I understand it's difficult for you to trust me after what I did. But I'm patient."

It would have been far easier if Penelope had tried to excuse what she'd done, if she'd demanded that I let her back into Bethany's life or if she'd lacked remorse. But the way she'd explained things, it painted the situation in an entirely different light. The anger and bitterness I had toward Penelope seeped away until I was left with nothing but sadness. For her. For Bethany. And for me.

I nodded. "Thank you for telling me this. I'm sorry . . . sorry for not noticing at the time. For not coming after you. And for hating you for all these years."

She smiled at my confession. "I hated me too," she said, tears forming in her eyes. "And some of that feeling still lingers."

I drew in a breath and pushed back my shoulders. Penelope wasn't a monster, and I wasn't about to keep her in a cage, protecting Bethany from someone who cared for her. There was no going back. We could only move forward. "We should tell Bethany that you're her mother."

A guttural sob broke from Penelope's throat and she nodded. "Thank you," she whispered.

It was the last thing I'd expected to come out of this lunch. I'd expected to be going through the motions so I could tell myself I'd done what Autumn had asked. Autumn couldn't have known Penelope's reasons for leaving and staying away, but she knew enough to understand that I should hear Penelope out. She was the wisest woman I knew.

"You should come to dinner later in the week," I said. "We can tell her together."

"You're a good man, Gabriel."

"I'm going to ask you for something in return."

"Anything," she asked, her eyes brightening.

"Don't take her from me, Penelope. I can't give her up." My jaw tightened and my fists clenched like I was ready to fight anyone who would even think about taking my daughter from me.

"Never," she replied, shaking her head. "I promise."

I reached across the table and put my hand over hers and my chest loosened at the softness of her familiar skin. We had to find a way forward. For Bethany and for ourselves. We had to move on from the hatred and anger, the shame and guilt. Contrary to everything I'd taught myself to believe, we all deserved a second chance.

THIRTY-NINE

Autumn

As I looked up at the bulging, undulating steps, it struck me. "It's like Barcelona is the younger, wayward sister of the grown-up Madrid."

"Madrid is Prada and Barcelona is Lacroix," Jackson said as we made our way up to the steps.

"La what now?" I asked. Every other sentence Jackson spoke needed translation. There was no way we had grown up in the same country. It felt like we inhabited different planets most of the time.

"*Christian* Lacroix," he said as if I might be the stupidest person to ever walk the earth. "They must have Lacroix in Oregon."

"In Oregon they might, but I'm certain Christian never entered the gates of the Sunshine Trailer Park."

He cackled and then spun three hundred and sixty degrees. "I mean, it's pretty. I'm just not sure it's very me. It's not that I don't appreciate the drama, because you know

I do. But I'll take the baroque glory of the Spanish steps over this any day."

I groaned. "No Rome references," I complained. "Not today."

I didn't have to see Jackson's face to know he was rolling his eyes. "Listen, I'm up before noon so we can spend an entire day in this place. I can't promise I can go the whole day without mentioning Rome. Anyway, it's where you first fell in love. It shouldn't make you grimace. It should make you smile."

I linked my arm into Jackson's. "No offense. I just wish I was spending the day with Gabriel today. He loves this park."

"No offence, but I've seen a picture of that man. I wish I was spending the day with him, too." Jackson was also in Spain nursing heartbreak. Hiding or running or distracting himself. We were in the same boat and had been each other's companions in misery for the last week.

I laughed. "We're both each other's consolation prizes."

"You never know. He might take you here for your honeymoon."

"That hopeless romanticism is what will get you into trouble next time," I said to him. "Gabriel won't be the man I go on honeymoon with. I honestly wonder if I even want to get married."

"And they say the gays are dramatic."

"I mean it. There wasn't anything I wouldn't have done for Gabriel. If he'd wanted to get married, I would have. For him. I just can't imagine feeling that way about anyone else."

"Give it time, sweet girl."

Time wasn't going to do it. Each day grew worse. It just

created space where I replayed our conversations over and over in my head. It made me crazy wondering if I'd done the right thing by leaving. Should I have stayed and fought? Why didn't I tell him I loved him? My heart grew heavier and heavier with aching for him. And Bethany.

I missed them.

"You're getting maudlin," he said. "I can see it in your eyes. And it's three hours before it's noon and acceptable to drink. Even in Europe."

"Should I send him a picture? We talked about this place." If he and Bethany were here, we could have brought a picnic and a Frisbee and raced up the steps. Gabriel would have put Bethany on his shoulders so she could see out onto the city. She would love it here.

"I know, honey. But don't do anything you're going to regret." He glanced around. "There," he said, pointing at an ice cream stand in the distance.

"I can't eat ice cream at this time of the morning."

"It's not an ice cream stall. It's a souvenir stand. Let's buy a postcard. You can write it with what you'd want to say to him and keep it until you've had time to think about whether you should send it."

"Are you this sensible when you break up with someone?" I asked. I didn't want to send a postcard. Or write one I knew I wouldn't send. Getting in contact with Gabriel wasn't the answer. He needed time to see if his family could be pieced back together. And I needed to give him that time.

"Nope. I'd be texting eleven times an hour and drinking in the shower in the mornings."

I didn't want to day drink. I wanted to make the most of the summer. Seeing Europe like this was a once-in-a-life-time opportunity and was the only kind of silver lining of an otherwise clouded sky. I needed to stay positive and make the best of things. "A postcard seems like a good option." Even if I never sent it, there was something deep inside me that told me he'd feel what I wrote. He'd know I was thinking about him. He'd understand that I loved him.

FORTY

Gabriel

It felt like we were about to begin a séance. "I hate this place," I said to Dexter, trying not to shudder as I took a seat at the round table of the private room where we often ended up if it was Dexter's turn to choose the venue for our regular evenings out.

He shot me a look. "It's one of the best private members clubs in Europe."

"Did you bring your cauldron?" Joshua asked.

"No," I replied. "But I brought some eye of newt."

"I think it's the red velvet curtains," Tristan said. "Or that low ceiling with the star cut into it. It's part witch's lair, part nineteenth-century Parisian brothel."

"I have no desire for a spell or a prostitute, so like I said, I hate this place." The lack of windows, the wooden paneling. The heavy velvet everywhere. It was claustrophobic and depressing.

"Well, we're planning *my* stag night, so I don't care if you like it here," Dexter said.

"Vegas!" Tristan exclaimed.

"Speaking of twenty-first-century brothels," Andrew chipped in.

"We're not going to Vegas," Dexter said. "Apart from it being a complete cliché, we all vowed never to go again after last time. Wherever we go, if you get arrested again, you're staying in prison, Joshua."

"That was a shit show," Joshua said. "Vegas is a terrible idea. Tallinn?"

A collective groan echoed in our velvet cave. "Way too predictable," Tristan said.

"What about Harry Potter world?" Joshua suggested. "We could rent the entire place out for the night. No one could get into trouble. It's original."

"Great idea . . . if this was my thirteenth birthday party," Dexter said.

I couldn't hold back a laugh. "What about Peppa Pig world?" I asked. Arguably, that could mean an overnight stay at my place.

"Or Legoland?" Andrew said.

"Okay, okay," Joshua said. "Message received. At least I'm coming up with ideas, even if they are all shit. Climb down from the cheap seats, get in the arena, and make some suggestions, Gabriel."

Why couldn't we just stay in London?

"Rome? Great food, great wine. Beautiful women," Joshua suggested. "All that passion. God, I love Italian women."

"This isn't about you getting laid," I snapped. There was no way I was going to Rome. "I'm vetoing Rome."

"Have you heard from her?" Tristan asked.

I shook my head. I'd not asked Dexter where she was or what she was doing. And I'd only seen Hollie once since

Autumn had left. I'd come close to asking after her, but I'd held myself back. There was no point. She'd been clear.

"And how are things going with Penelope?" Joshua asked.

"Good, actually."

Dexter's eyebrows shot up. He filled the expectant silence around the table by topping up my wineglass.

"We had lunch and talked things through a couple of weeks back. We've told Bethany she's her mother and she comes over to the house a few times a week."

"Well, that sounds mighty civilized," Dexter said. "And you seem okay about it."

"It is and I am. It's good for Bethany. Like Penelope said, she walked out, and it can be for three years or a lifetime. She'd prefer it to be three and . . ." I'd thought about it. I'd do anything for my daughter, and I wasn't going to be the man who denied her a mother. "And so would I. It's what's best for Bethany."

"So, she's back for good?" Joshua asked.

"Yes, I think she is. And if she walks out again . . . Well, I'll pick Bethany up and put her back together." I didn't think Penelope would leave again. She'd grown up. We both had. And she wouldn't want to miss out on Bethany any more than she already had done.

"What about the two of you?"

I shrugged. "I don't know. She's still the same woman I married but . . ." She wasn't Autumn. And when Autumn came back, I wanted to prove to her that I'd done everything I could to try with Penelope, even if that's not what I wanted. Autumn should have no doubt that I wanted her above all others.

"Too much water under the bridge?"

"I'm not sure I'm the same man she married." My

phone buzzed, interrupting my thoughts. I pulled it out of my pocket to find Mike's number flashing at me and I groaned before ignoring the call.

"Wait, did you just ignore a work call?" asked Tristan.

I shrugged. I was sick of Mike. Ever since Penelope and I had lunch and she'd been surprised that I was still lawyering, it had gotten me thinking. "I've been considering that I might not like my job."

"This is hardly breaking news," Joshua said. "What would be a surprise is if you said you were giving it up."

"Actually, I wanted you lot to talk me out of resigning." Since Primitivo's, I'd mulled over the idea of leaving the law. Penelope was right that, in theory, I didn't have to work. The family trust meant that my father hadn't worked a day in his life, and I wouldn't have to either. I'd been a lawyer a long time, dealing with shitty clients like Mike and whoever came before him or would come after him. At long last, it occurred to me that I didn't have to do something I hated to be a role model.

"Excuse me, did I hear you correctly?" Dexter asked.

"I'm not saying I'm about to resign from the partnership. I'm just thinking about it." The more I thought about it, the more appealing it seemed. "But obviously it's a terrible idea and I need to hear it. I wouldn't even know what else I could do. I don't want to sit around doing nothing and I don't want to do something I'm going to enjoy even less."

"You don't have to work, do you?" Tristan asked.

"No, but I *want* to. It's important that I'm a good role model for Bethany. And anyway, what would I do all day?"

"You could do charity work," Joshua suggested. "Set up a foundation. Raise money."

Didn't thousands of rich men do that? It always seemed

as much of an ego trip as a charitable endeavor. I'd rather just donate to someone else's foundation.

"Set up your own business," Andrew suggested, which was typical for him because he seemed to have a new business every time I saw him.

"Doing what?" I asked.

Silence stretched around the table. That was the problem with lawyers. No one could see them doing anything but being lawyers, including the lawyers themselves.

"You could go into politics," Dexter said. "You've got high moral standards and great decision-making skills."

"I think that disqualifies me," I said. "And anyway, I can't think of anything worse."

"You could sell tables," Tristan said. "Like the one you made for your kitchen."

Warmth gathered in my belly as I remembered Autumn describing how I gave furniture a new lease on life. I drummed my fingers on the table. "I didn't make it," I said.

"But you . . . polished it up or something, didn't you?" Tristan asked.

Or something. It had taken me six months of evenings to get that table into a useable state. "I do that for fun," I said. "To unwind."

"Right," Andrew said. "So make it into your job and you'll never feel like you're at work. But don't do it unless you feel it in your heart. In your gut."

"You're saying that you feel it in your heart every time you want to start a new business?" I asked, ready for him to say *of course not*.

"Absolutely," he replied. Andrew was a rich man. His family were well off, but Andrew was *rich*. And he'd done it himself, jumping from idea to idea, building successful business after successful business. So, although I wanted to dismiss his romantic idea that I needed some kind of visceral connection to a business, he'd already proved he did it the right way. "The question is, do you *love* working with secondhand furniture?"

"I *love* having sex with women. I'm not going to turn that into a business," Tristan said.

Tristan was a dick at times, but I saw his point.

"Never say never," Andrew replied. "You might need those gigolo stripes at some point in this economy."

Everyone around the table chuckled. Dexter opened his mouth to say something, and Tristan raised his hand to stop him.

"Spare me the obvious gags, Dexter. I know, I'll be bankrupt by the end of the week. Etcetera, etcetera."

"You know what, Tristan? I will spare you. What I was actually going to say to Gabriel was that he should do whatever makes him happy." Dexter turned to me. "Tune everything out. Ignore what you think you should do for Bethany. Ignore your reaction to your father's poor parenting and what you *think* people think about you. If it was entirely up to you, how would you spend your time?"

"In my workshop," I replied, without missing a beat. "But it's fun. Doesn't mean I'm good at it. And I know I'm a good lawyer."

"You'd be good at anything you set your mind to. It's who you are," Tristan said.

I playfully punched him on the arm and glanced around when I didn't hear the good-natured put-down coming from one of my brothers. Instead, they were all nodding.

"And no one's the best at anything straight off the bat," Joshua said. "Practice and you'll get better. That's just a fact."

They made it sound so simple. But I thought about it—Dexter loved his business. Loved jewelry. He always said it ran through his veins. There was nothing that lit a fire in Beck like redeveloping real estate. In fact, they were all like that. Tristan tried to pretend he wasn't, but he was a *passionate* geek. What exactly that he geeked out about I wasn't sure—something to do with technology. But they were lucky—they'd managed to find the holy grail where their passions and their careers aligned. Most people weren't so fortunate. I'd been vaguely considering resigning and maybe taking a couple of non-exec directorships of companies a bit like the older partners did when they retired. But these guys were telling me to rip up the rule book. "What? So I just resign and make the way I blow off steam my job?"

"Why not?" Joshua said.

"I'm a good lawyer. I've worked really hard for years and—"

"You might be a lawyer, but I know you understand your way around the business world enough to understand the concept of sunk costs," Joshua said. "If you're done, get out now. Don't give any more of your time to a career you don't enjoy."

"Right," Andrew said. "Not every business I invest in works. When it doesn't, I get out. And sometimes it works for a while and then I need to move on because I'm bored, or the business needs to move on because it needs someone else. What worked yesterday doesn't necessarily work today. Law served you for a while. If it doesn't any longer, move on."

Move on and give myself a chance at a second career? It seemed so out of character. But something was pulling me toward the idea.

"If you had to put food on the table for Bethany, it might be different," Dexter said. "But you're in a position that most people can only dream about. Don't waste it. You should role model *that* for Bethany—making the most out of life."

I hated to think of Bethany doing a job she didn't like, especially if she believed her father had taught her a "grin and bear it" mentality. With the amount of time everyone spent at work, it would mean she'd spend most of her life unhappy. I tried to picture myself in my workshop every day. I liked the idea of not having to put on a suit. Not having to wedge myself into an overcrowded tube train. More than that, the idea of getting to spend an entire day on a project was like the sun breaking through thunder clouds. My mind started to race with ideas of what I'd like to work on. I'd seen a Victorian bedframe online I'd love to have a go at. It would involve some cane work, but it was something I'd been meaning to try. And I'd always hoped that one day, I'd actually make something—a chair or a table—from scratch. "I wouldn't know how to start." A new venture sounded completely daunting, but at the same time there was a feeling of freedom that began to unlock the pressure around my heart.

"I'll tell you where to start," Joshua said. "Tell Mike to fuck off and find another lawyer to harass."

"Then resign from that firm," Dexter said.

"And pick up your axe and do something nice with wood," Tristan said.

"My axe?" They made it sound so simple. And in theory it was. In theory, there was nothing stopping me from handing my notice in.

"Worst-case scenario," Andrew said. "You can always go back to law."

Penelope had been right—I wasn't my father. I wouldn't make entertaining a series of nameless women my life's work. If I left the law, I'd read my daughter a bedtime story more often. I'd spend more time in my workshop. I'd make pieces I'd only let myself dream of. I could travel.

Why had it taken my estranged wife to bring these thoughts to the surface? Or maybe it hadn't been her at all. Autumn had been the one to insist I give myself a second chance at a future I'd dreamed of. Perhaps I'd just had time to examine those aspirations more closely and found that what I wanted had shifted.

"Great. Now we've figured out what Gabriel's going to do for the rest of his life, can we get back to planning my stag party?" Dexter asked.

"Yes, back to our cauldron," Joshua said. "What about Barcelona?"

FORTY-ONE

Autumn

It was raining, and I had no appetite for bad weather. Instead of being out sightseeing, making the most out of my last few hours in Croatia, I'd packed and repacked my case at least nine times. I was due to fly to Paris this afternoon, but I didn't want to go. How ridiculous was that? I was due to go to *Paris, France,* and I didn't want to go.

I was homesick. Not for Oregon. But for London. For my sister. For Gabriel. And Bethany.

"You called at the perfect time," Hollie said as she answered my videocall. "I'm deciding on napkins. To tell you the truth, Dexter decided on napkins and chose something ten times more expensive than we need, so I'm *rechoosing* napkins. Don't say anything if you speak to him."

"I promise. What are the options?" She held up two white napkins. "I prefer the plain ones."

"Great. Me too. The coordinator was pushing the scalloped edges, but I prefer the plain white." She collapsed onto the couch I recognized from her office. "So, haven't spoken to you since you left Greece. How's Zagreb?"

"Pretty. I wish you were here," I said, a little too weary to keep my smile from faltering.

"I wish I was there too. I could have come out. You want me to see if I can get flights?"

"Hollie, you're getting married in two weeks. You can't come out now. And anyway, I'll be back in London in six days."

"I've missed you so much," Hollie said.

"Same." I didn't have the energy to launch into how great the trip was, which was what I normally did when she told me she missed me. I didn't want her to worry.

"You don't sound like yourself. What's the matter?"

I wasn't sure whether or not Hollie was expecting me to have *gotten over* Gabriel by now, but we hadn't mentioned him since I'd left London. "I miss you. I miss London."

"Does that include Gabriel?" she asked.

I drew in a breath and prepared myself to disappoint my sister. "I'm so happy that I've had the chance to come to Europe, see all these amazing places. And I'll never regret leaving. You might not like this, but as much as I wish you'd been here with me, I wish Gabriel and Bethany had been here too."

She stared into the phone, her eyebrows pulled together, but didn't say a word.

"It's been weeks and I miss him more every day. Not less." I thought back to the dinners Gabriel and I had been to at Hollie and Dexter's place, and wondered how often he'd been there without me in the past month. It had taken me every ounce of willpower not to ask after him during every phone call. But just like I was out of energy, my self-control was at an all-time low.

Hollie's frown might have been disapproving but it also might have been sympathetic. Did she know something I didn't?

"Have you heard from him?" I asked.

"I was about to ask you the same question. I've been avoiding him," she said.

"I told him I didn't want to have any contact while I was away. I wanted him and Penelope to have a good shot at giving their marriage another chance." A thousand times a day I'd wondered if that had been the right decision. He might have moved on already. He might have thought I'd given up on him. "You haven't seen him at all?"

"Just once when I picked up Dexter. Wedding prep is a pain in my butt but it's a great excuse not to have people around for dinner."

"What about Dexter? Has he said anything?"

"About Gabriel? He's banned from telling me anything."

I understood why she didn't want to hear how Gabriel was—she was a loyal secret keeper, and while it was one of the things I loved most about her, I just wish her lips were a little looser when it came to Gabriel.

"You think he's back with Penelope?" I asked.

When Hollie didn't respond I assumed the screen had frozen. I held my phone toward my hotel room door. Damn WiFi.

"You know what?" she asked finally.

My heart pounded like I was waiting to hear my fate. She knew something, I knew she did, just like I knew she didn't want to tell me what it was. "What?" I braced myself to hear the truth. Better to find out here than watch him turn up to Dexter and Hollie's wedding with Penelope on his arm.

"I think I know you pretty well." That didn't sound good. "I've seen you go through your fair share of boyfriends."

We were veering off course. I wanted to know about Gabriel and Penelope. "Where are we going with this?"

"I'm saying that you've had lots of other boyfriends and I bet there's been a few you'd have difficulty recalling a surname for."

"Enough with the slut shaming, Hollie. You're supposed to be on my side." Was she saying I wasn't good enough for Gabriel?

"Like, you'd just move on, right? You'd leave them in your dust."

"Jesus, Hollie, you're making me sound like a monster."

"Sorry," she said, grinning into the camera. "I'm just saying that you've been through Europe on your own and you haven't met anyone. No crazy affairs, no Italian boyfriend, no flavor-of-the-week. You're still pining for Gabriel."

"Are you recapping all this for any particular reason or are you just testing the WiFi?"

"You're in love with him."

Hearing it from my sister was like being presented with evidence of an open and shut case. Of course I was in love with him—that wasn't new information. But knowing Hollie saw it too proved it wasn't going to be something I just got over.

"I know," I said, standing up from the bed and staring out over the city. I was in love with a man who might well be starting a new life with his wife. A man who used to love me and who I hadn't seen for weeks. A man who was hundreds of miles away, just where I'd left him. "What's your point, Hollie?"

"My point is that you've had the opportunity to spread your wings and you still love him, so you need to get the heck back here and fight for him."

I spun to face my suitcase. "You think?" Excitement fizzled in my chest before panic pushed past. Did she know something and wasn't telling me? "Who am I fighting? Is he back with Penelope?"

"Honestly I don't know. I told Dexter I didn't want to hear about any of it because it didn't seem fair. But if you love him, you need to tell him."

"I'm due to fly to Paris this afternoon. If he's decided to go back to Penelope, I'd rather stay there and lick my wounds."

"Fly to Paris," Hollie said. "If things are going to work out, a few days won't make much difference. Go distract yourself with the city and make a plan—I know you're good at those. If you weren't, Dexter and I wouldn't be about to get married. Then get your butt back here and fight for him. I'm sure there's a part of you that's scared to care about a guy but—"

"I'm not scared of loving him. I just don't want to get in the middle of him and Penelope if he can make a life with her. He's not good at giving people second chances."

"Sometimes they don't deserve them."

"That's not for me to decide. That's up to Gabriel."

"Right. It's up to Gabriel to decide if he wants you or not. Come back. Tell him you love him and then he can decide what he wants."

Was that what I should have done all along? I'd been so sure that me staying around would have muddied the waters for him and kept him from giving Penelope a second chance, but maybe she didn't deserve him? And although I wanted Gabriel to be happy, I wanted him to be happy with me. Because I knew he was the only man that I would ever want.

FORTY-TWO

Gabriel

There had been nothing wrong with the evening. The babysitter had turned up on time. Penelope and I had arrived at the restaurant within a few minutes of each other. We'd been seated at a nice table by the window that overlooked the park. The waiter was friendly when he took our order and the starter had been delicious. There had been nothing *wrong* with the evening, but it wasn't right either.

"How's work?" Penelope asked.

So far, our conversation had revolved entirely around Bethany. It was a neutral, common ground that didn't create any roadblocks or conflicts. And it didn't give anything of me away either, not that I'd been consciously holding myself back. I was trying. I'd promised Autumn I would spend time with Penelope and get to know her again, and I was fulfilling my promise. Which was why we were at dinner. And why I felt so uncomfortable, I wanted to crawl out of my skin.

"Same old, same old," I replied. She didn't need to know

that I was planning to resign. "What about you? Are you still writing?"

She shrugged. "I mean, in theory. I just don't enjoy it like I used to." Penelope had been a staff writer at a magazine when we split. She'd said she'd been doing freelance ever since.

"You've got something else in mind?" I asked.

"Not really," she said, moving the food around her plate. "I guess it depends on the next . . . however long."

"What do you mean?"

"You know. I obviously want to be around for Bethany. And you . . ." She said it as if it was a sentence she was expecting me to finish off.

"What does that mean?" I took a sip of my wine.

"Just that things are going well. We've been out to dinner a few times and Bethany and I are bonding. If things keep going along this route then hopefully . . . you know, it will get even better."

I finished off my lamb and sat back, watching her. Things were friendly between us but if I were watching our interaction, I wouldn't guess that we were married. Or dating. It wasn't flirtatious on either side. Penelope seemed on edge, as if she were going for a job interview, and I felt as if I were going through the motions at a business dinner.

"Where do you see yourself in five years?" I asked. I couldn't stop the images flooding my brain as soon as I'd asked the question. I was with Bethany. And Autumn. And we were sitting out in the garden on chairs that I'd made us.

She shrugged. "I guess, hopefully back with you and Bethany. As a family."

I didn't react, not because I didn't see that picture at all, but because we'd been talking about her career. "What do you see yourself doing professionally?"

"I really want to make it up to you and Bethany. I hope you let me do that."

"But that's not a job, Penelope."

"But being a full-time mother is," she replied. "And a wife. That's what I want to focus on. If you'll let me."

When I was a kid, there was a river we all played in during the summer months. It looked like a mud pit, so murky and brown that you couldn't see the bottom. One winter, long after I'd outgrown summer afternoons swimming in the water, I passed by when I was training for my Duke of Edinburgh Gold. At first, I hadn't recognized the place. The surface of the water was like a mirror, reflecting the trees and hedges on the bank. I stopped and looked more closely to find that the water was crystal clear—I could see right to the bottom. The bed was covered in smooth stone pebbles punctured by bits of weed and bigger rocks. It was an entirely different world that I'd never noticed beneath my feet. It wasn't that I hadn't been looking before —it was just a different time of year, which showed me something new.

I took a deep breath as I stared into Penelope's eyes. The water was crystal clear.

It was as if I'd never seen my wife until now. I'd never understood her drive or ambitions or what she wanted in life. When we were married, she just seemed to be excited by what I wanted—a life with her. A family with her. And despite her explanations, I hadn't really understood why she'd left. But now I saw clearly.

Penelope was desperately searching for something.

She hadn't found it in writing. And she hadn't found it in me. Or Bethany, or our life together. And that wasn't going to change the second time around. She needed to figure out her place in the world.

"I don't think that's going to work," I replied.

Terror slid across her face, but I continued as she started to protest.

"I'm not saying you can't be Bethany's mother, but I don't think that's going to be enough for you, Penelope. And you haven't been my wife for a very long time, despite what the law says. There's a lot of water under the bridge."

"But I'm still the same woman you married and you're still the man I married. We can try. I'm sorry I left and I'll work to regain your trust—"

"Lack of trust isn't the reason we're not going to work out," I said, my mind completely clear. "We're not compatible. I want someone who wants *me*. Not the idea of me. Not a husband. Not the father of her child. But me: Gabriel Chase. I'm not looking for someone who needs me to complete them."

I'd told Autumn I'd try with Penelope and I had. I could genuinely say that I'd spent time with her, wanting to understand why things hadn't worked between us. I'd looked carefully at that idealized image of family that I'd longed for. But I'd realized what I wanted wasn't simply the opposite of the life I'd had as a child. My dream had crystalized—had been for a while now but most especially in the past month.

I wasn't the same man I had been when I'd conjured up that ideal. I was a father now. I was older. I didn't want some fantasy. I wanted to be happy.

"I'm not asking you to leave our lives." I continued. "I'm not saying you can't be a mother to Bethany. But we can't be married anymore. And I think one day, you'll see that too. I don't think I'm what you're looking for."

"But I loved our life together."

"Are you sure?" I asked her, genuinely curious. "Some

of it worked, Penelope. But if it wasn't enough for you to stay then, is it enough now?"

Minutes ticked by as she gazed out the window.

"I want it to be," she said finally.

I reached across the table for her hand. "I know. But I'm not sure wishing something is enough makes it enough. If that was the case, you would never have left."

"I did love you." Her eyes pleaded with me to believe her.

Love seemed like such a meaningless word when it came to our marriage. I wasn't sure it had been about love for either of us. "I thought you were my forever but looking back . . . I should have known. Looking back, you were always searching for something. And you didn't find it in me. Or in Bethany."

A churning in my gut stirred memories of that cupboard where I used to hide. The shouting. The crying. I knew it then. I understood all those years ago that my father should have left. My mother should have kicked him out. We weren't enough for him. I didn't think Penelope had cheated on me. Maybe she had—it didn't matter. I was breaking this cycle. I wasn't going to take her back when I knew nothing was solved and so nothing would change. Maybe she'd stay, but if she did, she wouldn't be happy. We weren't enough. She had to figure out what she needed to make herself whole.

"I think I'm broken," she said. "You are the best of men. And Bethany's adorable. I don't know what's wrong with me."

Maybe it was me. Penelope had left and now Autumn was finding her fulfilment in Europe. I knew Autumn had left because she thought it was best for me. But she was young. Perhaps down the road, she'd realize I wouldn't be enough for her either. Something told me that it wasn't the same. What Autumn and I had was deeper somehow than what Penelope and I had. We hadn't talked about a future together, but I saw it as clear as I saw the plate in front of me. I knew we'd be together, knew it in my bones. "I don't think it's you. And I don't think it's me. You need to find you, rather than look for someone else to give you what you need."

"Please don't take Bethany away from me," she said, her voice full of panic. "I know I don't deserve a second chance, but I promise you, I'll do nothing to hurt her again."

I shook my head. "I'm not going to take her away. But she needs stability. We'll figure out how to put her first without putting you last. Let's agree now, in this moment, that we'll figure out something that works for all of us."

"Like I said, you're the best of men, Gabriel Chase." She took in a juddering breath. "I'm so sorry."

"I know." For the first time since she'd walked out on us three years ago, I felt at peace. Relieved. We weren't going to enter some kind of hell-loop where she came and went and we were both dragged into misery. Bethany wouldn't have to hide in cupboards, and I wouldn't waste my life wishing reality was something it wasn't. Penelope and I weren't meant to be. That had nothing to do with my anger or resentment, or not giving her a second chance. And it had nothing to do with Autumn.

FORTY-THREE

Gabriel

I couldn't remember the last time I'd been away from Bethany overnight, but I was surprisingly relaxed about it.

"Why don't they have these kinds of waitresses in London?" Tristan asked, glancing around at the women in white bikinis and nearly see-through cover-ups who were distributing cocktails to the patrons at the rooftop bar. It was a little weird for a five-star New York hotel, but it was hot as hell and this was America, so I wasn't about to complain. "Alcohol tastes better when served by a woman in a bikini."

"You're a sexist dick at times, Tristan," I said, kicking at his chair under the table.

"We're in a hotel bar. Not a strip club. Don't be a twat," Joshua said. "Keep your eyes on New York." The city stretched out all around us. Three hundred and sixty degrees of Manhattan. From up here we could see everything from the Chrysler building to the Brooklyn Bridge.

Dexter just shook his head. "I can't wait for you to fall

hook, line, and sinker for a girl. You'll realize what an idiot you've been."

"There's no way I'm settling down," Tristan replied.

"You will fall at the feet of the first woman who falls in love with you," Joshua said. "All your chat is just that. Chat."

"Whatever you say," Tristan replied. "At least I actually get laid. Unlike you."

"I have sex plenty," Joshua replied. "But I'm not a fifteen-year-old boy so I don't have to tell everyone about it."

"How's Bethany," Dexter asked, clearly wanting to change the subject.

"I spoke to her just before I came up. She's good. Excited that Penelope's staying over."

"Oh wow," Beck said. "Penelope is looking after her?"

"The nanny's there as well. But yeah, it's good for the two of them to have some time together."

"Sounds like things are still going well," Beck said.

I blew out a breath. "So far, so good." In many ways it would be easier if we could slip into our life before she left. Especially now when we knew each other and ourselves in a much deeper way than we had done before.

"She still want you back?" Beck asked.

I shrugged, swirling the whiskey in my glass. Penelope hadn't said anything more since we'd had dinner together. She'd been seeing more of Bethany, but she hadn't suggested dinner again and neither had I. "I don't think so."

"And you're not interested?"

I shook my head. "She wasn't the woman I thought I married. I'm not saying that to criticize her. It's more a reflection of me having an image in my head of what I wanted and trying to mold everything to fit. That image is gone. And Penelope and I are Bethany's parents, but we're not ever going to be husband and wife again."

"You sound okay about it," Andrew said.

"I am. But . . ." I wasn't a man who asked for help or advice. Tonight, I needed both. "I do have other things on my mind."

"You need to leave your job."

"Oh, I did that already. Just before I left for the airport."

Dexter beckoned one of the waitresses over. "A magnum of your best champagne, please."

"We have a double celebration on our hands," Beck said.

I winced. Dexter might cancel the champagne if he knew what I was about to say next. "I'm also in love with Autumn." I glanced at Dexter. "Sorry, mate."

"Yeah, I had a feeling," he replied. "You spoken to her?"

"Not since she left. She made me promise to give things a go with Penelope. But it's not my wife I want. It's Autumn. I never thought I could ever see myself trusting a woman, trusting myself to be with a woman again. Not like I had with Penelope. But I love Autumn. I trust her. I want to build a life with her."

"You can't help who you love," Beck said.

"You okay with this?" I asked, looking at Dexter.

"I'm with Beck on this. I can't speak for my future wife, but we'll win her round. She's very fond of you."

"Thanks, Dexter," I replied. "I appreciate it. I've got to focus on winning Autumn over first. I need something . . . big. To show her that I'm serious. She might have given up and moved on—it's been weeks, and she was determined I should get back together with Penelope—but I'll do what I need to do to get her back."

"Right," said Tristan. "The best brains in London are around this table. We can figure something out."

"A coven emergency, as Stella would describe it," Beck said.

"Stella thinks we're witches?"

He shrugged. "She's just jealous."

"But she comes to most of our drinks nights," Andrew said.

"I know," said Beck. "But she's not here tonight, so she's jealous."

"You should tell her that we'd prefer her company to yours any day," Joshua said.

"I'll make sure I pass the message on. And while we're passing messages on, get your fucking hair cut. You look like a student."

"I'm busy, and what can I say, Miss Tuesday Night likes something to run her fingers through."

"Miss Tuesday Night?" Beck asked. "You don't even have names for the women you fuck now? You're starting to sound like Tristan."

"Maybe I'm concealing her identity," Joshua said.

"You're both animals," I said.

"I've got it," Tristan said. "You go down on one knee during Dexter and Hollie's wedding breakfast. During the speeches or something."

"Firstly—no," Dexter said. "And secondly, no fucking way. What are you thinking, Tristan? Sometimes I wonder how you manage to dress yourself in the morning, let alone trick people into paying you to mess about with their computers."

"What's your problem? Proposing in front of everyone's a grand gesture," Tristan said, looking genuinely confused.

"That will take the focus off the bride and groom and

their wedding," I said as if I was explaining to Bethany that she shouldn't eat the sandwich she'd just dropped in the dirt.

Tristan shrugged. "Don't blame me that Dexter's a selfish narcissist who wants all the attention to himself. The brief was to think up a grand gesture to win back Autumn. I fulfilled the brief."

"When's she back in London?" Andrew asked. I couldn't answer him. I didn't know where Autumn was, who she was with, or when she was coming back.

"I guess she's coming back for the wedding." I glanced at Dexter.

"Yup. She's back next Wednesday."

My heart tumbled in my chest. In just days she'd be back in London.

"She's coming back on Eurostar."

That little piece of information planted a seed of an idea in my brain. "She's in Paris now?" I asked.

"I think that's what Hollie said."

Paris. We should be there together. I wanted to kiss her by the Seine. Hold her hand over *moules frites*. Watch her face when she saw the Venus di Milo for the first time. Plans started to form. I could go to Paris. Find her. Tell her I loved her.

"You know where she's staying?" I asked.

"No clue," Dexter said.

That wasn't a dealbreaker. I could ask Hollie, or I could call Autumn and just ask her. We might not have spoken in weeks, but it wasn't like she hated me. There'd be no reason for her not to pick up . . . unless. "She on her own?"

"I don't know." Dexter pulled his phone from his pocket. "Let me ask Hollie."

Did it matter if she was on her own? It wasn't like that

was going to stop me. If she'd met someone, I'd just have to fight for her. I could do that. She might not have told me she loved me, but I knew her well enough to be confident that what we had was special. The kind of thing that wasn't just replaced in a few weeks. She'd left *for me*. She'd stayed away *for me*. Well, I'd done as she'd asked, and I knew there wasn't a future with me and Penelope. There was no reason for Autumn to be anywhere but by my side. "It doesn't matter," I said standing. "I'm going to leave you guys to it. Sorry to miss the rest of your stag do, Dexter."

"What?" Andrew said.

"I'm going to get a flight to Paris." I beckoned the waiter over.

"Just like that?" Tristan asked.

I nodded. "Yeah. Just like that." I gave the waiter my card. "Put everything from tonight on here, please."

"Sometimes you've gotta do what you've gotta do," Dexter said.

"And I've got to go and get Autumn."

"Good for you, mate," Beck said. "Go for it. Keep us posted."

Beck got it. Dexter got it. The others would someday. I didn't want to be away from Autumn for another moment. I didn't even want to wait until next week. I didn't have to be back in London until the day after tomorrow. Hopefully it would be time enough to find Autumn and make her realize that I loved her, that she loved me, and that our futures were inextricably linked. There was no point in resisting it any longer.

FORTY-FOUR

Autumn

As I stood speechless, taking in the red windmill teetering on top of the building opposite, I couldn't help but wonder why someone before Baz Lurhmann hadn't made a musical about the place. Paris was all crimson and bright lights and optimism against the dull, grey sky. I pulled out my guide-book, complete with color coded Post-its and dogeared pages. Paris was always meant to be the first stop on my trip, and I'd spent so much time looking forward to being here that I was kind of nervous now I had finally landed. It was like the first day of a new job or a first date with . . .

If only he was here.

Hollie had told me to fight for him, but I wasn't sure what that meant. It didn't feel right to stand between a man and his wife, try to separate him from the life he'd always wanted. But being without him didn't seem right either.

What had been a bright blue sky until about five minutes ago had darkened, and as sure as night follows day, a sprinkle of drizzle began to speckle the pavement. The rain had followed me around in Europe. I pulled my tote from my shoulder and rummaged around trying to find my umbrella. But it wasn't in there. Damn it, I'd left it on the bed in my hotel room. I shouldn't have been so optimistic.

Never mind—it was getting late anyway, so I'd make this my final stop. I'd just wanted to see the lights of the Moulin Rouge at twilight. I zipped up my tote and straightened as the clouds above me darkened. I tipped my head back and saw not a cloud . . .

But an umbrella that someone was holding over my head.

I turned and came face-to-face with Gabriel. The man I'd thought constantly about for the last four weeks.

He grinned. "Need an umbrella?"

My heart lifted in my chest as if it was chasing the moon. "Gabriel? What are you doing here?"

"I thought I'd show you Paris. Unless you have other plans?"

I couldn't help but grin up at him like he was my sunshine breaking through the clouds. "Where's Bethany? Aren't you on Dexter's bachelor trip?" I gazed up at him and felt instantly like *right here* was where I was meant to be. How had I spent all these weeks away from him? I'd pushed so much aside—so much grief at having to leave him, so much love that I had for him, and now it all came crashing back in, threatening to overwhelm me. My knees weakened and I stumbled, but he caught me, his hand around my waist.

"You okay?"

Of course, I was more than okay. I was with the man I loved. "What are you doing here? How did you find me?"

"I didn't want you to see Paris without me," he said, like that explained everything. He hadn't moved to take his hand from my waist, and no matter how strong or strong-willed I was, not a single thing could have caused me to step away. "And I had a feeling you'd want to come here as soon as the light started to fade. You know, because of all that Baz Luhrmann genius."

He'd remembered. "It's so cute, right?"

"Cute?" He shrugged. "If you say so."

"What about Penelope? And Bethany?"

"Bethany's fine. She's in London. With Penelope as it happens. I did as you asked. I spent time with her."

My stomach churned at the thought of him dating someone else, even if it was his wife. He was mine. Did he know that?

"But she's not the woman I want. Not because I won't give her a second chance, but because we were never right for each other. When we married, we were both hoping we could find something in each other that was missing. But that's not the way life works."

"But your perfect family?" As much as I wanted him, I wanted him to be happy—to get what he'd always wanted.

"There's no such thing. I should have realized that a long time ago, rather than being bitter about mine falling apart. Being Bethany's father should have shown me that I'm a different man to either of my parents, but it took me so long to see it. I'm not about to repeat their mistakes. I don't need to prove that to anyone. Not even myself anymore."

He looked peaceful. The dark circles that sometimes ghosted his eyes had lifted, and the corners of his mouth twitched as if he were trying to hold back a grin.

"I've missed you," I said.

He cupped my face and gazed at me like I was treasure he'd been searching for his entire life. "I've missed you more than I thought possible. And I'm never going to let you go."

Relief swept through my body. "I never want you to."

"So, no French lover that I need to fight off?" he asked, brushing my hair from my face.

I slid my hand up his chest. "There's never been anyone for me except you." All those boyfriends before had been shadow boxing. I'd been waiting for Gabriel all along.

He pressed his lips against mine and my entire body sagged with relief. He was here. Kissing me. There would be no telling myself it was best for us to remain apart, or that I would be happy if he was happy. My life would be all silver linings and lemonade with Gabriel—no clouds, no lemons.

Finally, what seemed like hours later, our kiss ended. "I guess we should start your tour. I don't want you to miss anything."

I grinned as he took my hand and led the way. I realized this was how it was between us—him wanting to make me happy, me wanting to make him happy. It was a perfect balance.

"How did you manage to get the time off work to be here?" I asked, suddenly worried that we had to make the most of every moment rather than saunter down the street, dodging the mopeds.

"You're taking up with an unemployed lay-about. I resigned."

I came to an abrupt halt. "You quit? Did Mike push you over the edge?"

He shook his head. "Nope. Meeting you and then losing you made me look at my life with new eyes. I'd been working for similar reasons that I got married—to make sure I bore no resemblance to my father. I want to hang out with Bethany more. With you. It means we can travel and—"

"I know I don't have a job yet, Gabriel. But I want a career."

"Right. And if you have to take an assignment somewhere else in Europe or back in the U.S., we can come with you."

My heart threatened to explode in my chest. Could life really be this simple? This good?

"Are you not going to work?" I asked.

"I'm going to give second chances for a living. You're a wise woman, Autumn Lumen." His smile was infectious.

"I am?"

"The furniture. Restoring and renewing things. It makes me happy."

Just watching his face as he talked made it obvious that his mind was set. He had been renewed by the prospect of a different life.

"That's wonderful. And bonus for me, I get to enjoy the fruits of that labor." I squeezed his bicep, my thoughts already spinning with images of Gabriel hard at work.

"All of me is yours," he said, his eyes darkening. He pressed his lips to mine and pulled away abruptly. "I need to stop that. Or I'll be dragging you back to the hotel. I promised you a tour."

I'd be happy to skip the tour and spend the next week in bed, but Paris was calling, and we had a lifetime to be naked.

As we wandered along the Seine, the sun dimmed further and sky turned darker, the drizzle turning to huge, fat raindrops that thudded against the sidewalks, splashed onto our cheeks, and dented the surface of the river. "The rain has been following me around," I said.

"It's raining? Really? From where I stand, the sun is shining all over the place."

If I didn't already know that Gabriel Chase was the man for me, that sealed it. "Did you just quote my favorite movie at me?"

He shrugged. "What can I say? I'm so in love with you that I don't even notice the rain."

I wasn't sure what I'd done to deserve Gabriel, but I was going to spend the rest of my life grateful that I'd found him.

FORTY-FIVE

Gabriel

I didn't approve of the jumpsuit Autumn was wearing.

"Stop growling," she said, grinning at me. "It's a wedding. It's not like we can get frisky during the ceremony."

"It's not quick to get out of. Or into. It's a ridiculous piece of clothing."

"It's gorgeous."

"You're gorgeous," I corrected. "You could wear anything and make it look incredible."

"Back at you," she said, kissing my cheek and smoothing her hands down my suit. "I'm going to miss you being in a suit every day."

"If you like, I can dress up once in a while."

"Ohhh, roleplay. Interesting." She nudged me with her hip.

"I'm not sure we need roleplay to keep things interesting," I said, grabbing her bottom and pressing my hips against hers.

She pushed me away. "We have five minutes to get downstairs. And I haven't finished my hair because you've *interested* me plenty already this morning."

I watched as she had to do exactly nothing to her hair for it to look completely amazing. She stepped into her strappy black heels. "Yeah, I'm going to need you to wear those for me later when everything else is off."

"That can be arranged." She glanced at me as she dropped her phone into her bag. "In the meantime, let's go and watch our best friends get married."

I held out my hand and she took it. "Us next, right?"

"Us next, what?"

I pulled the hotel room door closed and we started down the hallway. "You know—getting married."

She shook her head. "You're crazy. I've been back in London a week. We've only just told Bethany."

"I'm not saying we need to start thinking about it next week, but I want to marry you. That's not a surprise, is it?" I wanted to do it all with Autumn. I wanted to make love with her, wake up with her, cook, travel, father her children, and spend my life with her. I'd wait if that's what she wanted, but I had no doubt about where I stood.

"I guess not. And I'm not saying no, obviously. I need to find a job and figure out where I'm going to live—"

"What do you mean, figure out where you're going to live? Are you thinking that we might not be living together?" I was clearly making assumptions about our future that I shouldn't have been. A pit opened up in my gut, but I took a breath and waited for her answer. I was beyond jumping to conclusions.

She shrugged. "We haven't talked about any of this stuff. But we'll work it out. It's not like we don't have the rest of our lives together."

Relief and warmth and sunshine flooded through me, closing up the pit again.

"I love you," I said.

"I love you too," she replied. "And I want to live with you . . ."

"But?" I could hear the unspoken word echoing down the hallway. We got to the lift and she turned to face me.

"But honestly, I don't want to live in the house where your ex-wife picked out the wallpaper."

"That's just as well, because the house is up for sale."

She tilted her head as a smile crept across her face. "It is?"

"I want a fresh start with you. I don't want to live in the past anymore. And I want to live in *our* house. Not my house. You're not going to be an overnight guest or the nanny. You're going to be my wife. My best friend. My partner. We should pick out the place we're going to raise our family together."

"Raise a family?" she said, looking like I just asked her the difference between a turret lathe and a toolroom lathe.

"I hate to tell you, but Bethany comes as part of the deal." I knew that's not what she meant, but she was so easy to tease.

"Of course," she replied. "But . . . Gabriel . . . I'm not ready for—"

I slid my hand around her waist and pulled her closer. "I know. I'm thinking too far ahead. I just want to future-proof the house. We'll wait as long as you want. I want you to be happy."

"You always know the perfect thing to say," she said, and we stepped into the lift.

"Now you know that's not true. I'm going to get it wrong a lot. I'm impatient and surly at times. But promise me you'll always know that you are at the center of every-thing I do. You and Bethany. You two are everything I think about, everything I am. I might need you to help me back on track from time to time but know that I love you, even when I veer off course."

The lift doors pinged open, and we made our way toward the suite where Dexter and Hollie were getting married. "Gabriel Chase, I love the way you love me. I love you just as hard. And I'm going to make mistakes too. But I know that we'll be with each other until one of us isn't in this world anymore."

I nodded, knowing what she was saying because it was exactly how I felt. We had just strolled through the corri-dors of a hotel on the way to a wedding, but it was as if we were the ones who had just been married. Our promises wouldn't get any stronger for being made in public or put on a register somewhere.

This woman was my soulmate. There hadn't been a ceremony invented that would bind us any closer than we already were.

"Shall we go watch your sister marry one of the best men I know?"

"What's wild about today is that I think she feels for Dexter the same kind of forever love that I have for you."

"What makes that wild?" I asked.

"I just never thought we could both be so lucky."

I pulled her closer to me as we came to the door to the suite, content to let her believe that of the two of us, she was the lucky one.

EPILOGUE

Three Months Later

Autumn

I glanced around at the huge kitchen, dining, and living areas arranged around the central outdoor courtyard encased in glass. It was so big. So grand. I loved it but it also made me a little uneasy.

"You'll get used to it," Hollie said, reading my mind as she uncorked a bottle of champagne.

"I hope so," I replied. "I know I live here but I'm not sure I can quite believe it at the same time. Does that make sense?" My life had changed so completely in the last few months. Not only had I moved continents, but I'd discovered my future, and I knew who I was going to share it with.

"You're still the same person. Just remember that. It's not so different to our trailer back in Oregon."

We both burst into laughter. Gabriel and my new home couldn't have been further from where and how we'd grown up. But she was right. It didn't make us different people. We loved the men we loved, regardless of whether they were rich or poor.

"I'm still bummed I couldn't get you to move to Knightsbridge."

"I like Smithfield," I replied. "And it's a super easy commute." The investment bank where I'd interviewed just before I'd flown to Madrid had offered me an entry-level investment analyst job. I'd been there about a month and I was *loving* it. I felt like I was living in an eighties movie. I wasn't sure how, but life just kept getting better and better.

"I'm so proud of you," she said, slinging her arm around my shoulders. "Your career is going to be amazing. I feel like you've taken flight since moving to London. There's something about this place. We've both come here and spread our wings and we're living our best lives."

Hollie had always believed it was possible. Her vision of the world out there had meant she'd pushed me to focus and study and not make the wrong choices. She'd shaped the woman I was today—the life I had, and how happy I was. "I love you," I said.

"I love you too," she said. "I'll love you even more if you pour me a glass of that champagne."

The crash in the hallway made me spill the alcohol over the glass. "What the hell?"

We poked our heads out to find Gabriel, Dexter, Tristan, and Joshua carrying in a huge . . . grandfather clock.

"Don't worry, it's not ours," Gabriel said. "It's so bloody ugly."

Gabriel spent hours trawling websites and auction houses, trying to find new projects. One of the reasons we'd bought this house was because of the huge workshop next door. But he managed to fill the cavernous space with desks, chairs, bureaus, tables, and really, any piece of wood looking for a little TLC and a second chance. At least this clock hadn't been adopted.

"Whose is it?" Hollie asked suspiciously.

"Glad you asked," Dexter said, grinning. "I thought it would look great in my office."

"As long as it's going somewhere I don't have to look at it," Hollie said.

The four of them heaved the monolithic timepiece upright. "Don't think you're keeping it," Dexter said to Gabriel.

"Believe me, I don't want it," replied Gabriel.

"That makes two of us," I said.

"Make that three of us," Hollie said.

"Marriage is about compromise," Dexter said, lifting Hollie into his arms and kissing her.

"It's a good thing I love you," she said.

"Stop with the PDA," Tristan said. "It's making my stomach churn."

"You're just jealous that I have a hot wife," Dexter said.

Tristan rolled his eyes. "Get me a drink."

Tristan tried to pretend he wanted nothing to do with a committed relationship, but I couldn't help but think he just hadn't met the right girl yet. He was always focused on who was hot rather than who he liked. Joshua wasn't a lot better, but he was a little more discreet and a better flirt.

They all circled the kitchen island, where I was filling a row of champagne flutes. Gabriel went straight to the wine fridge and pulled out another bottle.

When everyone had a full glass in their hand, I raised mine. "Here's to Tristan finding the love of his life when he's least expecting it. May she torture and tease him until he begs for mercy."

Joshua chuckled and I pointed at him. "And here's to Joshua finding a woman who's as good a flirt as he is."

"Gabriel, I don't know how you managed to trick Autumn into falling for you, but congratulations," Joshua said, ever the charmer. "If anyone deserves to be happy, it's the two of you."

We all clinked our glasses and it felt somehow as if we were cementing together our extended family. Beck, Dexter, Joshua, Tristan, Andrew, and Gabriel had known each other forever and were brothers in all but name. It was heartwarming to see such strong men support each other through the turbulent ups and downs of life, but the icing on the cake was how they had welcomed me, Hollie, and Stella into their lives as if we were long-lost sisters. The group really did feel like family.

"Oh, and did I tell you, I'm moving in," Joshua said. "Your house is so bloody cool."

The corner of Gabriel's mouth twitched. He loved this house. It had taken a bit of persuasion for me to agree to it being our home—it was just so big. But the workshop next door was ideal, and the short commute had sealed the deal.

"You'd be welcome," I said.

"No, he wouldn't," Gabriel said, looking at me as if I'd lost my mind. "We already have Bethany to look after. And unlike my daughter, I'm not sure Joshua is housetrained."

"He's more than housetrained," Dexter said. "He organizes his lovers by the days of the week."

"That's just because he has a terrible memory and can't remember their names," Tristan said.

"You're out of line, Tristan," Joshua replied.

"Okay, tell me Miss Sunday Afternoon's name?"

Joshua flushed scarlet with rage, but before they could come to blows, my sister interrupted.

"My prediction is that Joshua will find someone special soon and he'll be moving in with her, so no need to panic," Hollie said as she patted Gabriel on the back.

"How much champagne have you had?" Joshua asked. "You're way off base. I'm never going to live with a woman. I don't like to share my space."

Hollie grinned at him like he had no idea what was coming. And if I knew anything about my sister's determination and single-mindedness, she'd have Joshua in love and married within a year.

I pulled Gabriel to one side as Hollie and Joshua continued to bicker, and Dexter and Tristan looked on, delighted at Joshua being tortured.

"I love you," I said. "And your wild, dysfunctional group of friends."

"I love you too," he said. "And as much as I loved this house as soon as I saw it, I love it even more, now I see you in it."

That's how life would always be with Gabriel and me. Life was made better by being together. The dark moments in life wouldn't be so scary when I was holding his hand and good times would just be made better by being side by side, step-by-step with this beautiful soul next to me.

A few weeks later still...

Gabriel

A twitch in my trousers told me that maybe this blindfold I'd just secured around Autumn's eyes would come in handy a little later this evening.

"Gabriel," she said, her tone hushed. She brought her fingers up to the edge of the black silk bandana.

"Take my hand," I said. "You're fine." I led her from the

hallway into the dining room, which had a clear view of the internal courtyard.

When I had her in position, I stepped back. I wanted to take in her reaction when she saw what I was about to show her. "Autumn Lumen, I wanted to do something special as this is an anniversary."

Her hand shot to the blindfold. "Anniversary?"

"Don't take it off yet," I said. "Yes, it's the fifteenth month anniversary of the first time I ever laid eyes on you, wearing pajamas and eating ice cream with your sister at Dexter's place."

Autumn tipped her head to the side. "You are too sweet."

"You know that's not true."

She laughed and I took a deep breath, relishing the sound that filled my soul every time I heard it. "You're sweet with a side of dirty between the sheets."

"I wanted to mark it," I continued. "So I made you something."

Her delicious pout widened into a smile as if just hearing the words was enough of a gift.

I pulled the tie fastening the blindfold and it fell to the ground. Her eyes grew large as she took in the two Adirondack chairs set out in the courtyard. "A classic American design made with the strength of English oak," I said, watching her reaction as she stepped out into the courtyard.

"They're beautiful," she said, smoothing her hands over the wood. "You made these?"

She turned to me and I stalked toward her, wanting to hold her expression of pride and happiness in my memory forever.

"After the jewelry box, I thought maybe I'd do another project from scratch," I said. "I thought that when we're too old to travel, we can sit in these chairs and reminisce over the times we went to a thousand faraway places."

"I love that idea." She slid her palm over my cheek, and I circled my arms around her waist. "And the stool," she said pointing to the matching one I'd also made. "That's for Bethany," she said, knowing exactly what I'd been thinking. "And you can make more for our other children."

"When the time comes," I said. There was no rush to add to our family, but we both hoped more children were in our future.

"I miss her when she's not here," she said.

"Me too," I replied. "But it's good that Penelope's in her life." Penelope had started a fine art course and found a place to live between the college and Smithfield. She had shown no signs of abandoning Bethany and they'd grown closer. I hoped she found whatever she was looking for in Bethany and in her art. If Penelope was happy, that was good for our daughter.

"She's going to love it," Autumn said. "You're so talented."

"I'm so lucky," I said, squeezing her tight. "Oh, and another thing." I nodded at the white envelopes on her chair.

"More anniversary gifts?" She picked up the envelopes and I took a seat, pulling her onto my lap. "I don't need anything more. What could be better than these beautiful chairs?"

"What about somewhere to go that we can reminisce over while we sit in them?"

"Are you serious?" she said, ripping open the envelope. "India?" She glanced over the paperwork.

"Did you know that the Taj Mahal was built as a monument of love?"

She pressed her lips to my cheek. "I did know that." She kissed me again—my jaw this time.

"I'm thinking I might propose," I said, holding my breath for her reaction. She was still so young, and I didn't want to put her under any pressure, but I knew that I'd be with her until my dying breath. I saw no reason why we weren't as publicly committed as we were privately.

She pulled away, checking to see if I was serious. She trailed her fingers along my neck. "Will it involve karaoke?" she asked. "Because if it does, I'm definitely saying yes."

"Karaoke? At the Taj Mahal?"

She pulled back to meet my eye, her expression deadly serious. "There's never a bad place for karaoke."

"And if I say there will be strictly no karaoke involved when I propose marriage to you, are you going to say no?"

She huffed out a breath and glanced at the ceiling, like she was really having to consider it. "It won't be a *definite* no."

I chuckled and shook my head. "You're ridiculous. You're totally going to say yes."

She shrugged. "Maybe I'll propose to you. On the plane on the way over. When the seatbelt signs go off, I'll jump into the aisle and belt out 'Defying Gravity' at the top of my lungs and end on one knee, bearing a ring."

"Okay, if you're going to threaten me with stuff like that, I'm never travelling with you. Not ever. And the proposal is off."

She looped her arms around my neck. "No deal. You're totally going to propose. And so long as there's karaoke at the wedding, I can cope with a song-free proposal."

"You sure you're ready?" I asked, serious again. I didn't want her to feel rushed.

"It doesn't matter how young or old I am. I'm going to

spend the rest of my life with you. If we get married now or in ten years, what difference does it make?"

She was right of course, because she was the wisest woman I knew. Autumn was someone who'd always seen the light in me and whose darkness didn't scare me. She was my forever—horrific singing voice and all.

Joshua's book, **Mr. Park Lane** is available for pre order **NOW**

My **NEXT** release is **Private Player**. Pre-order **NOW**! Keep reading for a sneak peek.

Have you read
Beck and Stella in **Mr. Mayfair**
Dexter and Hollie in **Mr. Knightsbridge**

Sign up to my newsletter and receive all my latest news, book updates, giveaways and freebies!
www.louisebay.com/newsletter

BOOKS BY LOUISE BAY

The Mister Series

Mr. Mayfair

Mr. Knightsbridge

Mr. Smithfield

Mr. Park Lane

Standalones

International Player

Hollywood Scandal

Love Unexpected

Hopeful

The Empire State Series

Gentleman Series

The Wrong Gentleman

The Ruthless Gentleman

The Royals Series

The Earl of London

The British Knight

Duke of Manhattan

Park Avenue Prince

King of Wall Street

Sign up to the Louise Bay mailing list at
www.louisebay/mailinglist

Read more at www.louisebay.com

PRIVATE PLAYER - CHAPTER ONE

Nathan

I watched from the edges of the lawn where guests were gathered. The groom, one of my oldest friends, grinned like his team had just won the FA cup. The photographer scurried after him and his bride as the happy couple flitted among groups of guests enjoying their canapes and champagne.

Everyone was full of smiles, air kisses, and congratulations.

Everyone except me. I hated weddings.

It came down to small talk. Some people were good at chatting about the weather, or Wimbledon, or whatever else it was that small-talkers talked about.

I wasn't that guy.

Add in the bad wine, cold food, and prolonged speeches, and weddings became my personal hell medley. And that was *before* the soon-to-explode bomb landed in my lap last night.

I should have been in London. Working. Planning. Strategizing. Defusing. Instead, I was listening to the *tick,*

tick, tick—powerless to stop the explosion I knew would come. I glanced at my phone. Gretel was supposed to come back to me by four with details of some last-minute story the *Sunday Mercury* intended to run about me tomorrow—it was the kind of thing that normally didn't concern me, but given my current relationship with my board, I couldn't afford to ignore anything. Three fifty-eight. She had two minutes.

Tick, tick, tick.

My phone buzzed in my hand. Well, at least she wasn't late. I moved toward the trees and pressed Accept. "Go ahead."

"They have photos of you with Audrey Alpern. Is that Mark Alpern's wife?" she asked.

The news stuck in my throat like I'd swallowed a mouthful of wood chippings. Fuck, fuck, fuck.

Since I'd floated Astro Holdings, there had been murmurs about whether my focus was on the job . . . or elsewhere. The murmurs were turning into shrieks. The market didn't think I could work hard and play hard. But I'd always been that way. My two passions in life were work and play—business and pleasure. It had always served me well.

Until now.

Until I'd taken Astro public.

Now, instead of answering to myself alone, I had pension funds, investors, and the business press—not to mention the board—scrutinizing everything I did.

Apparently, the rest of the world didn't think you could run a FTSE 100 company *and* enjoy yourself.

"Yes," I replied and I cleared my throat. "I've been friends with both of them since before they were married. We all met at university."

"Was Mark there last night?" she asked.

"Nope." Of course he wasn't. Audrey had come to me for help. Advice. Support. Bomb disposal expertise. Her husband had betrayed her—betrayed everyone. Mark was the last person who would have been there last night.

"Well, the *Mercury* is lobbing words like *playboy* and *cheater* and—"

"And none of those words are accurate when describing me, so what's your plan?" The board had forced me to hire a PR person to repair my reputation as a playboy who was more focused on women than his business, so she needed to do her job.

"My plan is for you to tell me why you were with another man's wife at Annabel's at three in the morning. It's usually better to start with the truth."

"She's a friend. We went out for some drinks."

Gretel groaned on the other end of the line. She assumed I was lying. If I'd been trying to cover up something sordid, maybe I would have. But I was telling the truth. It just wasn't the whole truth.

"Well, Houston, we have a problem," she said.

"I'm not sleeping with Audrey Alpern." At least the *Mercury* hadn't uncovered the real reason we were together last night.

"I don't care whether or not you're fucking her," Gretel said. "I care that it *looks* like you're fucking her."

"And I don't care *what* it looks like," I said. "I care about the truth. And the truth is, she's just a friend. We were having drinks. There's no story." Another lie. There was a story, but it was far bigger than me being out with a married woman. It just wasn't mine to tell.

"Unfortunately, that kind of truth doesn't sell newspapers. We need to give them some explanation."

"You want me to make something up?" I asked.

Gretel sighed. I'd not been making her life easy since she joined, but I resented the board questioning my commitment to the job when they were the ones around the table seeing the business thrive. Astro was outperforming its targets on every measure. "We need to offer an alternative perspective to the image of you that's out there," she said.

Despite Astro's success, I was dangerously close to being fired by the board I'd created. If they thought I was sleeping with another man's wife, especially a man who happened to be one of the biggest wealth managers in London, *and* I'd ignored PR, the guillotine would inch closer to my neck.

"All anyone knows about you is that you're a surly play-boy," Gretel continued. "Someone who doesn't like them. People like to feel liked."

"I don't give a shit about being liked." Being popular was overrated. I cared about results. Loyalty. Getting things done. Not making it onto people's Christmas card lists.

"Well, you're an anomaly in many ways," she said in a sing-song voice, as if she were telling a child their painting deserved to hang in the National Gallery. "I'm trying to help you. And if you want my help, you need to work with me to show the world the best side of yourself. Show them why you're the youngest CEO the FTSE 100 has ever seen. Show them you're sharp, focused, decisive, and most of all —open."

I didn't want to *need* Gretel, but I did. Astro Holdings was my life's work, my passion, and I'd do whatever it took to ensure my position there was safe. Then again, the prospect of being fired by the board I had created wasn't even the worst prospect coming down the line in the coming weeks. Being thought of as a moody womanizer was likely to be the least of my problems if what Audrey told me last night was even half right. For the second time in my life, being Mark Alpern's friend was likely to cost me and the people I cared about. This time, I had to protect myself. Protect Audrey.

"Do you have something in mind?" These photographs the *Mercury* had were like cutting my hand and going out surfing. If I ignored them, I'd be asking for trouble. When the Mark Alpern bomb eventually dropped, the sharks would circle and finish me off.

"We need an entire campaign designed to cast you in a new light. At the center of it would be an in-depth profile of you in a national broadsheet, like the *Post*. You give them an all-access pass—no questions or parts of your life or business off-limits."

That sounded like my worst nightmare. I was far from reclusive, but I liked my privacy. Though I'd never considered myself a playboy, my private life involved me getting naked with women fairly regularly. "I'm not sure that will work."

"It's the only thing that will—complete transparency," she insisted. "Then we'll build in some charity work, some corporate social responsibility. You'll have to wine and dine some influential people in the City, but if keeping your position as CEO at Astro is important to you, I'm telling you, this is what it will take."

Bloody Mark Alpern. If he weren't the subject of an active police investigation, Audrey and I wouldn't have been meeting last night and I wouldn't be having this conversation. This was all his fault.

Assignments of blame aside, my business was at stake. I wasn't prepared to sacrifice everything I'd worked so hard for. I'd done that once before for Mark, and it wasn't going to happen a second time.

"Set it up," I said.

"Consider it done," she replied. "I have a journalist in mind who's likely to be a little softer on you. She—"

"I'm at a wedding. I'll expect something in my diary for Monday." I didn't need to know the details. This was Gretel's opportunity to prove she was as good as everyone said she was. And if she was right, it was also my do-or-die chance to prove I was as good as I'd always believed.

Made in the USA
Middletown, DE
17 June 2021